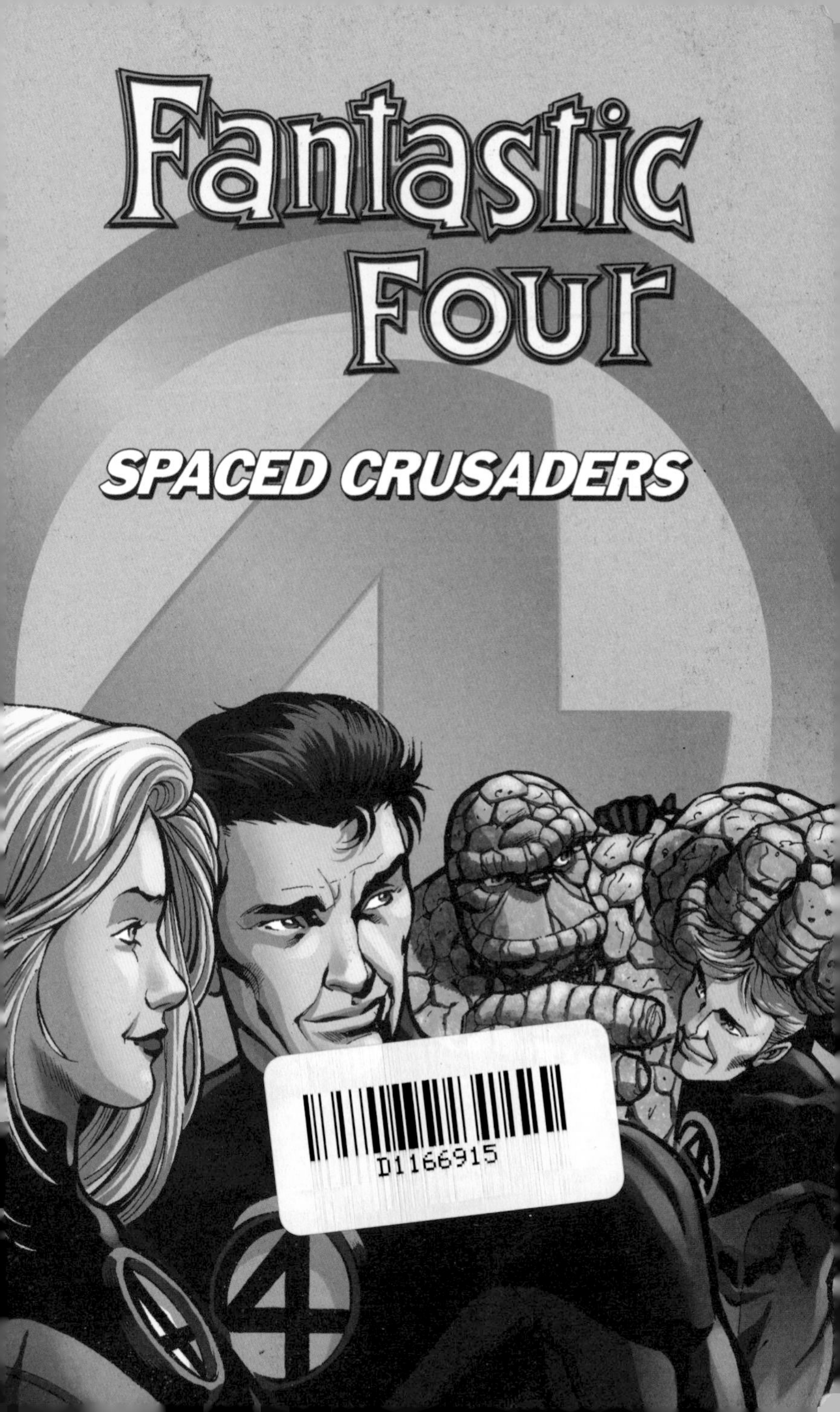
Fantastic Four
SPACED CRUSADERS

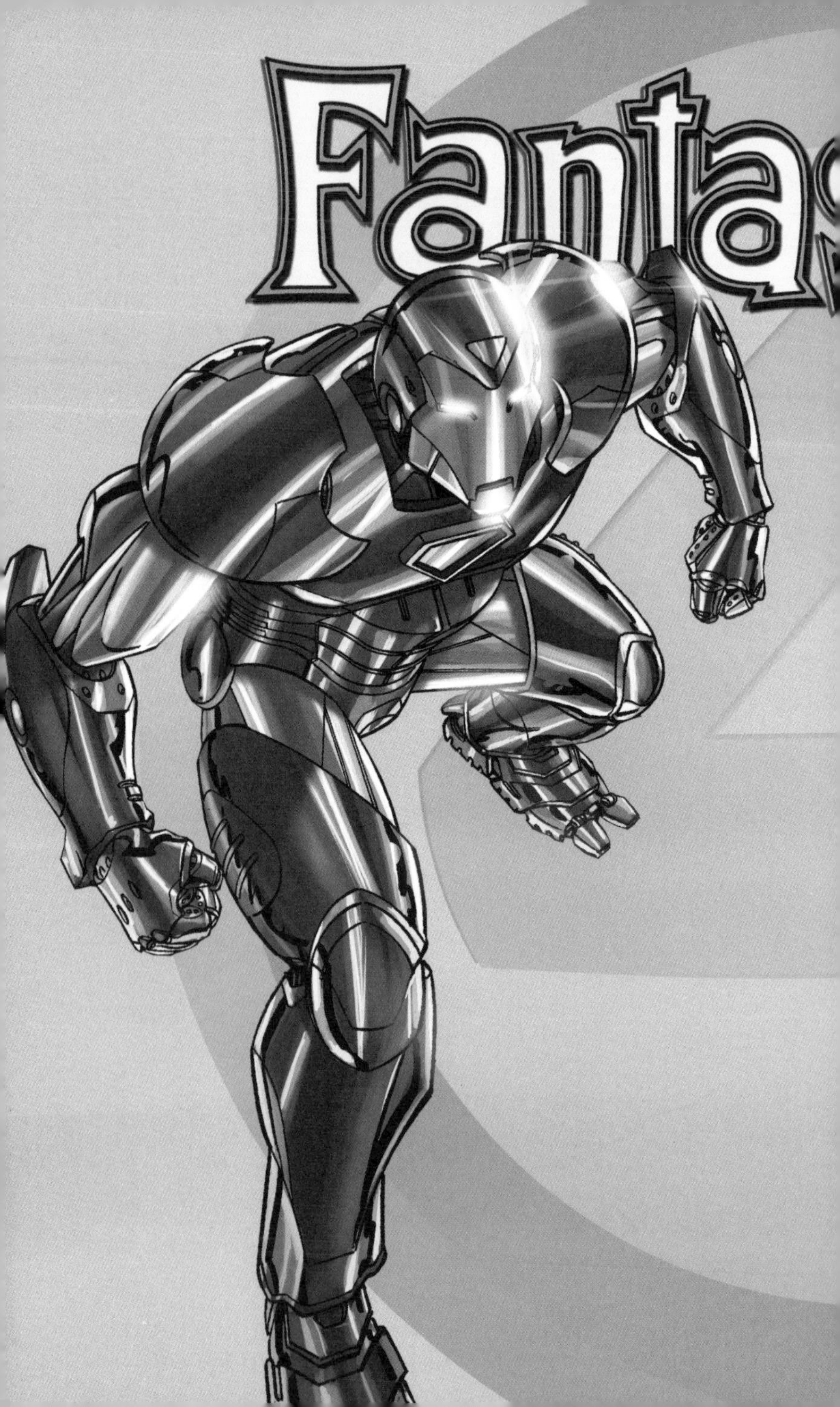
Fantas

tic Four

SPACED CRUSADERS

Writers:
Chris Eliopoulos
with **Joe Caramagna**
Pencilers:
**Ronan Cliquet, Graham Nolan
& Scott Koblish** with **Matteo Lolli**
Inkers:
**Amilton Santos, Graham Nolan &
Scott Koblish** with **Christian Vecchia**

Colorists: **Guillem Mari & Ulises Arreola**
Letterer: **Blambot's Nate Piekos**
Cover Art: **Graham Nolan & Brad Anderson; Carlo
Pagulayan, Jeffrey Huet & Guru eFX; Salvador Espin &
Brad Anderson; and Clayton Henry & Guru eFX**
Consulting Editor: **Mark Paniccia**
Editor: **Nathan Cosby**

Collection Editor: **Jennifer Grünwald**
Editorial Assistant: **Alex Starbuck**
Assistant Editors: **Cory Levine & John Denning**
Editor, Special Projects: **Mark D. Beazley**
Senior Editor, Special Projects: **Jeff Youngquist**
Senior Vice President of Sales: **David Gabriel**
Vice President of Creative: **Tom Marvelli**

Editor in Chief: **Joe Quesada**
Publisher: **Dan Buckley**

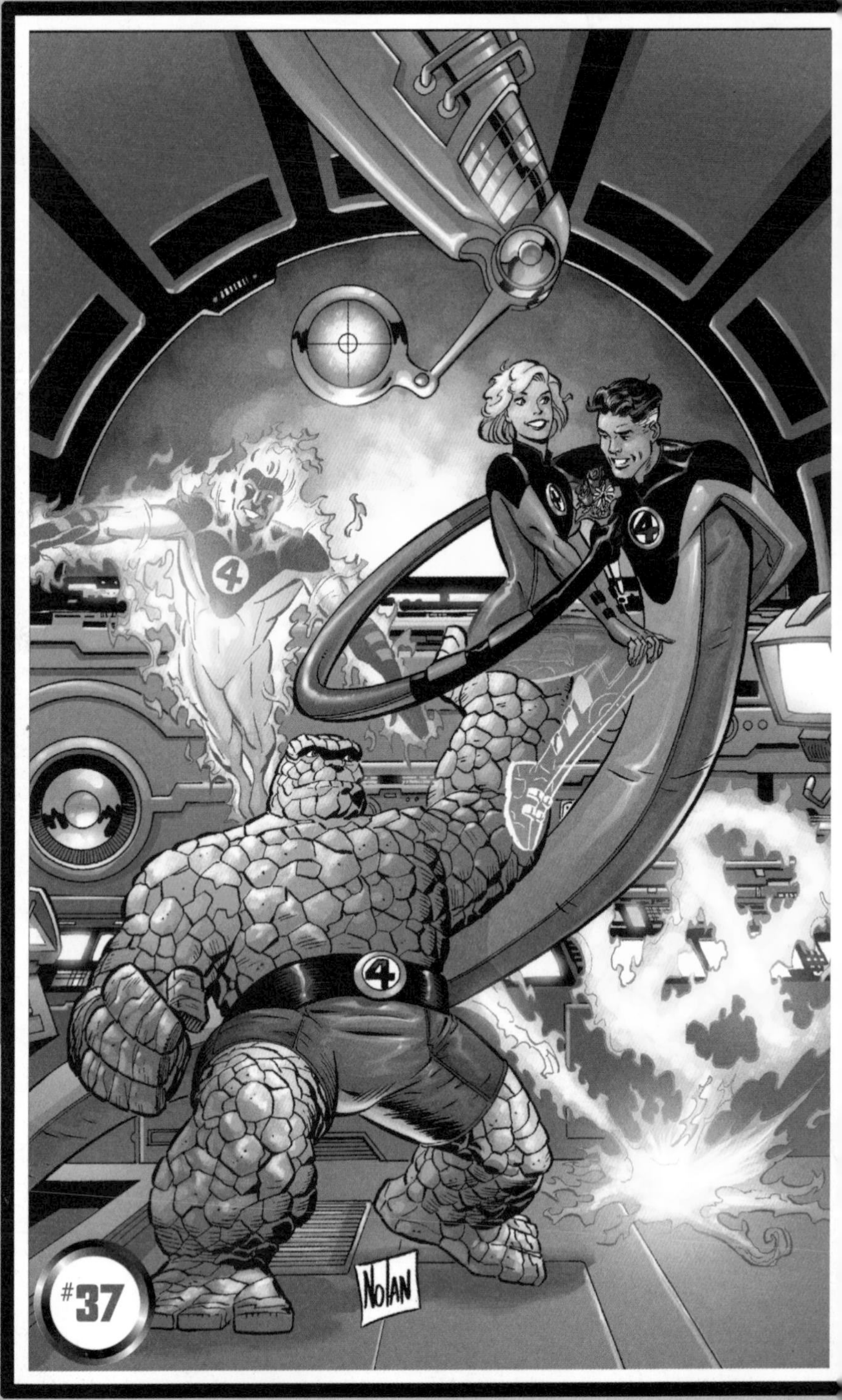
#37
NOLAN

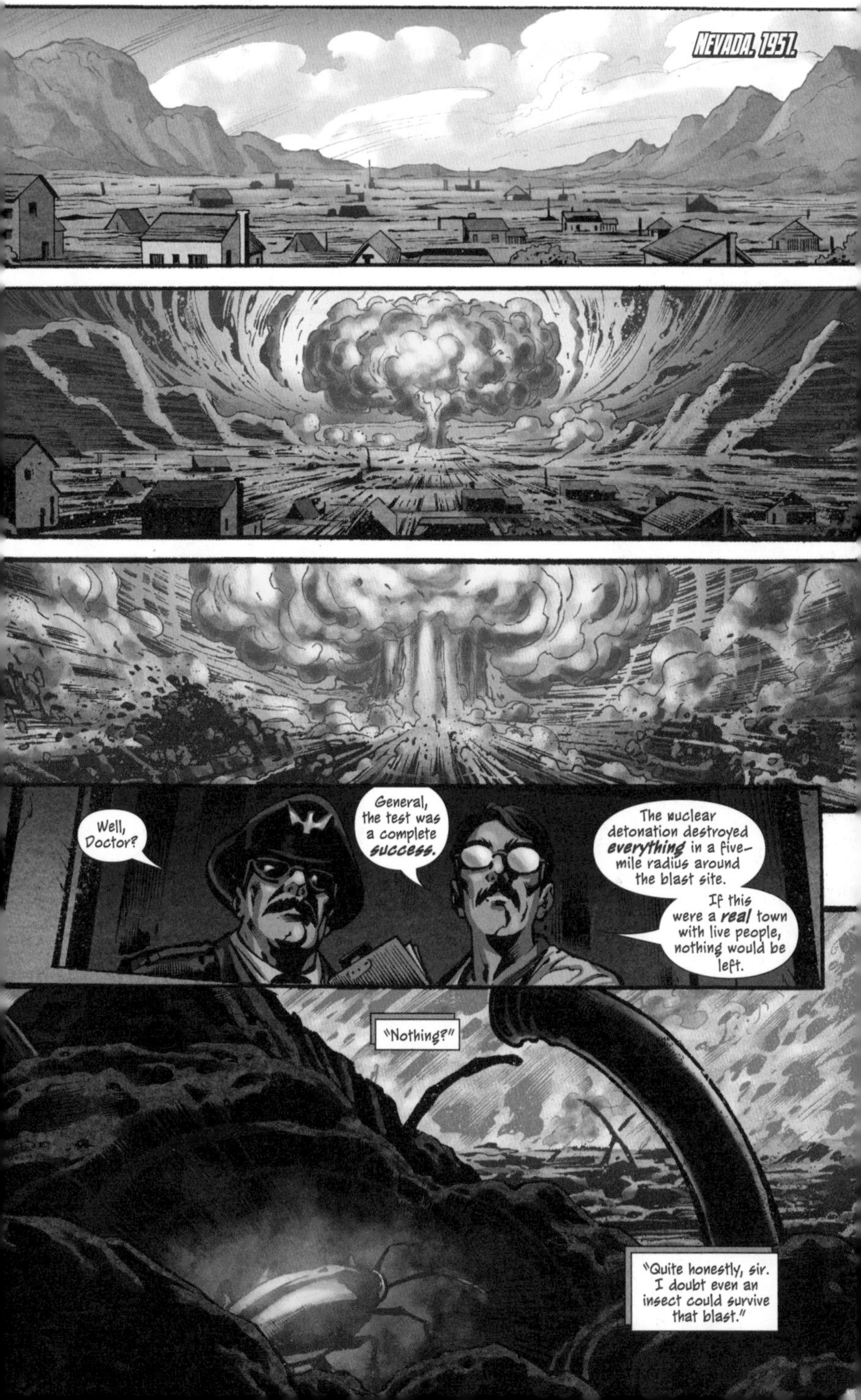
NEVADA, 1951.
Well, Doctor?
General, the test was a complete success.
The nuclear detonation destroyed everything in a five-mile radius around the blast site.
If this were a real town with live people, nothing would be left.
"Nothing?"
"Quite honestly, sir. I doubt even an insect could survive that blast."

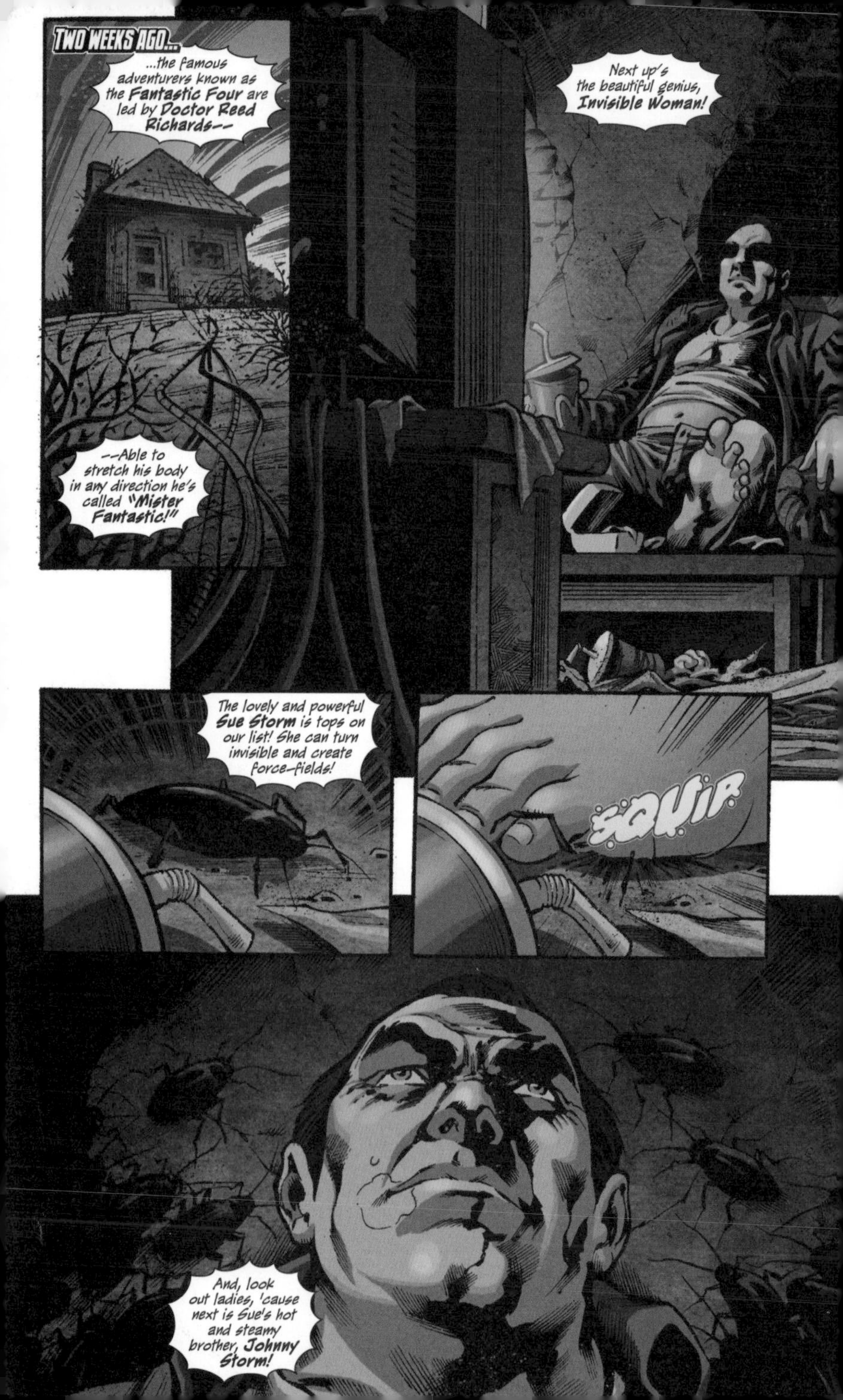
TWO WEEKS AGO...
...the famous adventurers known as the Fantastic Four are led by Doctor Reed Richards--
--Able to stretch his body in any direction he's called "Mister Fantastic!"
Next up's the beautiful genius, Invisible Woman!
The lovely and powerful Sue Storm is tops on our list! She can turn invisible and create force-fields!
SQUIP
And, look out ladies, 'cause next is Sue's hot and steamy brother, Johnny Storm!

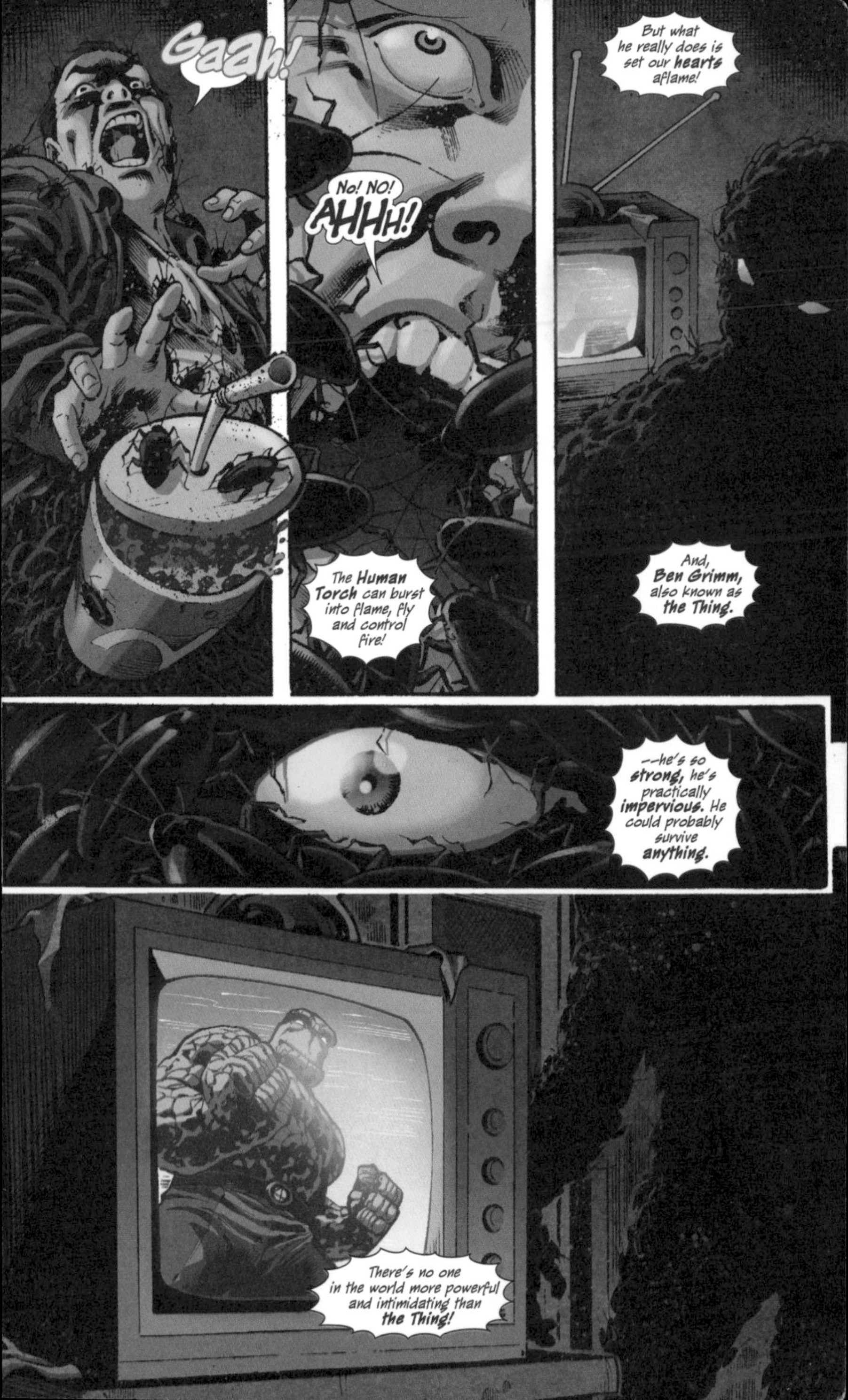
Gaah!
No! NO! AHHH!
The Human Torch can burst into flame, fly and control fire!
But what he really does is set our hearts aflame!
And, Ben Grimm, also known as the Thing.
--he's so strong, he's practically impervious. He could probably survive anything.
There's no one in the world more powerful and intimidating than the Thing!

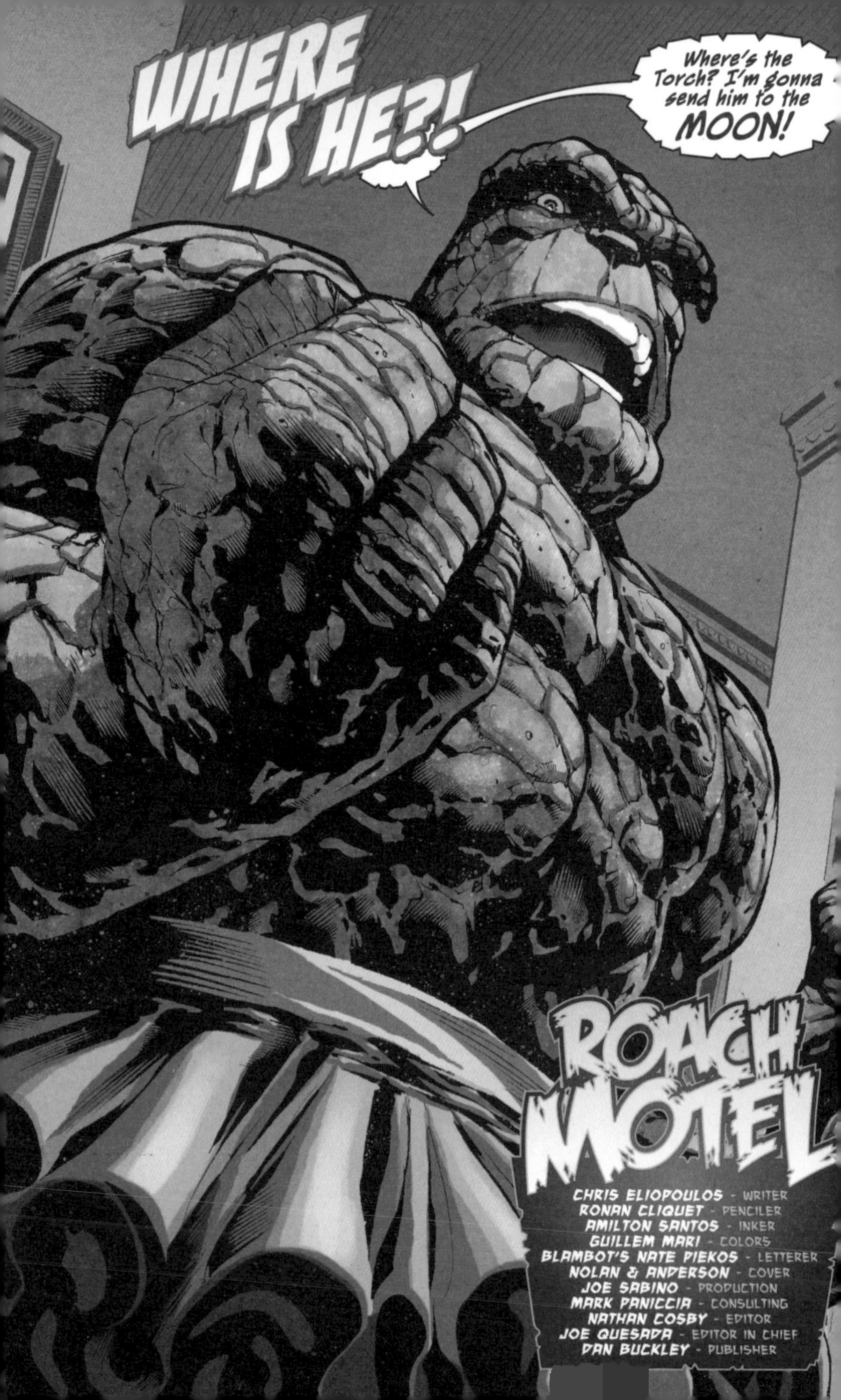
WHERE IS HE?!
Where's the Torch? I'm gonna send him to the MOON!
ROACH MOTEL
CHRIS ELIOPOULOS - WRITER
RONAN CLIQUET - PENCILER
AMILTON SANTOS - INKER
GUILLEM MARI - COLORS
BLAMBOT'S NATE PIEKOS - LETTERER
NOLAN & ANDERSON - COVER
JOE SABINO - PRODUCTION
MARK PANICCIA - CONSULTING
NATHAN COSBY - EDITOR
JOE QUESADA - EDITOR IN CHIEF
DAN BUCKLEY - PUBLISHER

Oh, Ben, I didn't know you were *so* into the ballet.

How'd Johnny trick you into that costume *this* time?

I don't wanna *talk* about it. I'm just gonna *pound* him.

That punk doesn't care about anyone but himself and his *cheap laughs.*

Come on, Ben. You know when push comes to shove, Johnny would do *anything* for you. He's just having a little--

beep

Pardon me, Mr. Grimm.

This is Roberta in reception. There is a gentleman here to see you.

I ain't expecting anyone.

He says he does not have an appointment, but says he *must* see you. It is of *vital* importance.

All his credentials check out, sir, and all scans indicate he is *not* a danger or threat.

Ah. Awright. Send 'im up. I'll meet 'im in a minute...

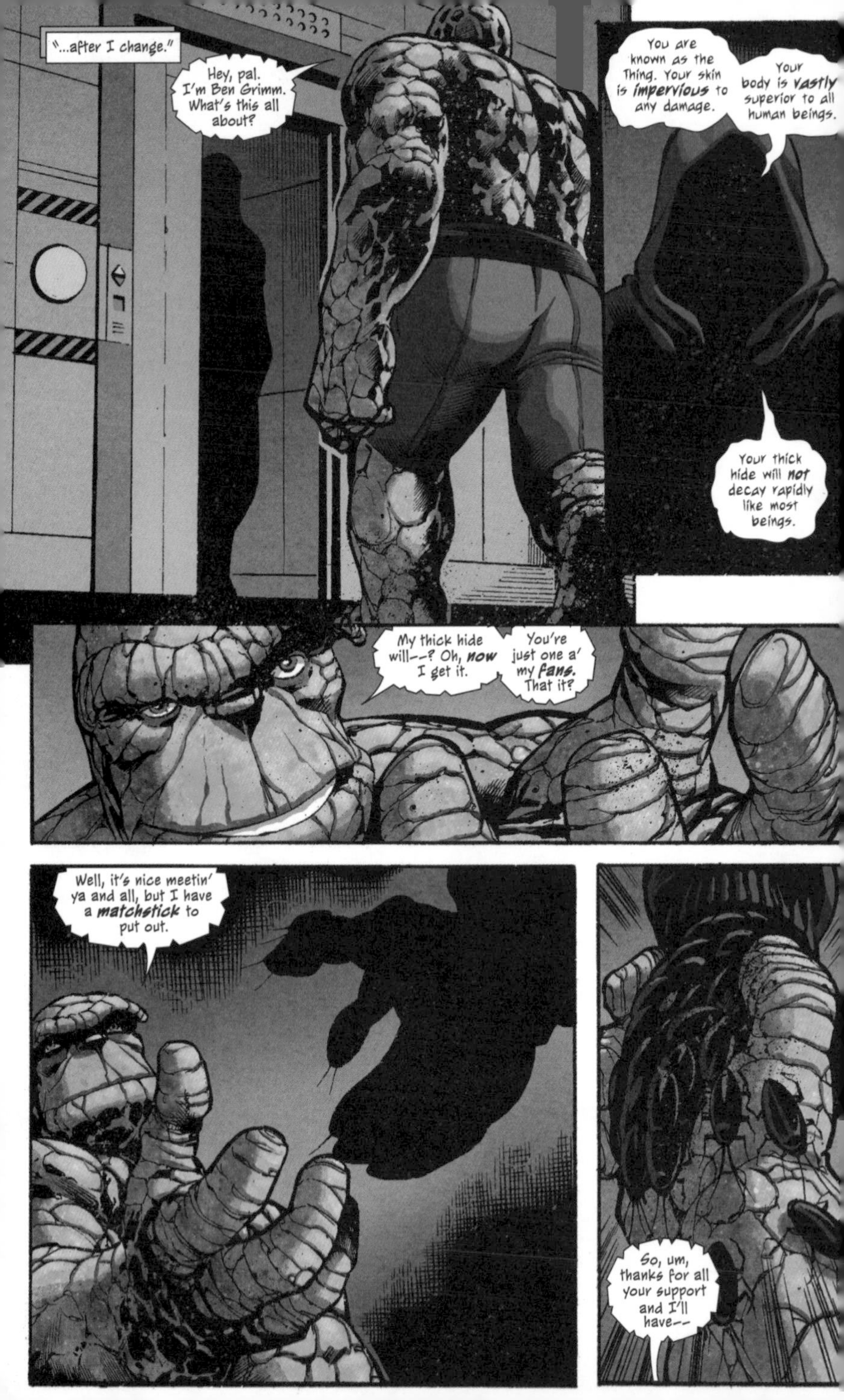
"...after I change."
Hey, pal. I'm Ben Grimm. What's this all about?
You are known as the Thing. Your skin is impervious to any damage.
Your body is vastly superior to all human beings.
Your thick hide will not decay rapidly like most beings.
My thick hide will--? Oh, now I get it.
You're just one a' my fans. That it?
Well, it's nice meetin' ya and all, but I have a matchstick to put out.
So, um, thanks for all your support and I'll have--

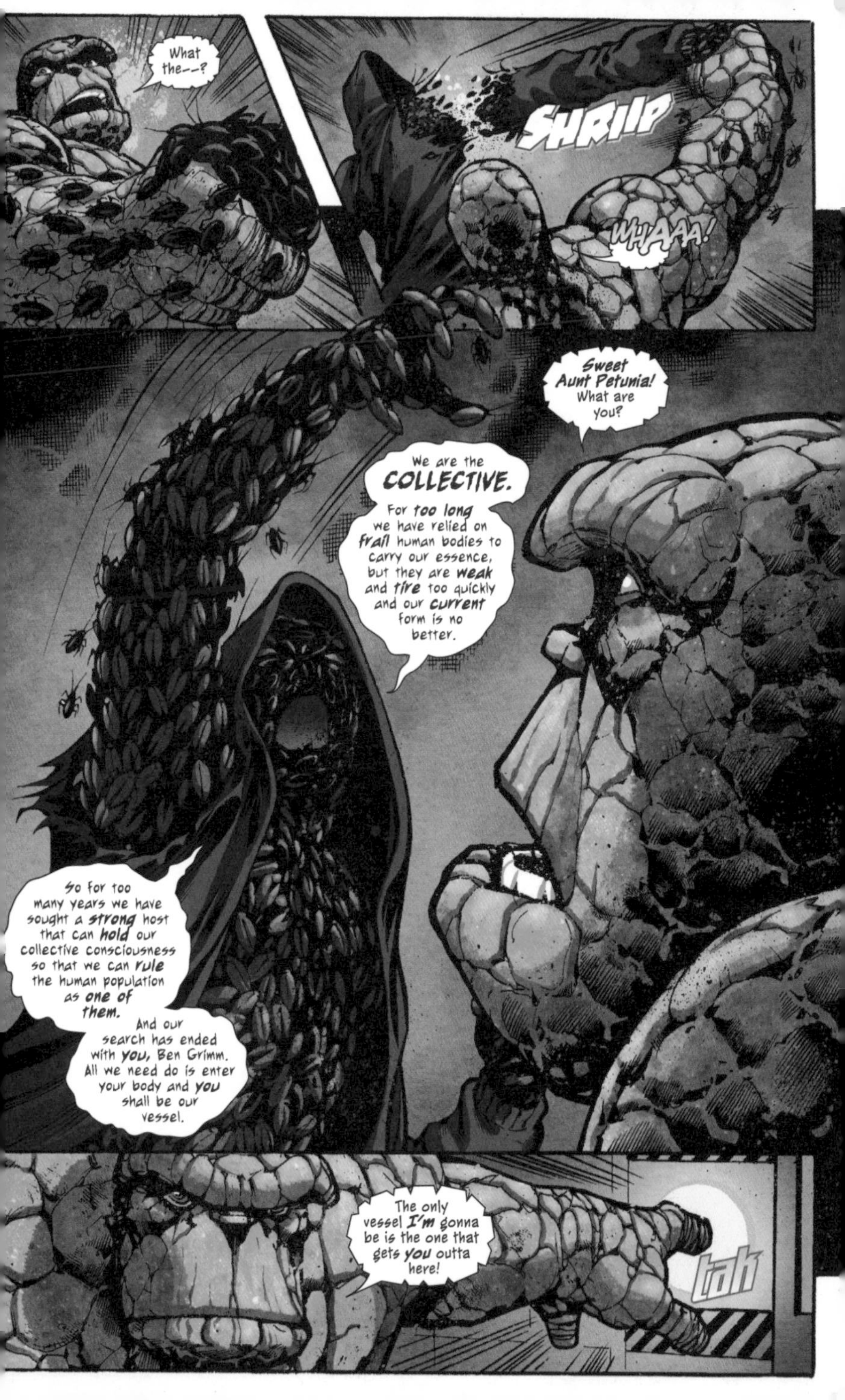
What the--?
SHRIIP
WHAAA!
Sweet Aunt Petunia! What are you?
We are the COLLECTIVE.
For too long we have relied on frail human bodies to carry our essence, but they are weak and tire too quickly and our current form is no better.
So for too many years we have sought a strong host that can hold our collective consciousness so that we can rule the human population as one of them.
And our search has ended with you, Ben Grimm. All we need do is enter your body and you shall be our vessel.
The only vessel I'm gonna be is the one that gets you outta here!
tak

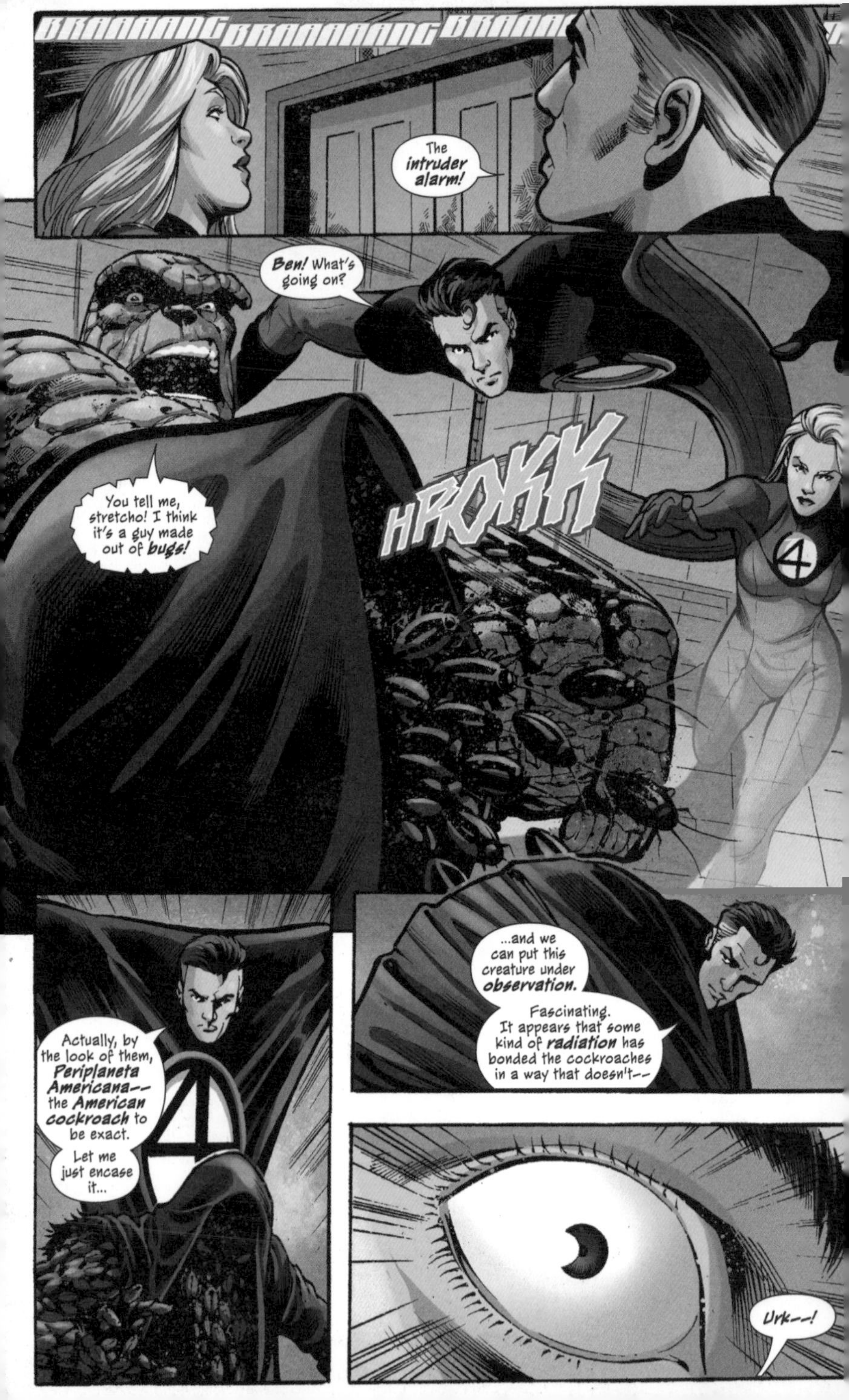

BRAAAAANG BRAAAAANG BRAAAA
The intruder alarm!
Ben! What's going on?
You tell me, stretcho! I think it's a guy made out of bugs!
HROKK
Actually, by the look of them, Periplaneta Americana-- the American cockroach to be exact.
Let me just encase it...
...and we can put this creature under observation.
Fascinating. It appears that some kind of radiation has bonded the cockroaches in a way that doesn't--
Urk--!

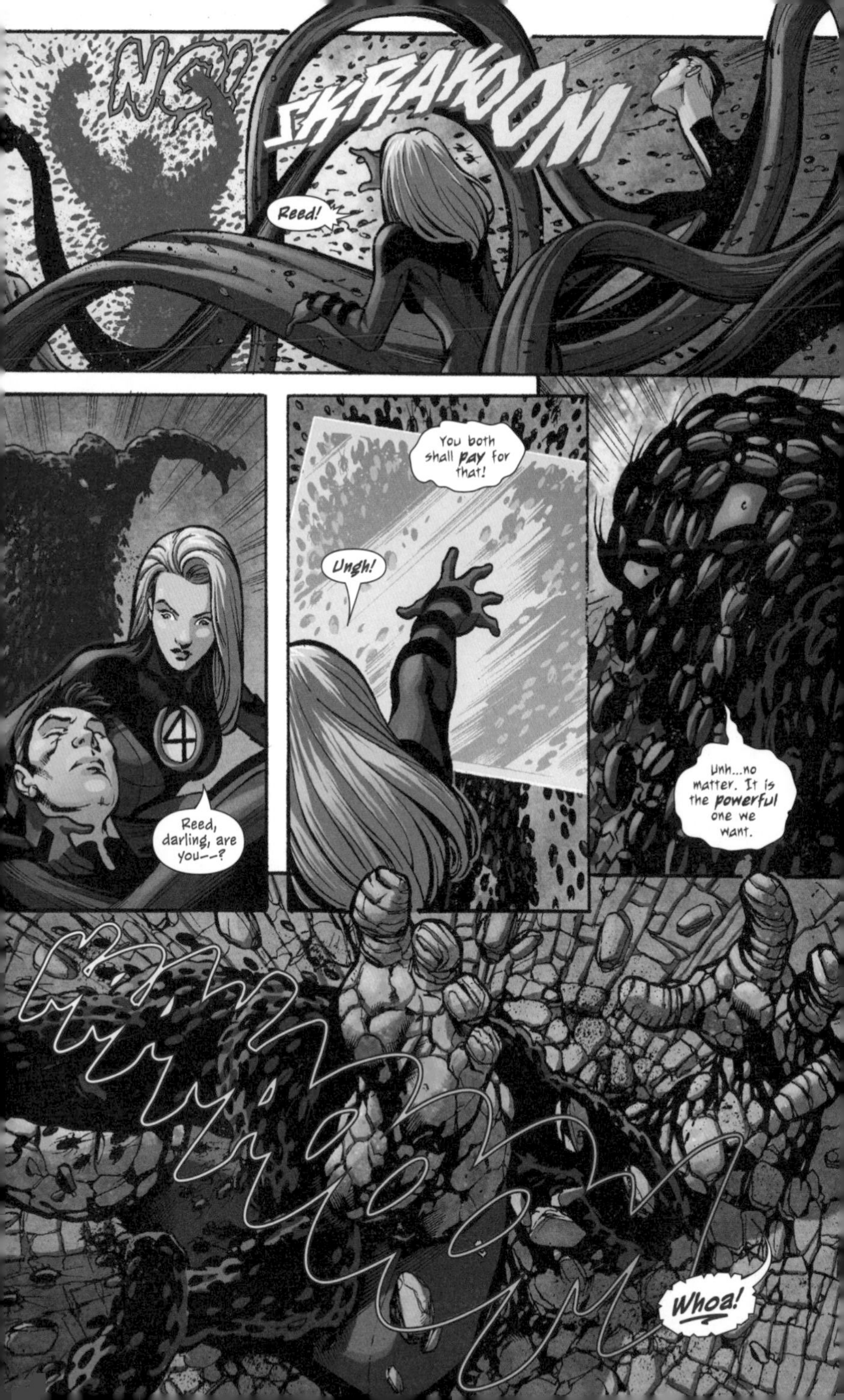
NO
SKRAKOOM
Reed!
Reed, darling, are you--?
You both shall pay for that!
Ungh!
Unh...no matter. It is the powerful one we want.
Whoa!

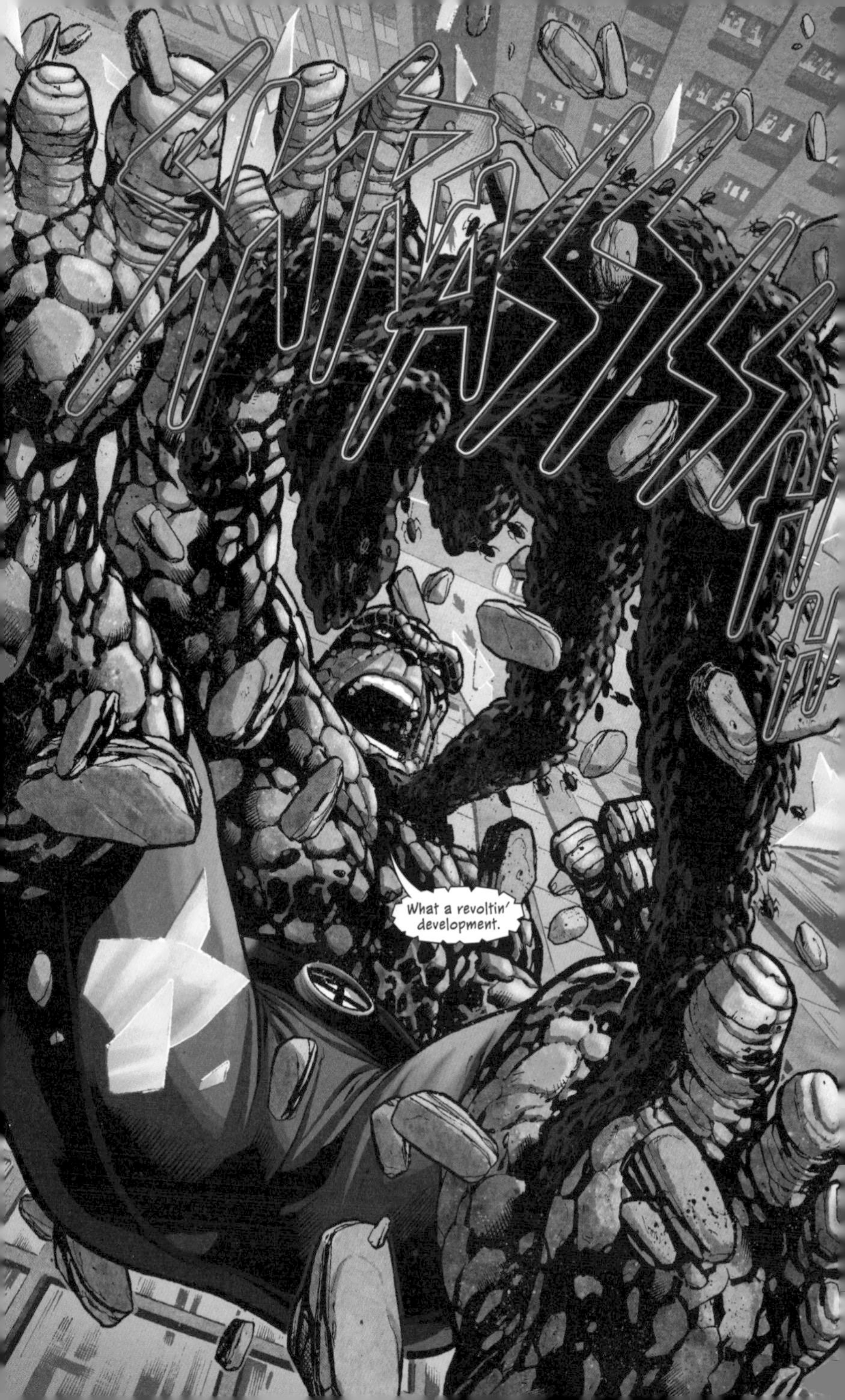
What a revoltin' development.

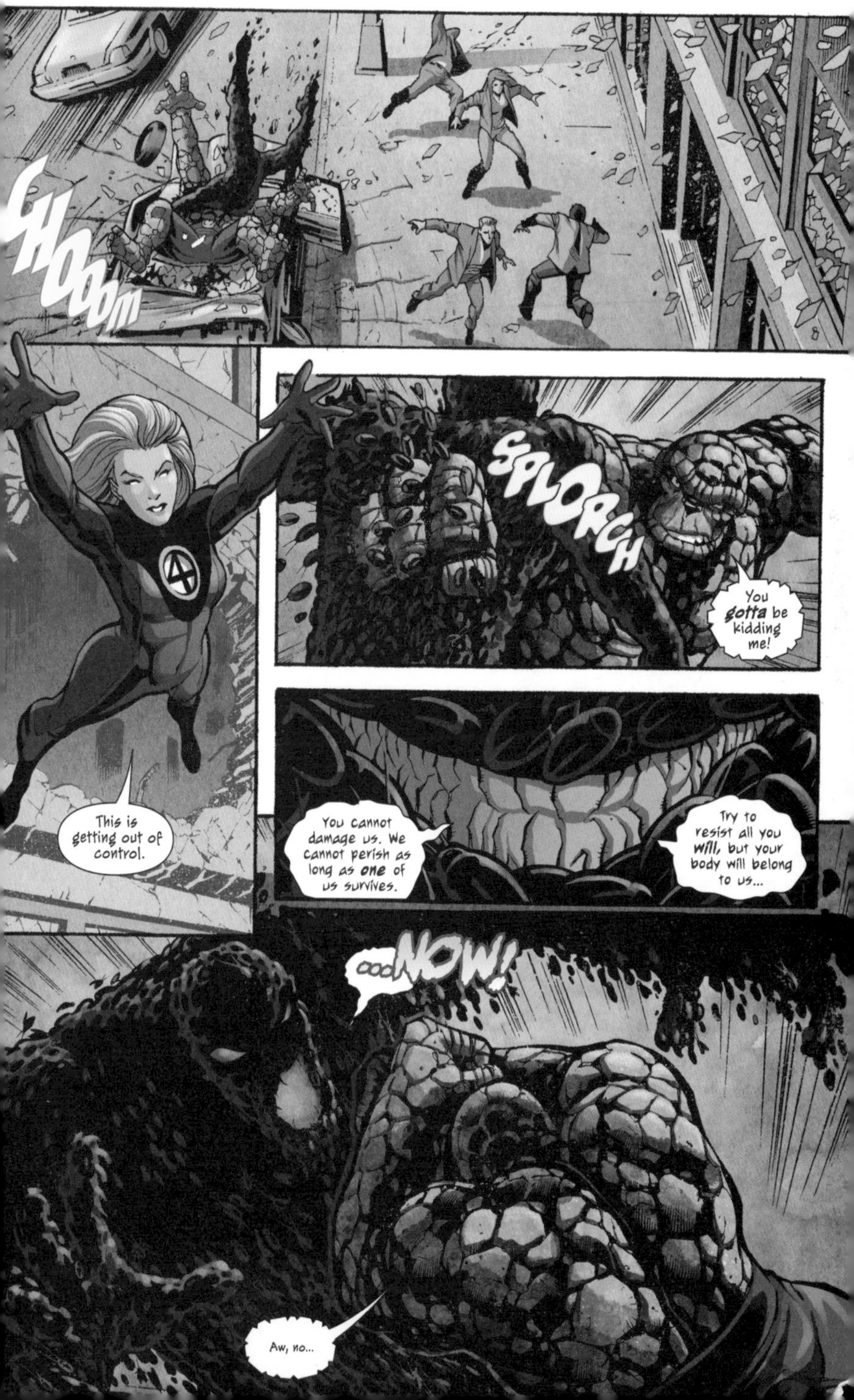
CHOOOOM
SPLORCH
You gotta be kidding me!
This is getting out of control.
You cannot damage us. We cannot perish as long as one of us survives.
Try to resist all you will, but your body will belong to us...
oooNOW!
Aw, no...

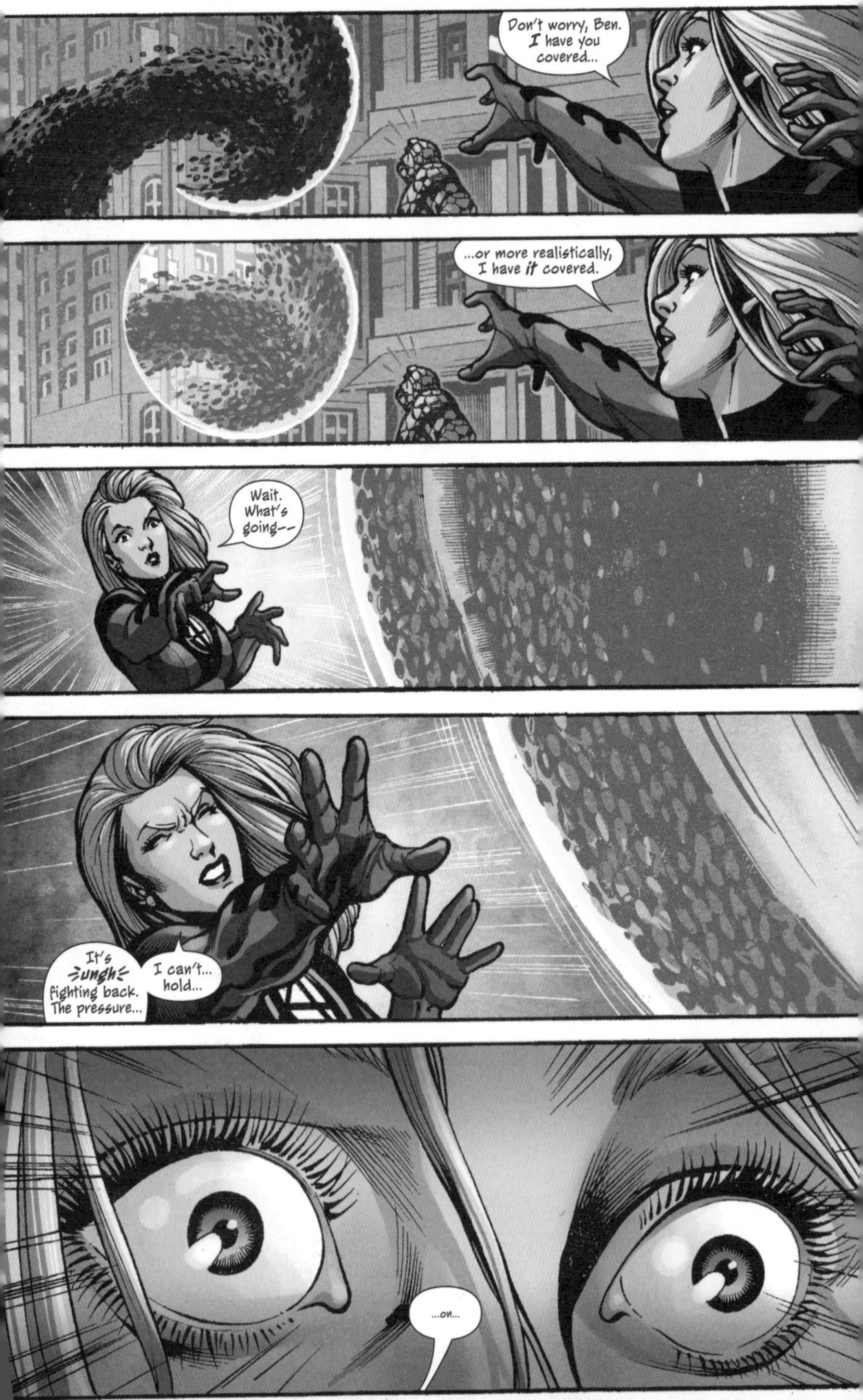
Don't worry, Ben. I have you covered...
...or more realistically, I have it covered.
Wait. What's going--
It's ungh fighting back. The pressure...
I can't... hold...
...on...

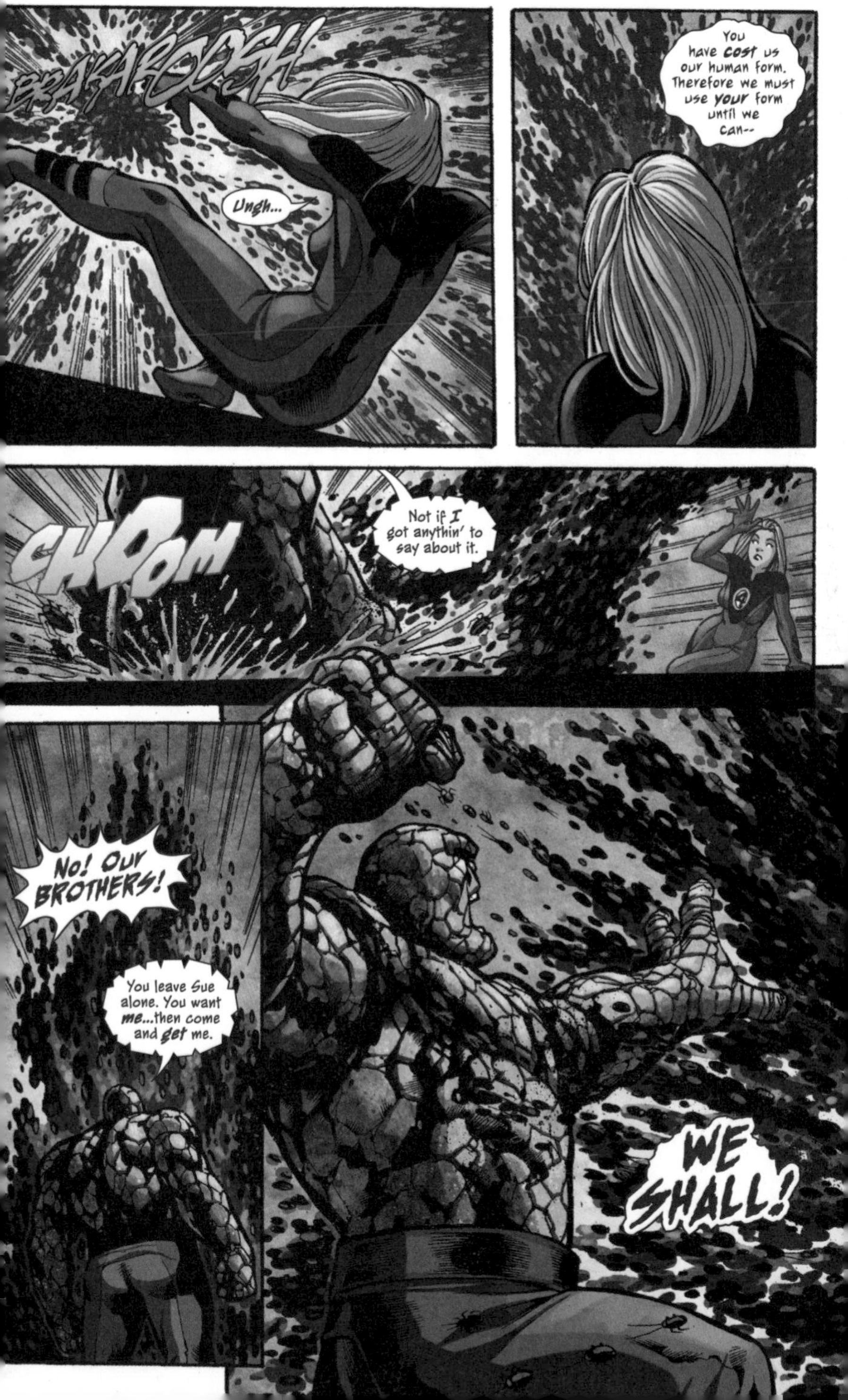
BRAKAROOSH
Ungh...
You have cost us our human form. Therefore we must use your form until we can--
CHOOM
Not if I got anythin' to say about it.
No! Our BROTHERS!
You leave Sue alone. You want me...then come and get me.
WE SHALL!

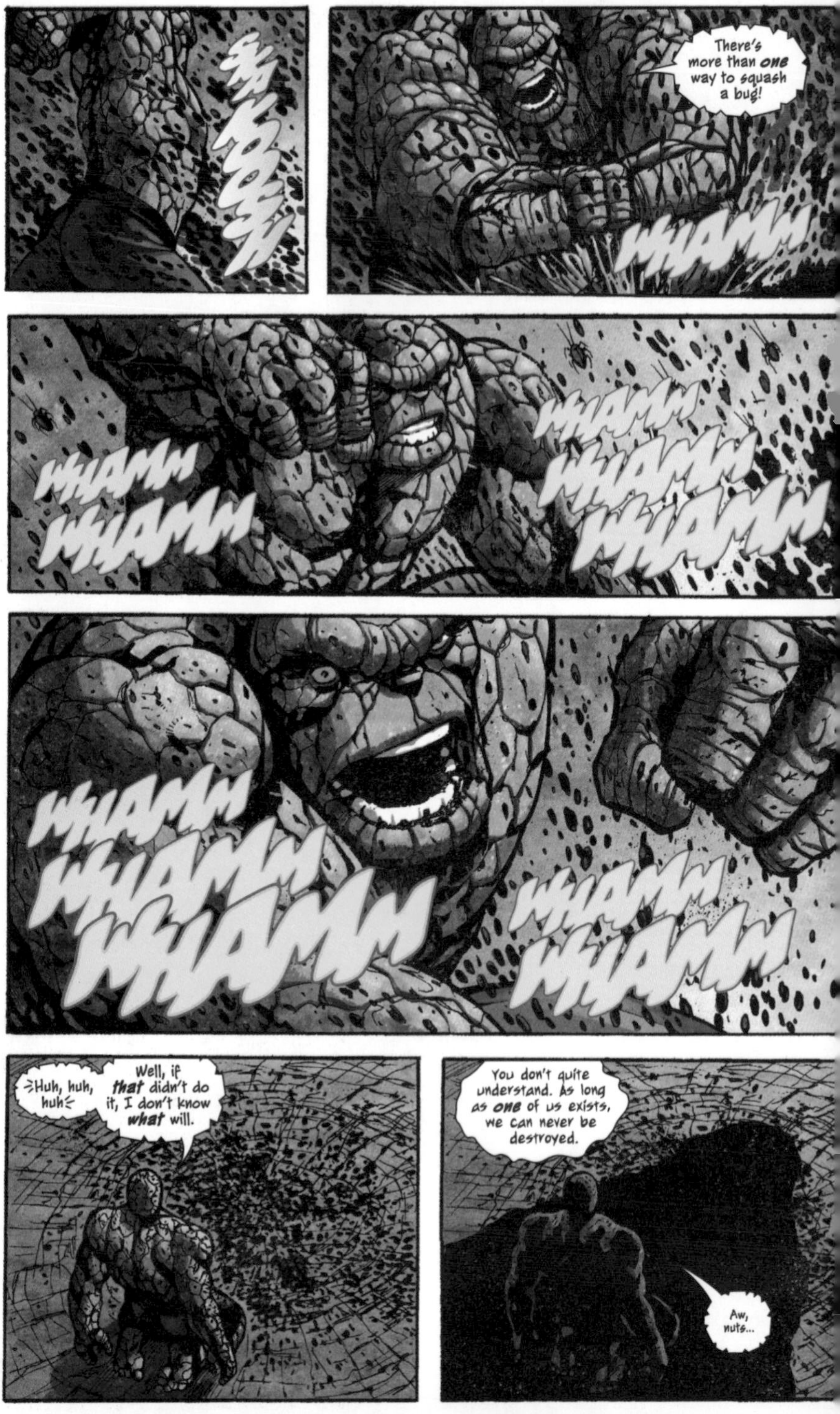

WHOOOSH
There's more than ONE way to squash a bug!
WHAMM
WHAMM
WHAMM
WHAMM
WHAMM
WHAMM
WHAMM
WHAMM
WHAMM
WHAMM
WHAMM
Huh, huh, huh
Well, if THAT didn't do it, I don't know WHAT will.
You don't quite understand. As long as ONE of us exists, we can never be destroyed.
Aw, nuts...

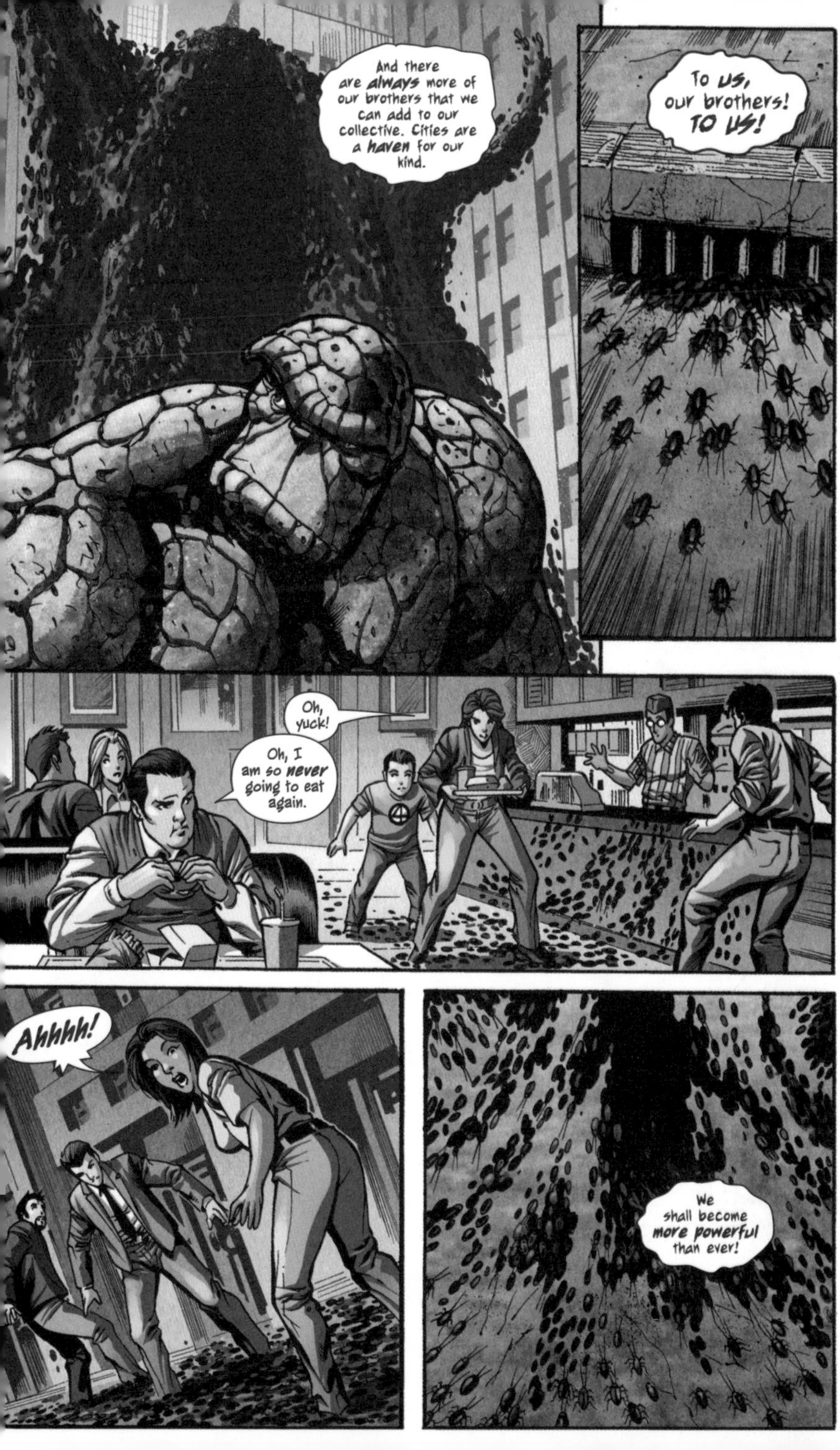
And there are always more of our brothers that we can add to our collective. Cities are a haven for our kind.
To us, our brothers! TO US!
Oh, yuck!
Oh, I am so never going to eat again.
Ahhhh!
We shall become more powerful than ever!

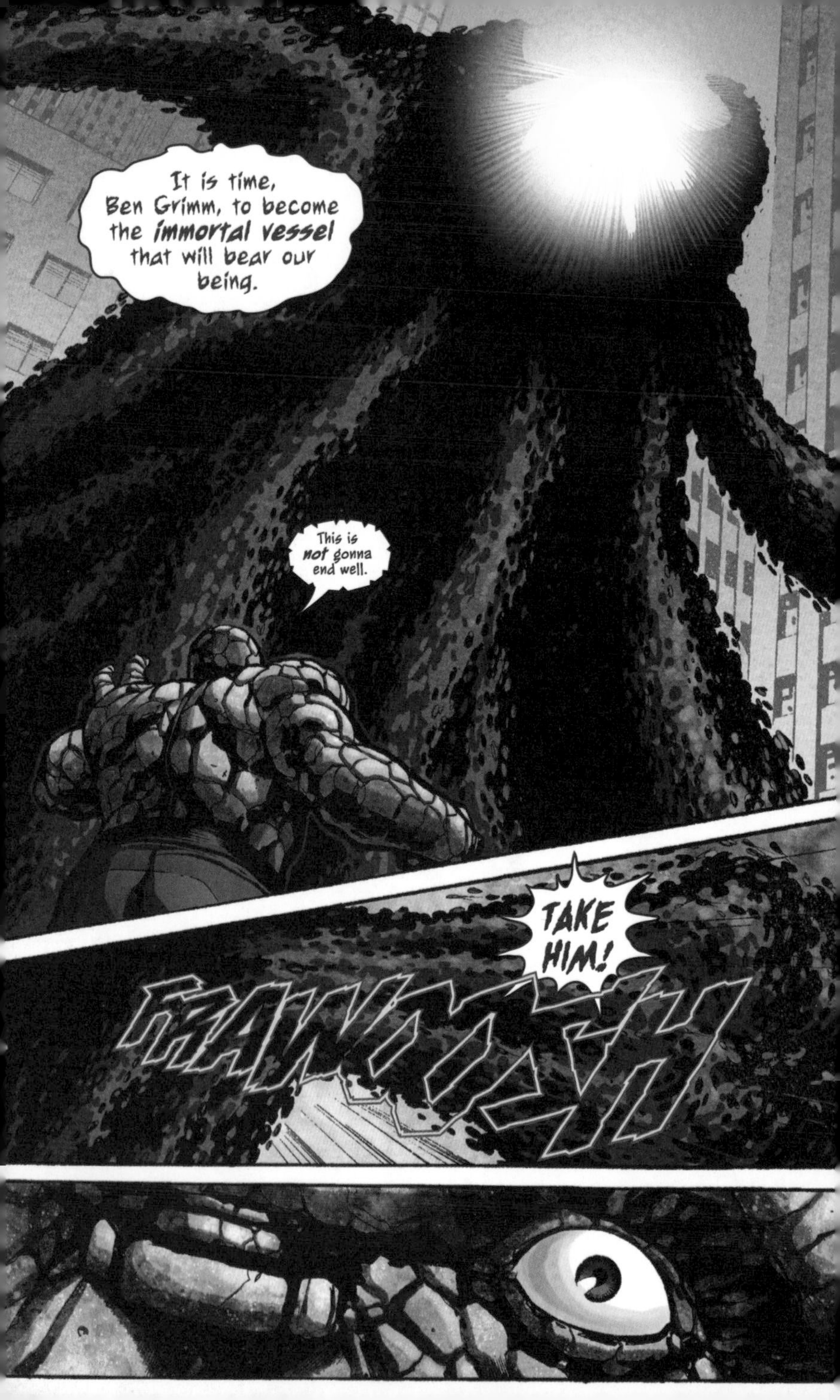
It is time, Ben Grimm, to become the *immortal vessel* that will bear our being.
This is *not* gonna end well.
TAKE HIM!
FRAKOOOSH

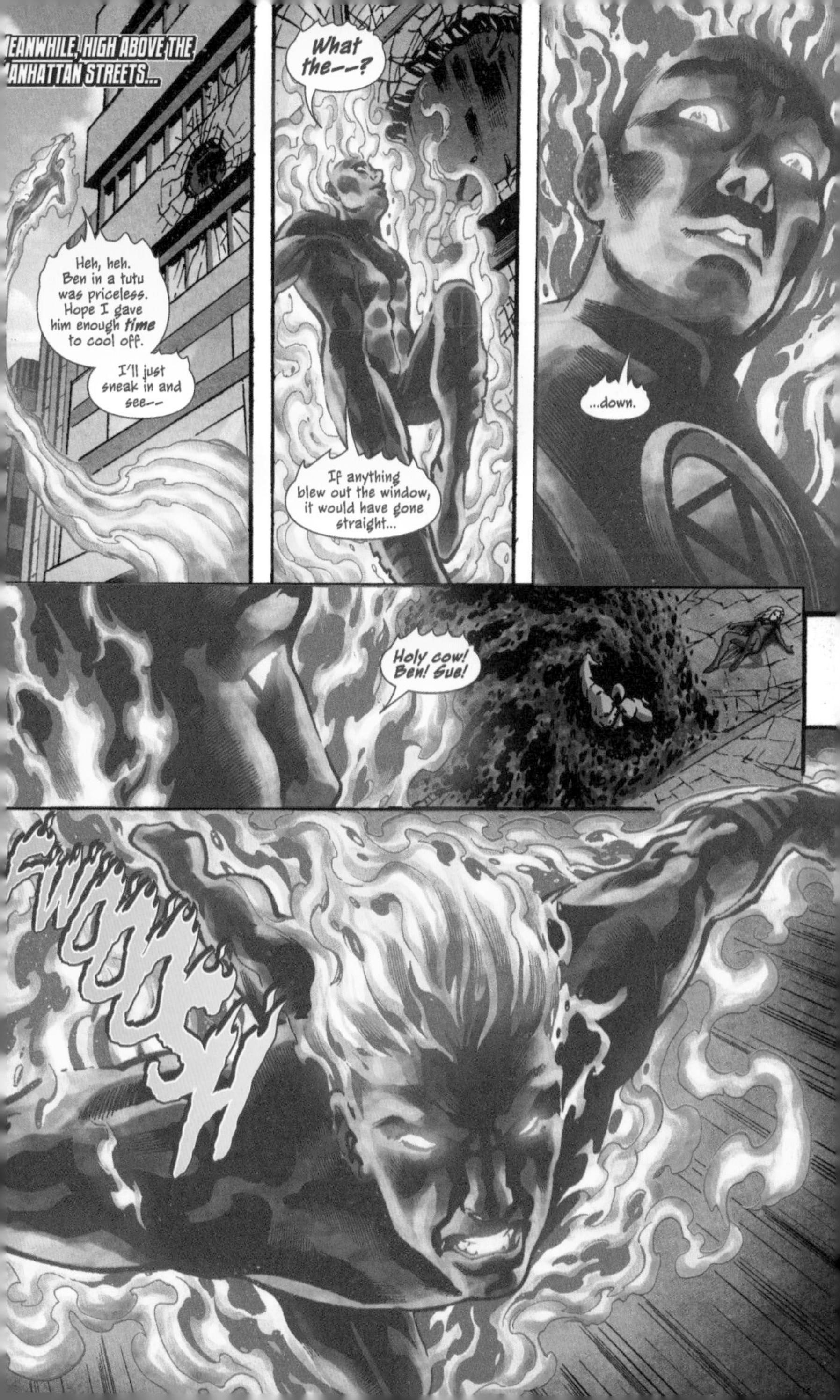
EANWHILE, HIGH ABOVE THE ANHATTAN STREETS...
Heh, heh. Ben in a tutu was priceless. Hope I gave him enough *time* to cool off.
I'll just sneak in and see--
What the--?
If anything blew out the window, it would have gone straight...
...down.
Holy cow! Ben! Sue!

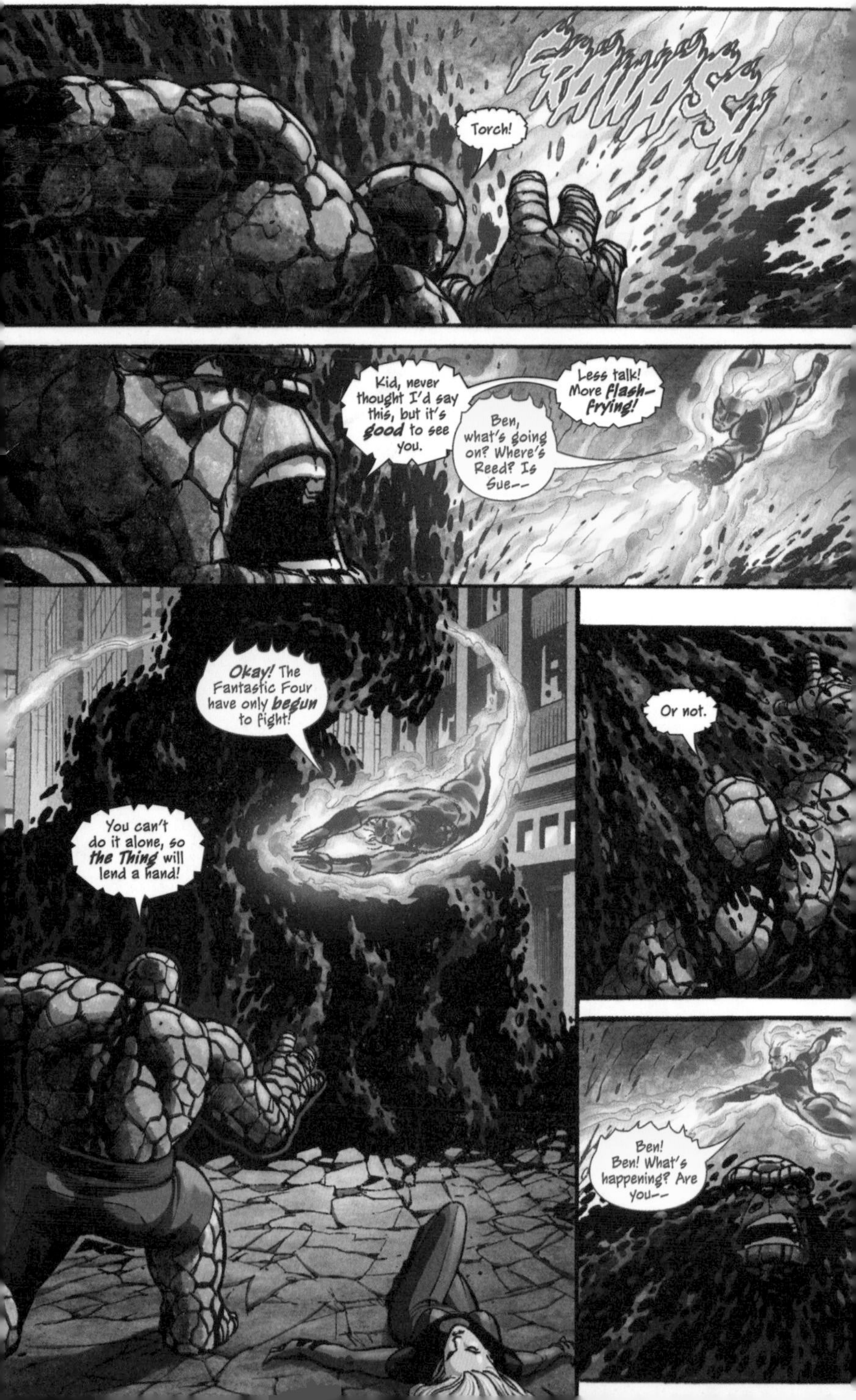
FRAWASH
Torch!
Kid, never thought I'd say this, but it's good to see you.
Less talk! More flash-frying!
Ben, what's going on? Where's Reed? Is Sue--
Okay! The Fantastic Four have only begun to fight!
You can't do it alone, so the Thing will lend a hand!
Or not.
Ben! Ben! What's happening? Are you--

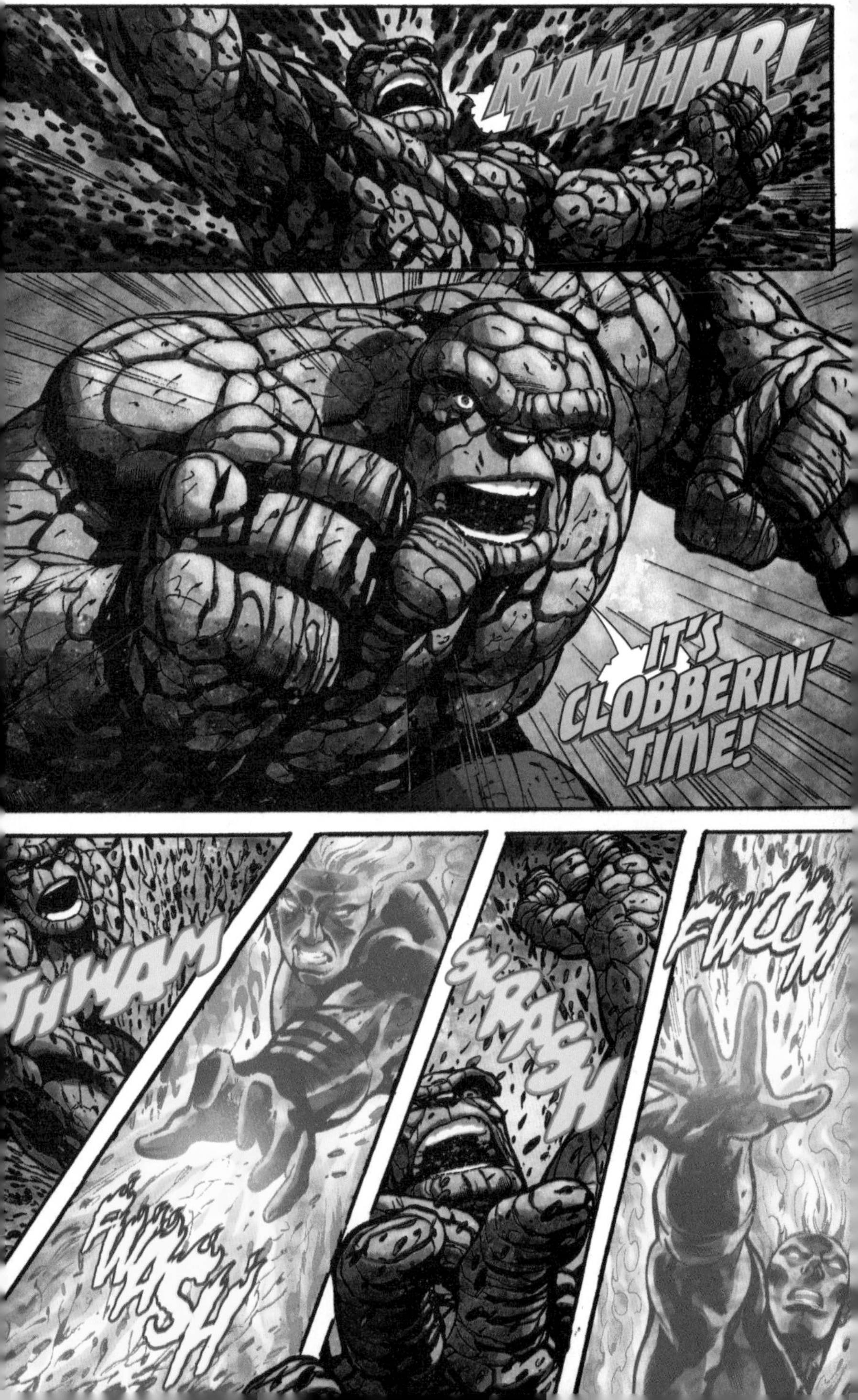
RAAAHHHR!
IT'S CLOBBERIN' TIME!
THWAM
FWASH
SKRASH
FWOOM

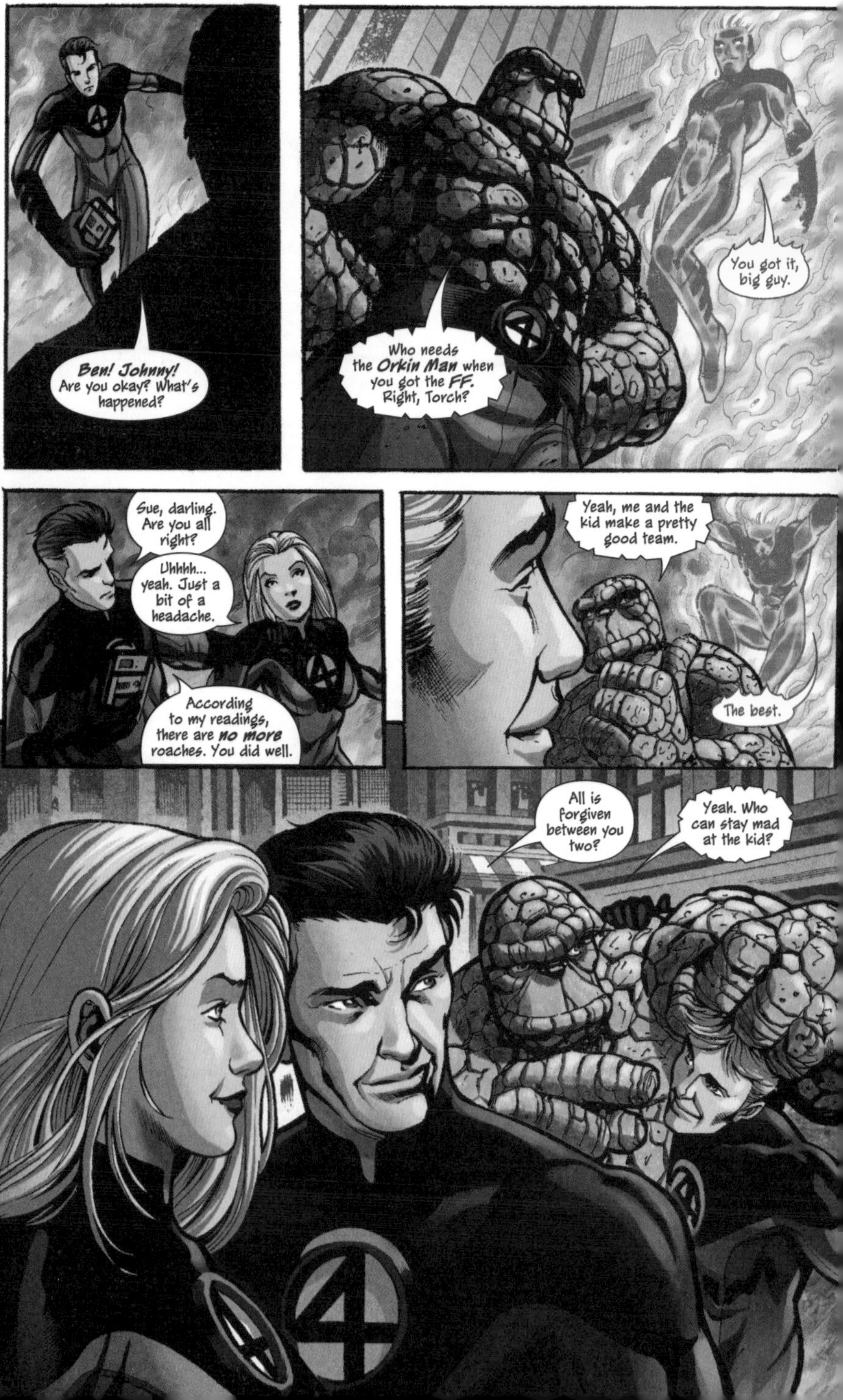

Ben! Johnny! Are you okay? What's happened?
Who needs the Orkin Man when you got the FF. Right, Torch?
You got it, big guy.
Sue, darling. Are you all right?
Uhhhh... yeah. Just a bit of a headache.
According to my readings, there are no more roaches. You did well.
Yeah, me and the kid make a pretty good team.
The best.
All is forgiven between you two?
Yeah. Who can stay mad at the kid?

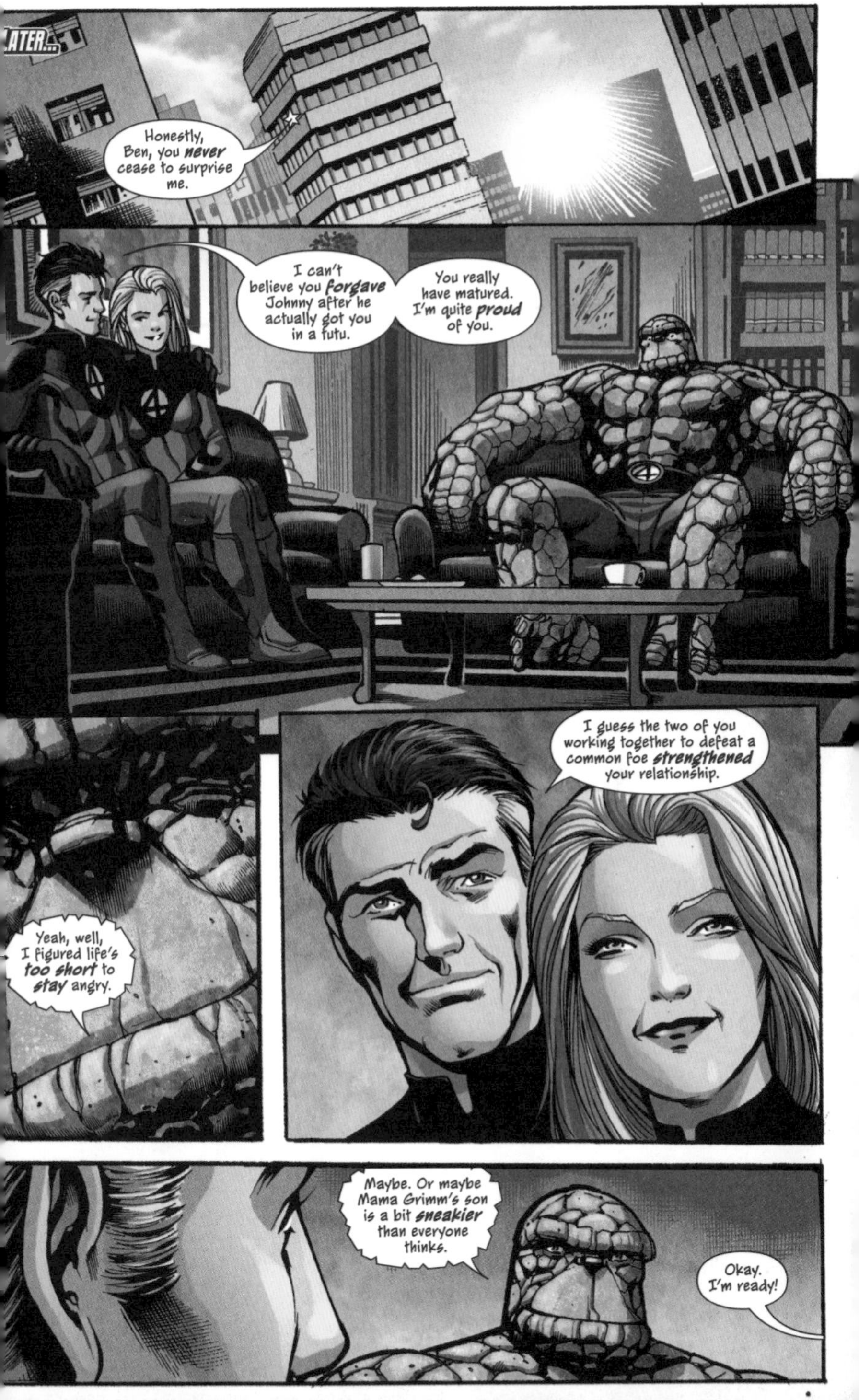
LATER...
Honestly, Ben, you never cease to surprise me.
I can't believe you forgave Johnny after he actually got you in a tutu.
You really have matured. I'm quite proud of you.
Yeah, well, I figured life's too short to stay angry.
I guess the two of you working together to defeat a common foe strengthened your relationship.
Maybe. Or maybe Mama Grimm's son is a bit sneakier than everyone thinks.
Okay. I'm ready!

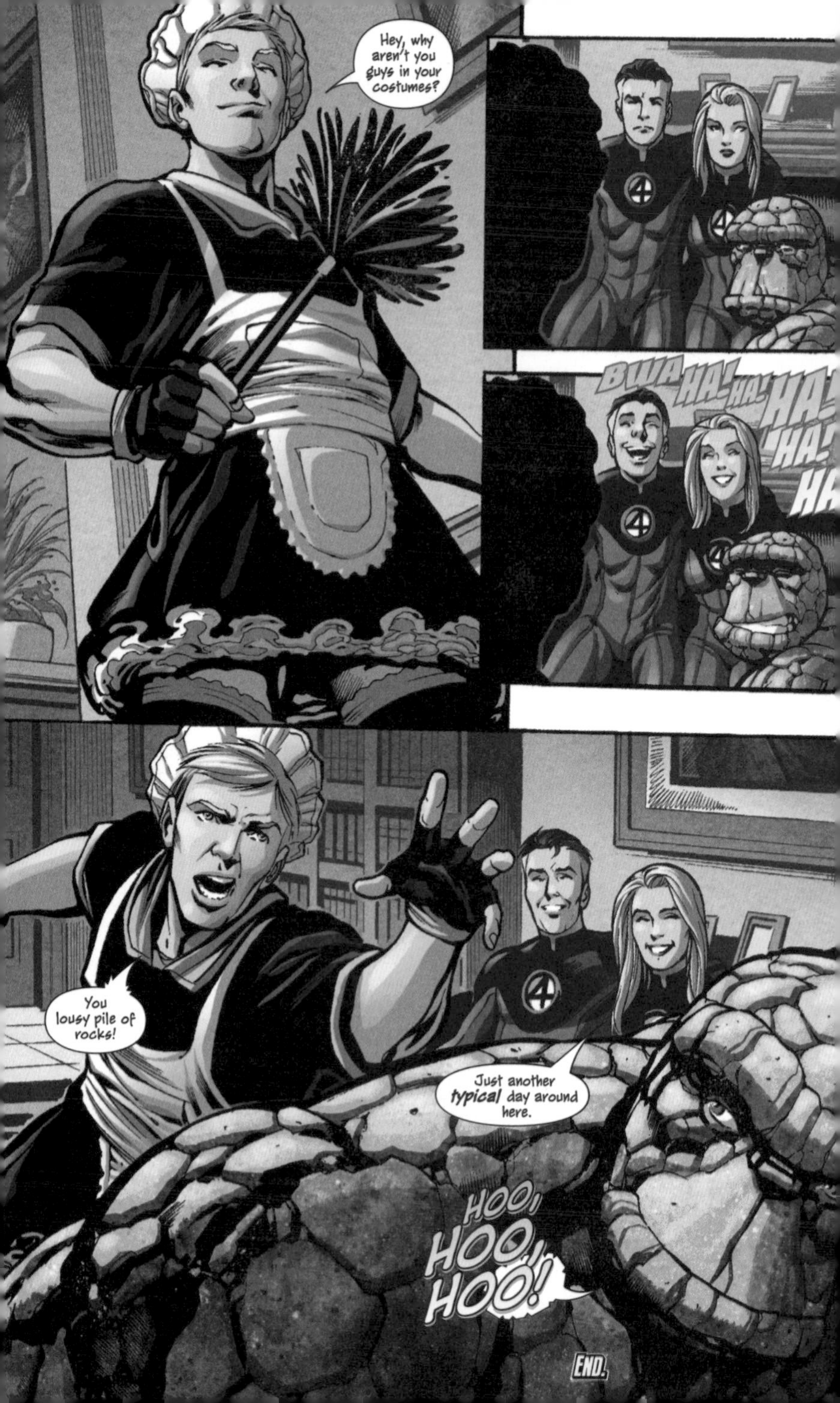
Hey, why aren't you guys in your costumes?
BWA HA! HA! HA! HA! HA
You lousy pile of rocks!
Just another *typical* day around here.
HOO, HOO, HOO!
END.

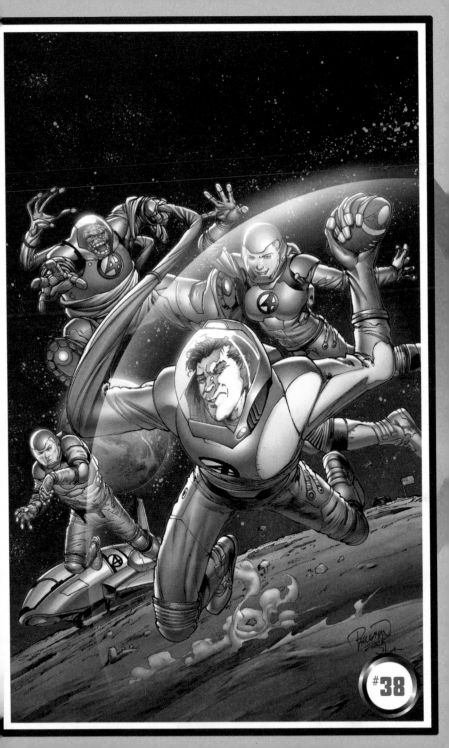

#38

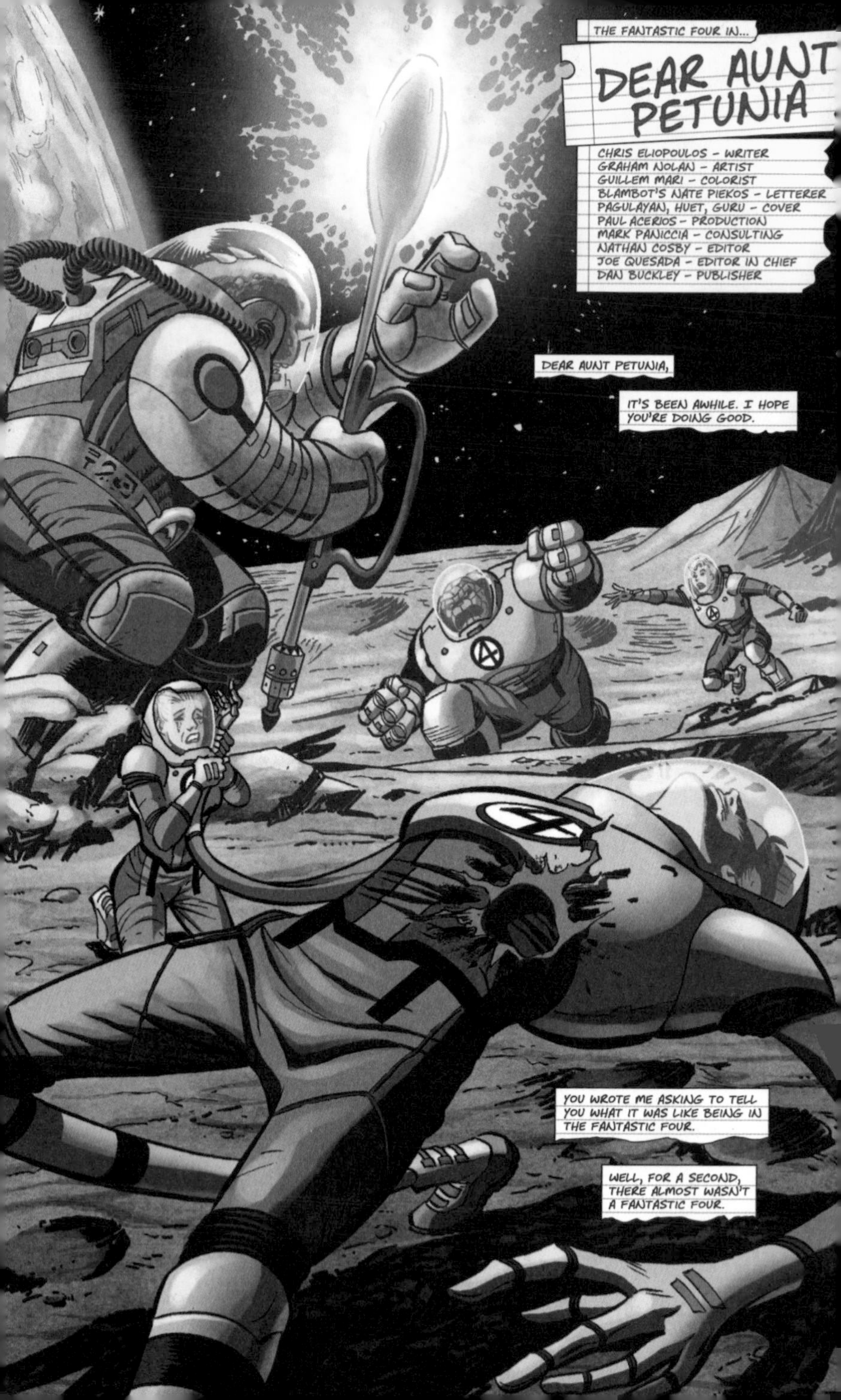

THE FANTASTIC FOUR IN...
DEAR AUNT PETUNIA
CHRIS ELIOPOULOS - WRITER
GRAHAM NOLAN - ARTIST
GUILLEM MARI - COLORIST
BLAMBOT'S NATE PIEKOS - LETTERER
PAGULAYAN, HUET, GURU - COVER
PAUL ACERIOS - PRODUCTION
MARK PANICCIA - CONSULTING
NATHAN COSBY - EDITOR
JOE QUESADA - EDITOR IN CHIEF
DAN BUCKLEY - PUBLISHER
DEAR AUNT PETUNIA,
IT'S BEEN AWHILE. I HOPE YOU'RE DOING GOOD.
YOU WROTE ME ASKING TO TELL YOU WHAT IT WAS LIKE BEING IN THE FANTASTIC FOUR.
WELL, FOR A SECOND, THERE ALMOST WASN'T A FANTASTIC FOUR.

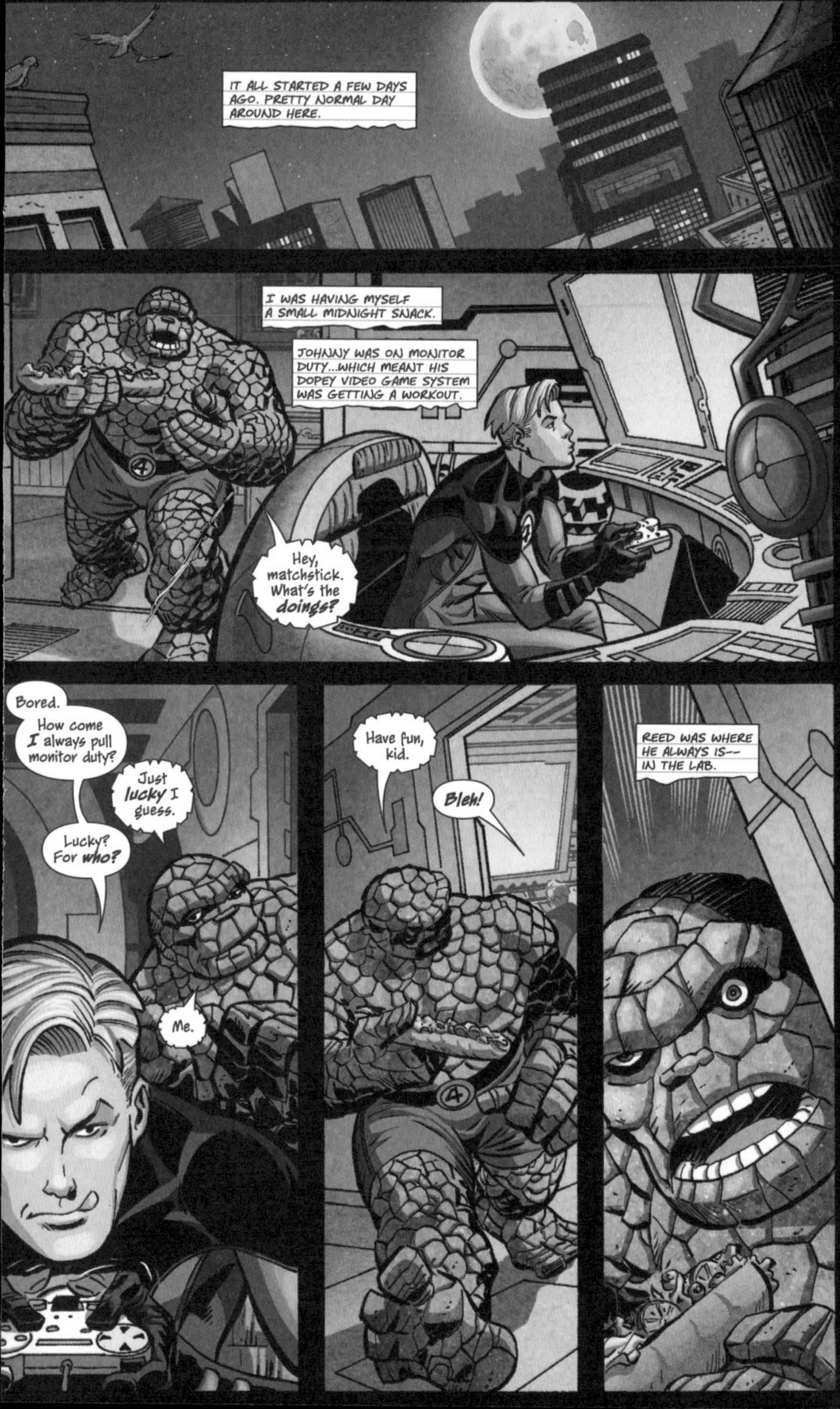
IT ALL STARTED A FEW DAYS AGO. PRETTY NORMAL DAY AROUND HERE.
I WAS HAVING MYSELF A SMALL MIDNIGHT SNACK.
JOHNNY WAS ON MONITOR DUTY...WHICH MEANT HIS DOPEY VIDEO GAME SYSTEM WAS GETTING A WORKOUT.
Hey, matchstick. What's the doings?
Bored.
How come I always pull monitor duty?
Just lucky I guess.
Lucky? For who?
Me.
Have fun, kid.
Bleh!
REED WAS WHERE HE ALWAYS IS-- IN THE LAB.

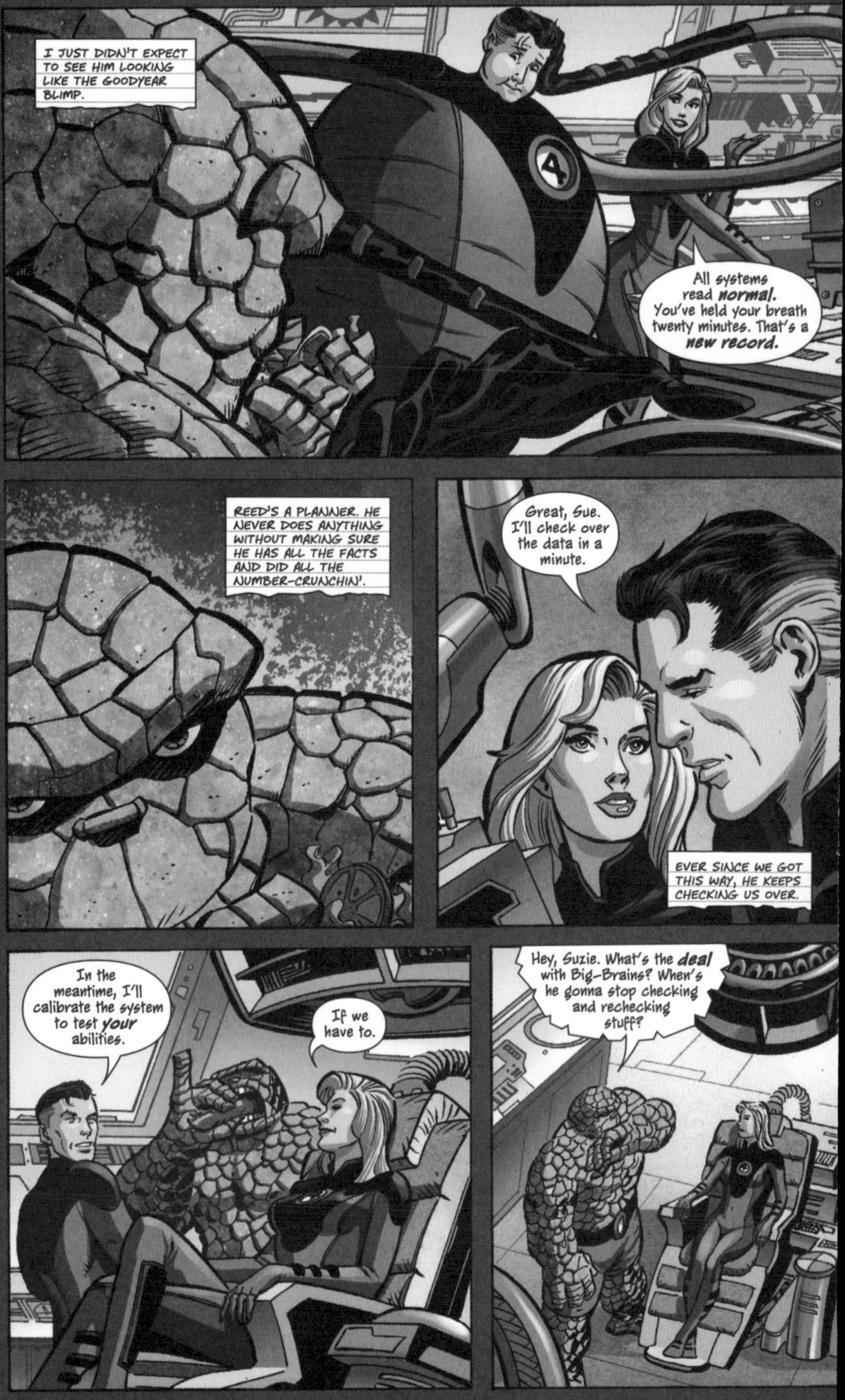

I JUST DIDN'T EXPECT TO SEE HIM LOOKING LIKE THE GOODYEAR BLIMP.
All systems read normal. You've held your breath twenty minutes. That's a new record.
REED'S A PLANNER. HE NEVER DOES ANYTHING WITHOUT MAKING SURE HE HAS ALL THE FACTS AND DID ALL THE NUMBER-CRUNCHIN'.
Great, Sue. I'll check over the data in a minute.
EVER SINCE WE GOT THIS WAY, HE KEEPS CHECKING US OVER.
In the meantime, I'll calibrate the system to test your abilities.
If we have to.
Hey, Suzie. What's the deal with Big-Brains? When's he gonna stop checking and rechecking stuff?

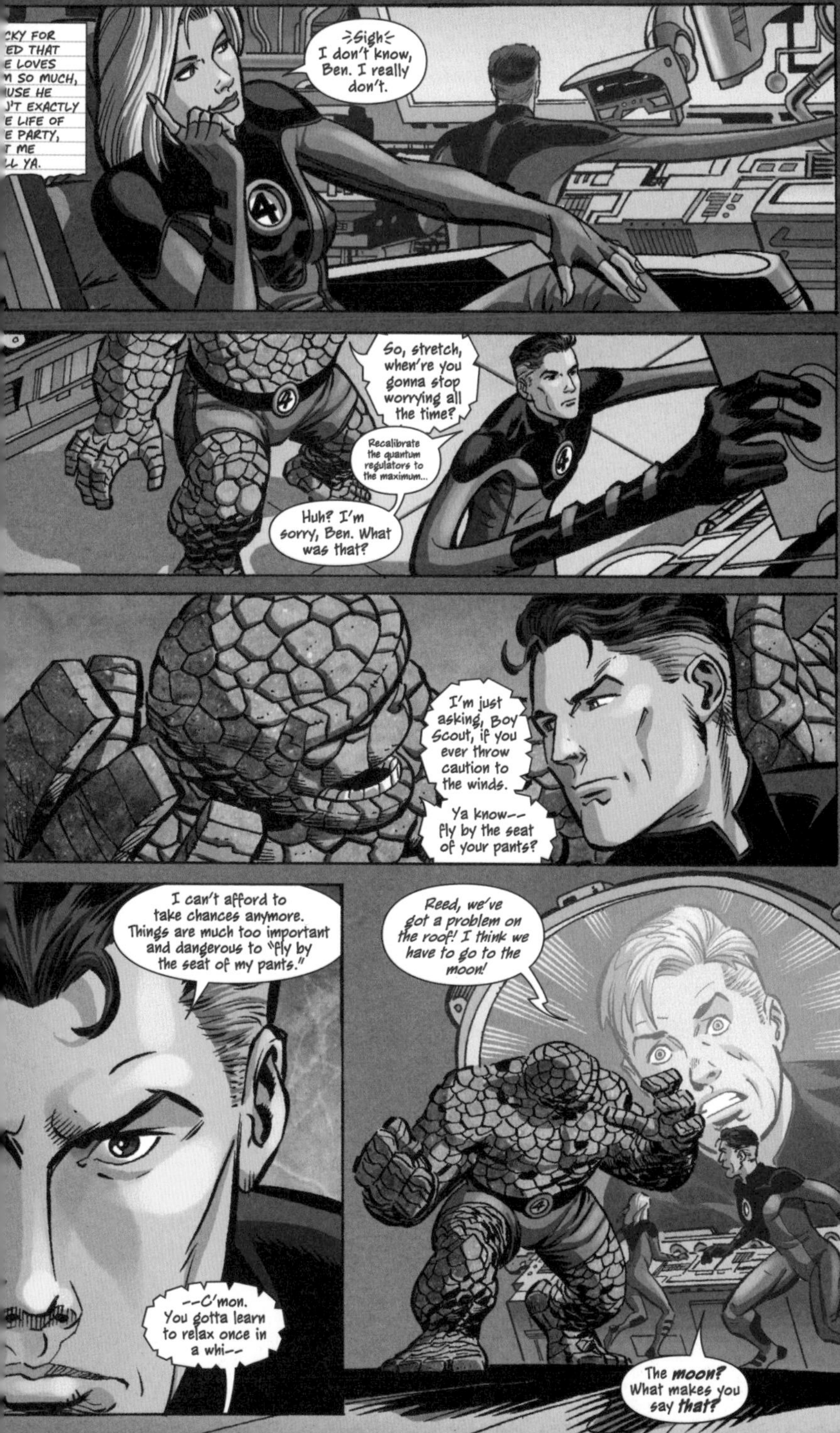

CKY FOR ED THAT E LOVES M SO MUCH, USE HE 'T EXACTLY E LIFE OF E PARTY, T ME L YA.
Sigh I don't know, Ben. I really don't.
So, stretch, when're you gonna stop worrying all the time?
Recalibrate the quantum regulators to the maximum...
Huh? I'm sorry, Ben. What was that?
I'm just asking, Boy Scout, if you ever throw caution to the winds.
Ya know-- fly by the seat of your pants?
I can't afford to take chances anymore. Things are much too important and dangerous to "fly by the seat of my pants."
--C'mon. You gotta learn to relax once in a whi--
Reed, we've got a problem on the roof! I think we have to go to the moon!
The moon? What makes you say that?

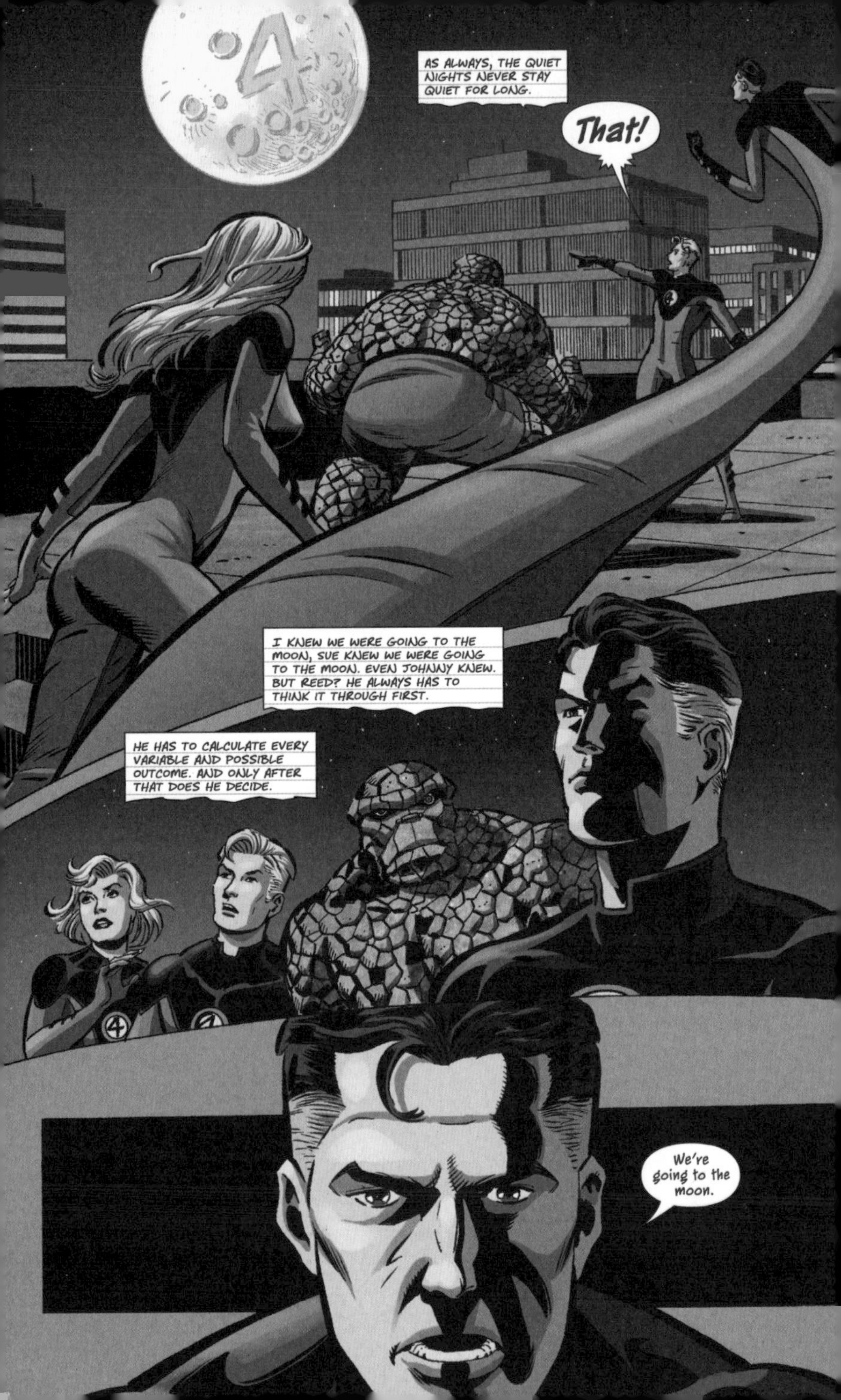

4
AS ALWAYS, THE QUIET NIGHTS NEVER STAY QUIET FOR LONG.
That!
I KNEW WE WERE GOING TO THE MOON, SUE KNEW WE WERE GOING TO THE MOON. EVEN JOHNNY KNEW. BUT REED? HE ALWAYS HAS TO THINK IT THROUGH FIRST.
HE HAS TO CALCULATE EVERY VARIABLE AND POSSIBLE OUTCOME. AND ONLY AFTER THAT DOES HE DECIDE.
We're going to the moon.

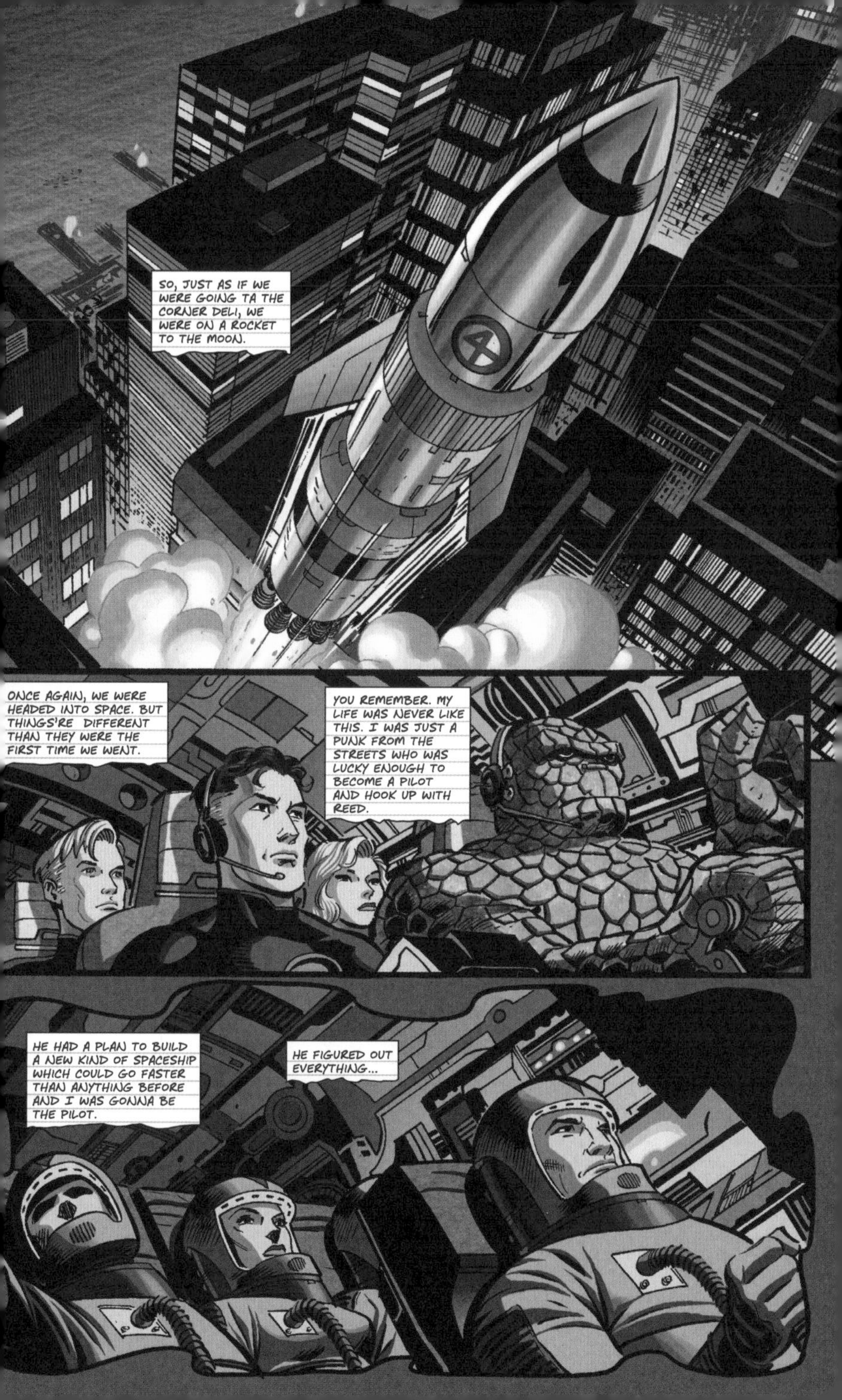
SO, JUST AS IF WE WERE GOING TA THE CORNER DELI, WE WERE ON A ROCKET TO THE MOON.
ONCE AGAIN, WE WERE HEADED INTO SPACE. BUT THINGS'RE DIFFERENT THAN THEY WERE THE FIRST TIME WE WENT.
YOU REMEMBER. MY LIFE WAS NEVER LIKE THIS. I WAS JUST A PUNK FROM THE STREETS WHO WAS LUCKY ENOUGH TO BECOME A PILOT AND HOOK UP WITH REED.
HE HAD A PLAN TO BUILD A NEW KIND OF SPACESHIP WHICH COULD GO FASTER THAN ANYTHING BEFORE AND I WAS GONNA BE THE PILOT.
HE FIGURED OUT EVERYTHING...

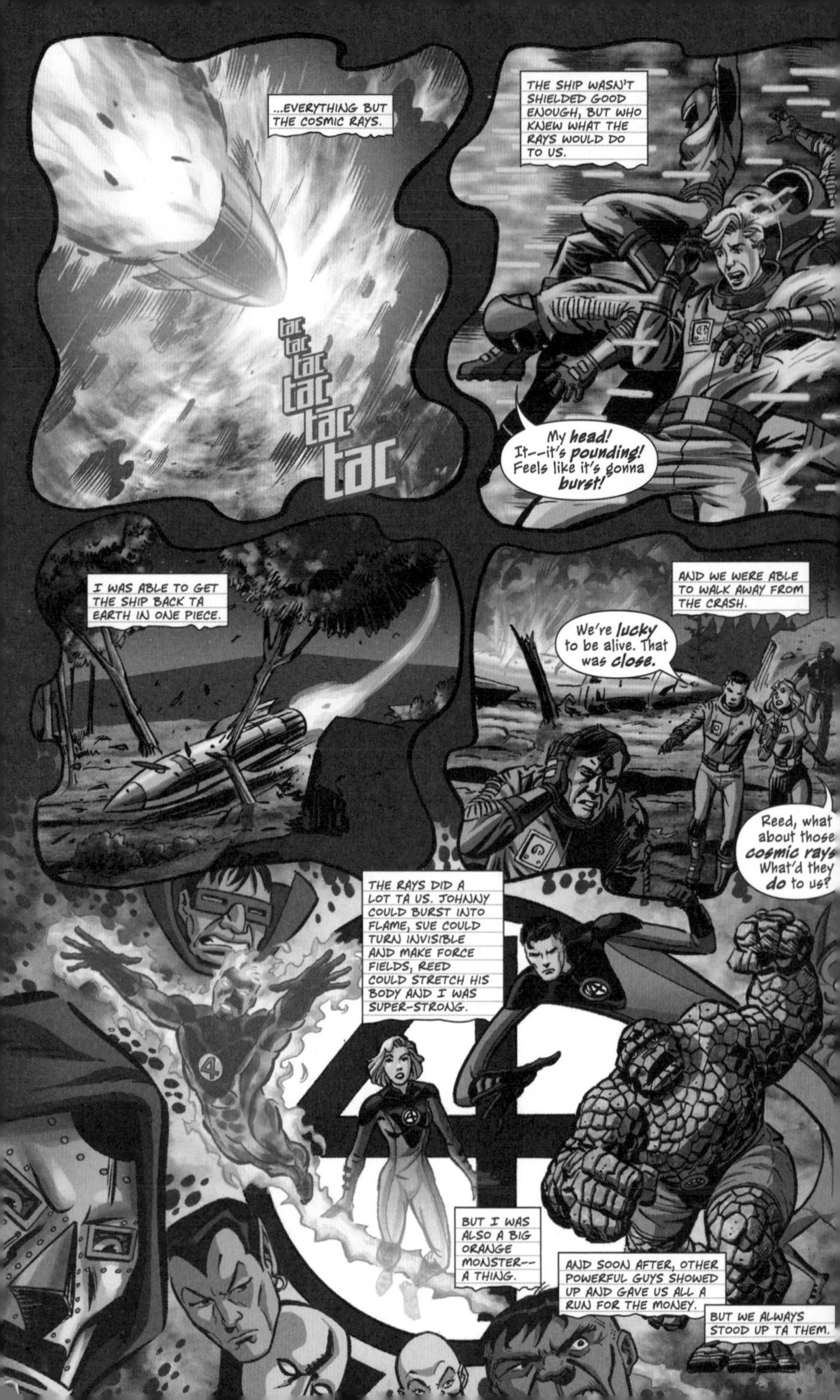
...EVERYTHING BUT THE COSMIC RAYS.
tac tac tac tac tac tac
THE SHIP WASN'T SHIELDED GOOD ENOUGH, BUT WHO KNEW WHAT THE RAYS WOULD DO TO US.
My head! It--it's pounding! Feels like it's gonna burst!
I WAS ABLE TO GET THE SHIP BACK TA EARTH IN ONE PIECE.
AND WE WERE ABLE TO WALK AWAY FROM THE CRASH.
We're lucky to be alive. That was close.
Reed, what about those cosmic rays What'd they do to us?
THE RAYS DID A LOT TA US. JOHNNY COULD BURST INTO FLAME, SUE COULD TURN INVISIBLE AND MAKE FORCE FIELDS, REED COULD STRETCH HIS BODY AND I WAS SUPER-STRONG.
BUT I WAS ALSO A BIG ORANGE MONSTER-- A THING.
AND SOON AFTER, OTHER POWERFUL GUYS SHOWED UP AND GAVE US ALL A RUN FOR THE MONEY.
BUT WE ALWAYS STOOD UP TA THEM.

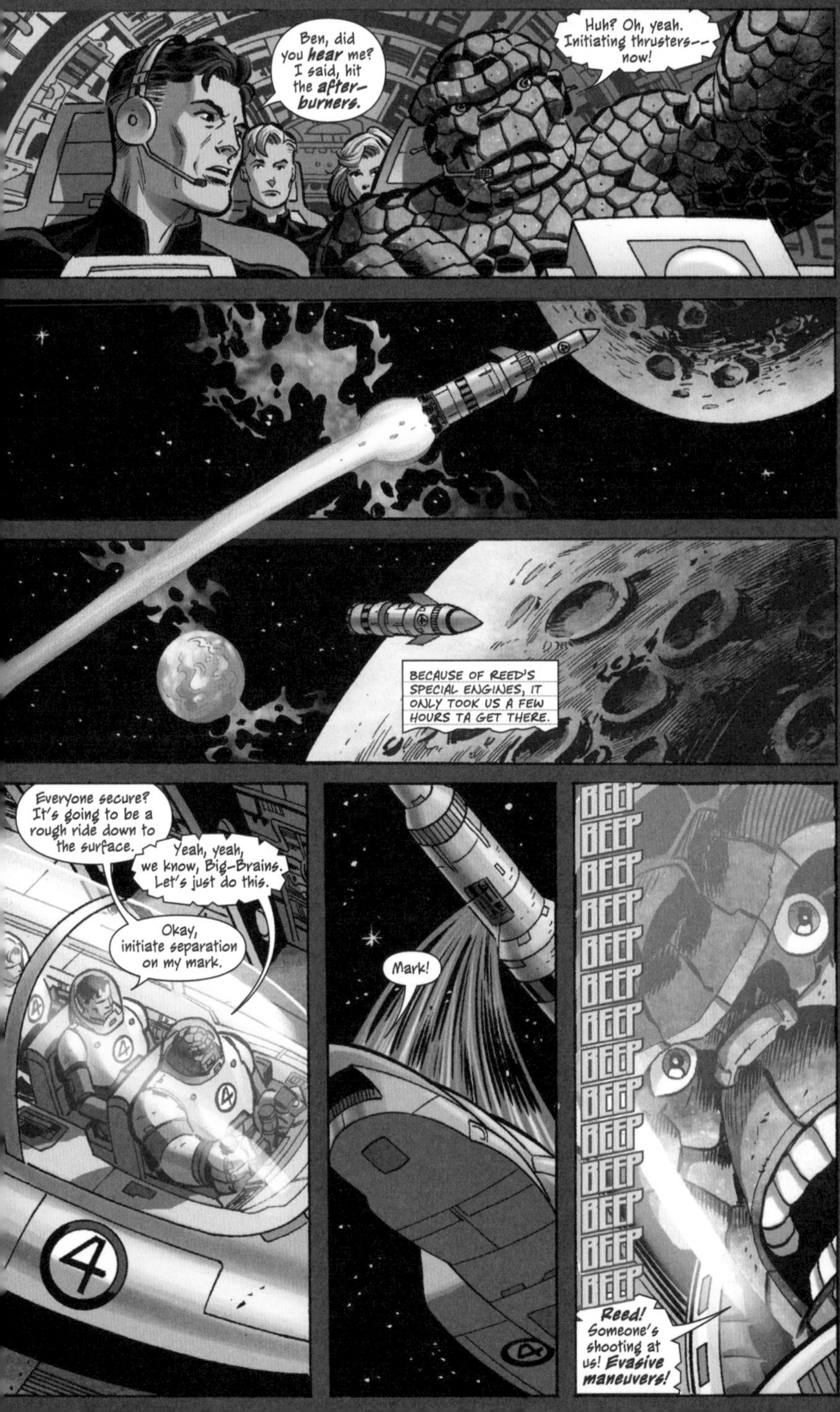

Ben, did you hear me? I said, hit the after-burners.
Huh? Oh, yeah. Initiating thrusters-- now!
BECAUSE OF REED'S SPECIAL ENGINES, IT ONLY TOOK US A FEW HOURS TA GET THERE.
Everyone secure? It's going to be a rough ride down to the surface.
Yeah, yeah, we know, Big-Brains. Let's just do this.
Okay, initiate separation on my mark.
Mark!
BEEP BEEP BEEP BEEP BEEP BEEP BEEP BEEP BEEP BEEP BEEP BEEP BEEP BEEP BEEP BEEP BEEP
Reed! Someone's shooting at us! Evasive maneuvers!

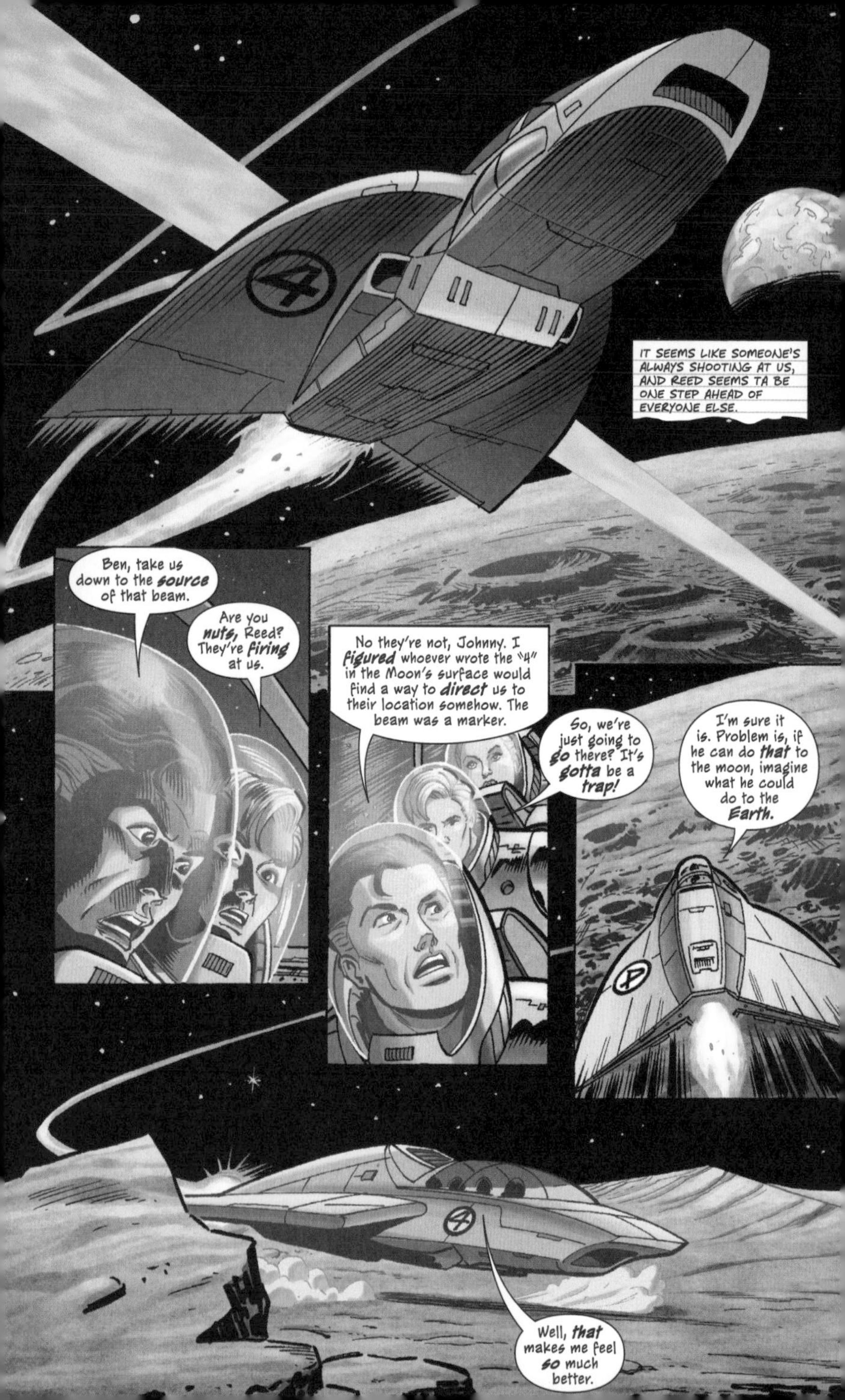
IT SEEMS LIKE SOMEONE'S ALWAYS SHOOTING AT US, AND REED SEEMS TA BE ONE STEP AHEAD OF EVERYONE ELSE.
Ben, take us down to the source of that beam.
Are you nuts, Reed? They're firing at us.
No they're not, Johnny. I figured whoever wrote the "4" in the Moon's surface would find a way to direct us to their location somehow. The beam was a marker.
So, we're just going to go there? It's gotta be a trap!
I'm sure it is. Problem is, if he can do that to the moon, imagine what he could do to the Earth.
Well, that makes me feel so much better.

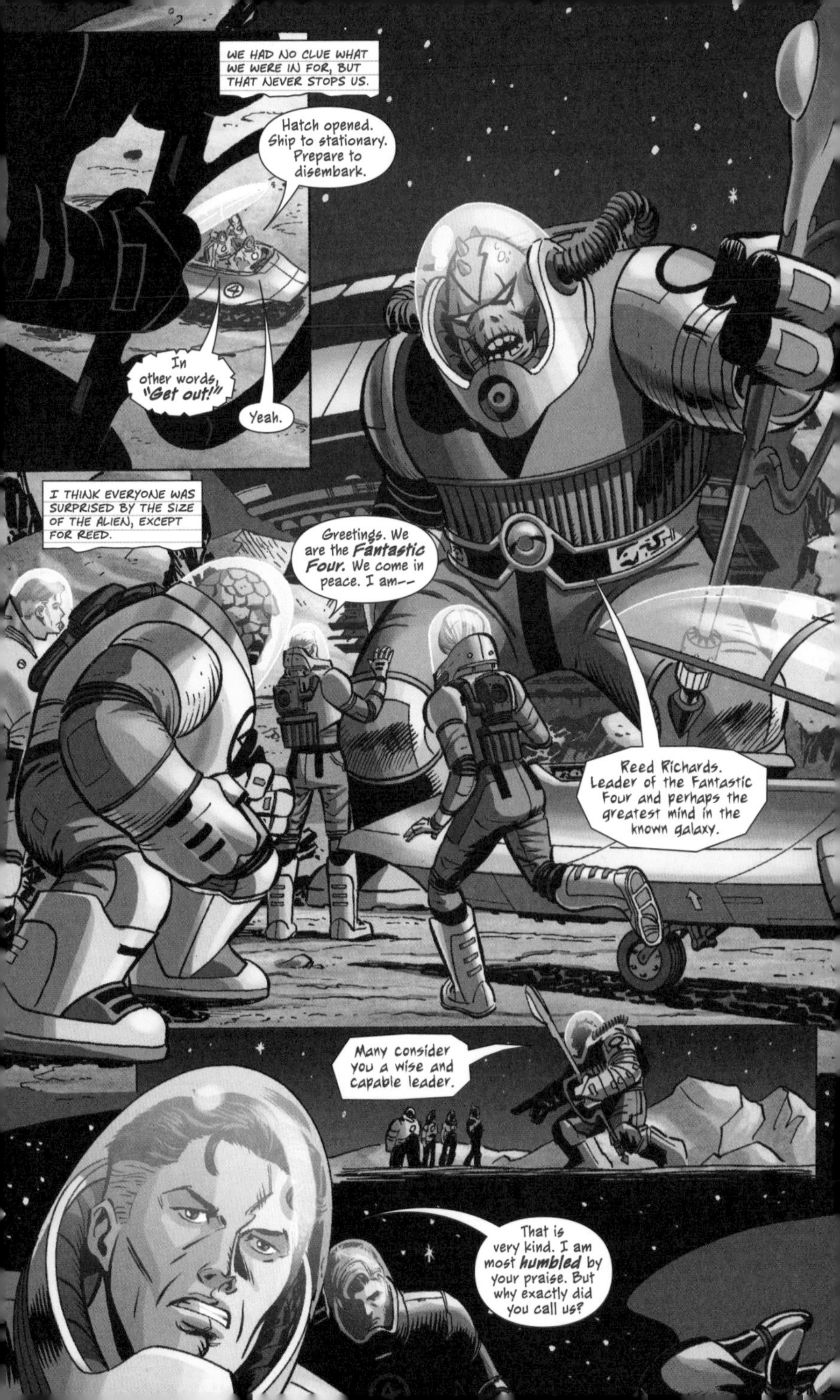

WE HAD NO CLUE WHAT WE WERE IN FOR, BUT THAT NEVER STOPS US.
Hatch opened. Ship to stationary. Prepare to disembark.
In other words, "Get out!"
Yeah.
I THINK EVERYONE WAS SURPRISED BY THE SIZE OF THE ALIEN, EXCEPT FOR REED.
Greetings. We are the Fantastic Four. We come in peace. I am--
Reed Richards. Leader of the Fantastic Four and perhaps the greatest mind in the known galaxy.
Many consider you a wise and capable leader.
That is very kind. I am most humbled by your praise. But why exactly did you call us?

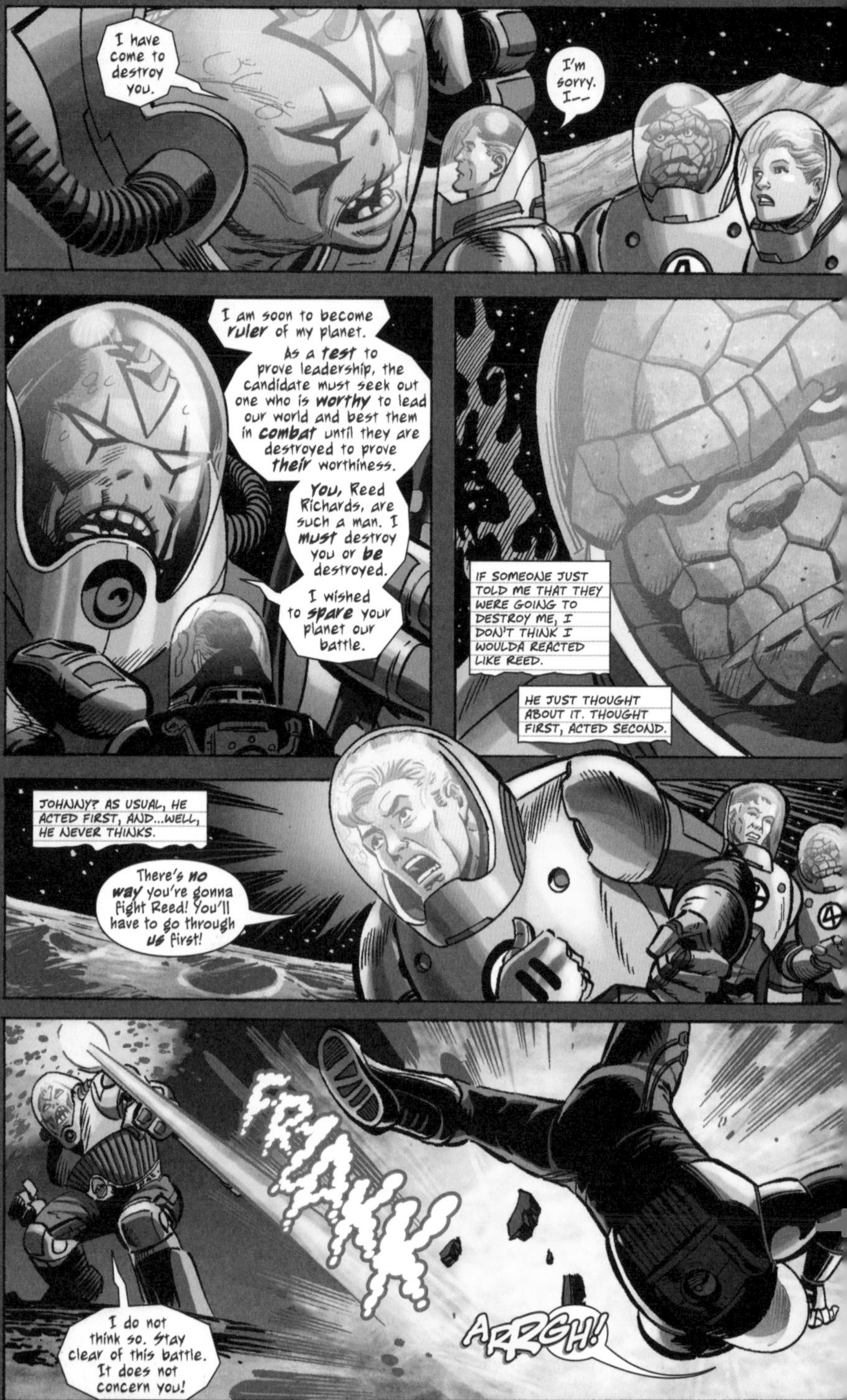
I have come to destroy you.
I'm sorry. I--
I am soon to become ruler of my planet.
As a test to prove leadership, the candidate must seek out one who is worthy to lead our world and best them in combat until they are destroyed to prove their worthiness.
You, Reed Richards, are such a man. I must destroy you or be destroyed.
I wished to spare your planet our battle.
IF SOMEONE JUST TOLD ME THAT THEY WERE GOING TO DESTROY ME, I DON'T THINK I WOULDA REACTED LIKE REED.
HE JUST THOUGHT ABOUT IT. THOUGHT FIRST, ACTED SECOND.
JOHNNY? AS USUAL, HE ACTED FIRST, AND...WELL, HE NEVER THINKS.
There's no way you're gonna fight Reed! You'll have to go through us first!
FRAKK!
ARRGH!
I do not think so. Stay clear of this battle. It does not concern you!

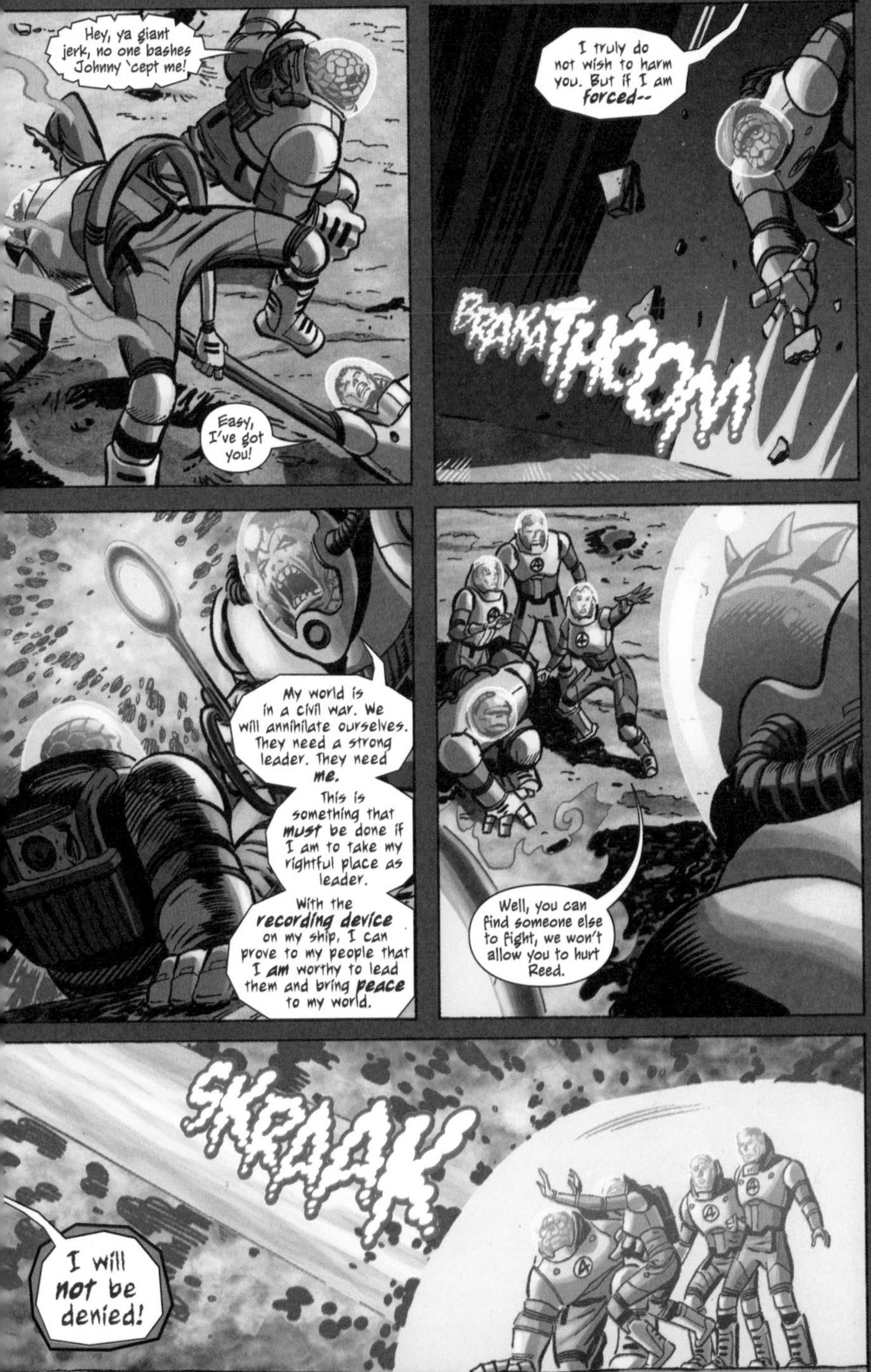
Hey, ya giant jerk, no one bashes Johnny 'cept me!
Easy, I've got you!
I truly do not wish to harm you. But if I am forced--
BRAKATHOOM
My world is in a civil war. We will annihilate ourselves. They need a strong leader. They need me.
This is something that must be done if I am to take my rightful place as leader.
With the recording device on my ship, I can prove to my people that I am worthy to lead them and bring peace to my world.
Well, you can find someone else to fight, we won't allow you to hurt Reed.
SKRAAK
I will not be denied!

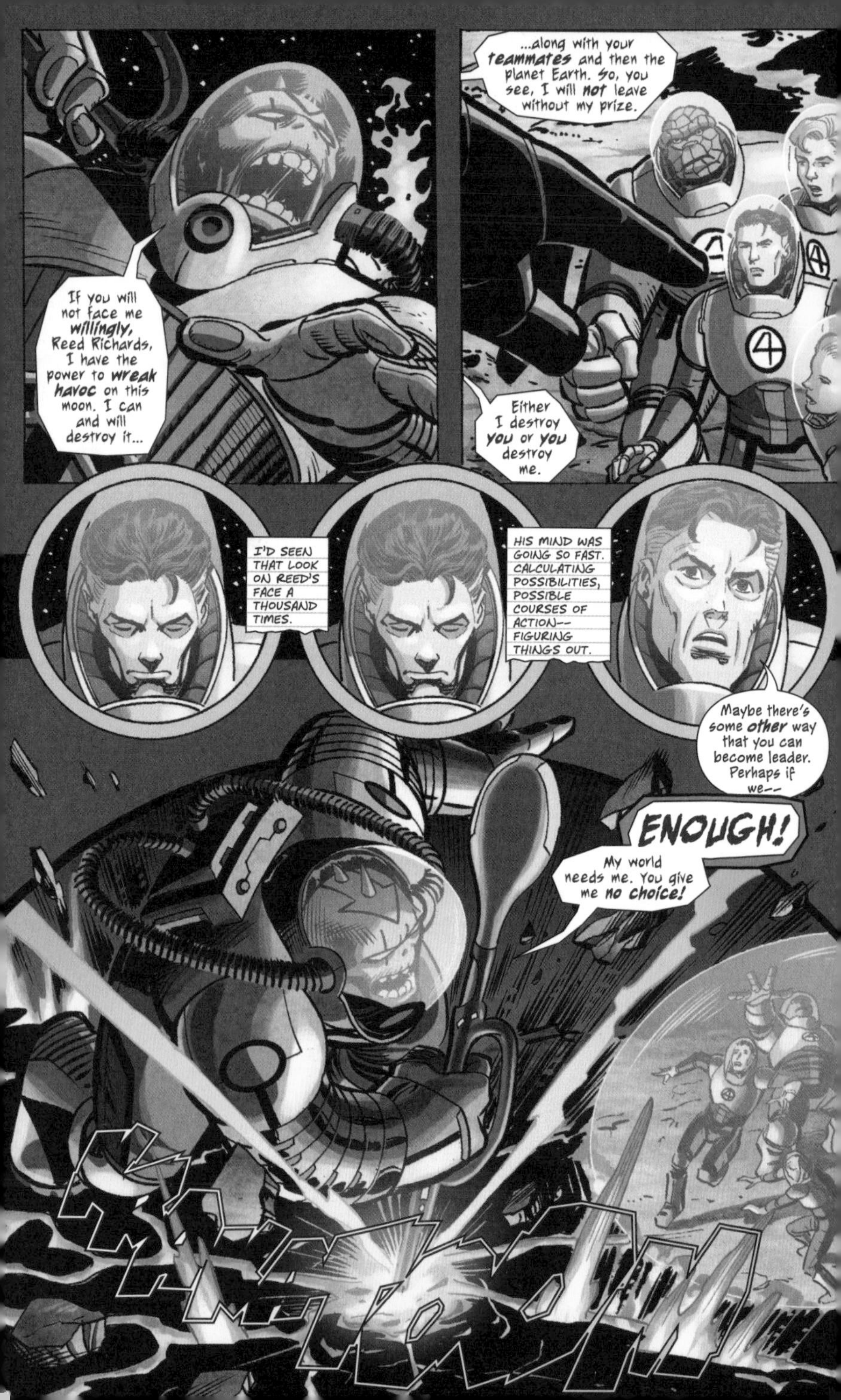

If you will not face me willingly, Reed Richards, I have the power to wreak havoc on this moon. I can and will destroy it...
...along with your teammates and then the planet Earth. So, you see, I will not leave without my prize.
Either I destroy you or you destroy me.
I'D SEEN THAT LOOK ON REED'S FACE A THOUSAND TIMES.
HIS MIND WAS GOING SO FAST. CALCULATING POSSIBILITIES, POSSIBLE COURSES OF ACTION-- FIGURING THINGS OUT.
Maybe there's some other way that you can become leader. Perhaps if we--
ENOUGH!
My world needs me. You give me no choice!

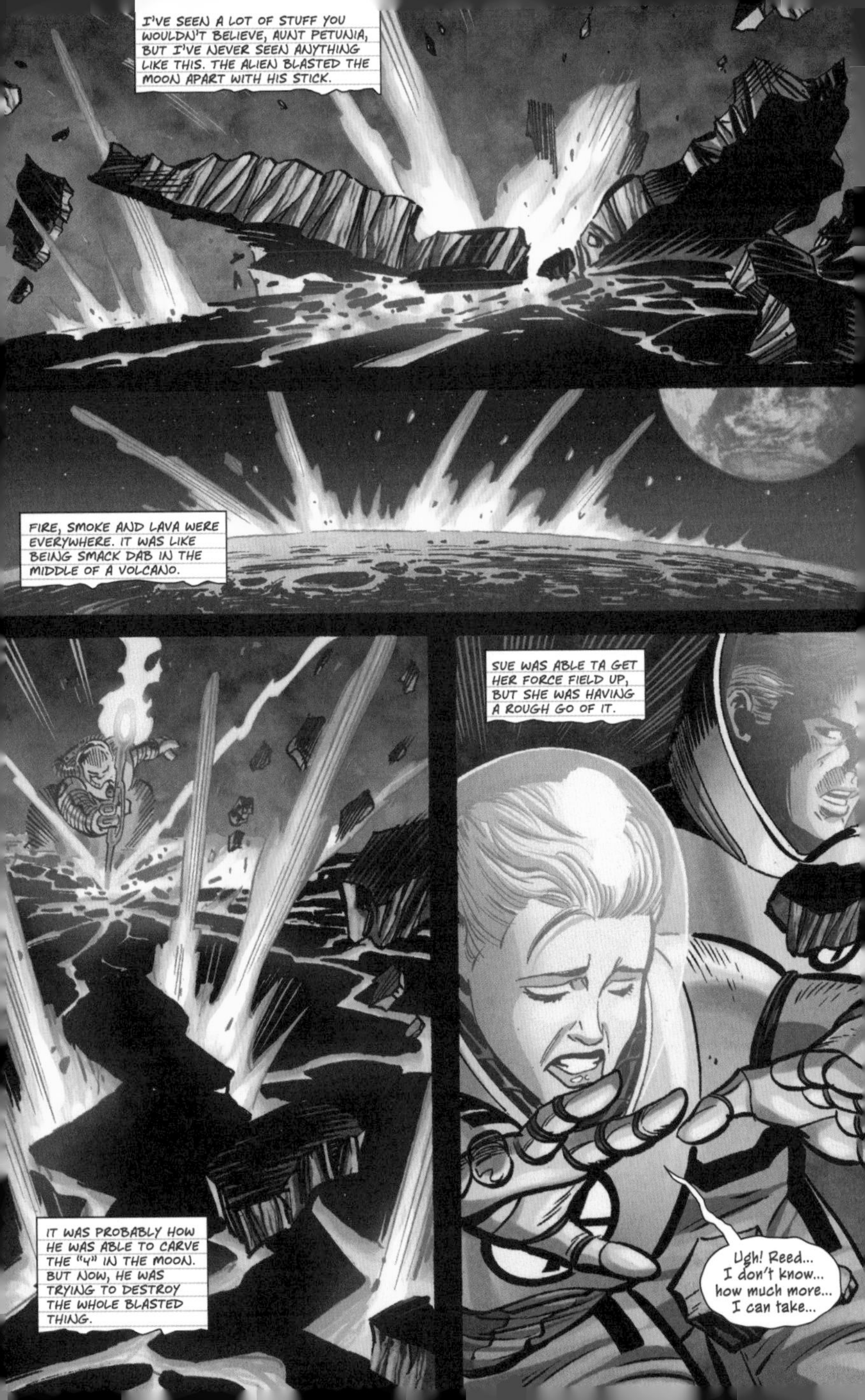
I'VE SEEN A LOT OF STUFF YOU WOULDN'T BELIEVE, AUNT PETUNIA, BUT I'VE NEVER SEEN ANYTHING LIKE THIS. THE ALIEN BLASTED THE MOON APART WITH HIS STICK.
FIRE, SMOKE AND LAVA WERE EVERYWHERE. IT WAS LIKE BEING SMACK DAB IN THE MIDDLE OF A VOLCANO.
IT WAS PROBABLY HOW HE WAS ABLE TO CARVE THE "4" IN THE MOON. BUT NOW, HE WAS TRYING TO DESTROY THE WHOLE BLASTED THING.
SUE WAS ABLE TA GET HER FORCE FIELD UP, BUT SHE WAS HAVING A ROUGH GO OF IT.
Ugh! Reed... I don't know... how much more... I can take...

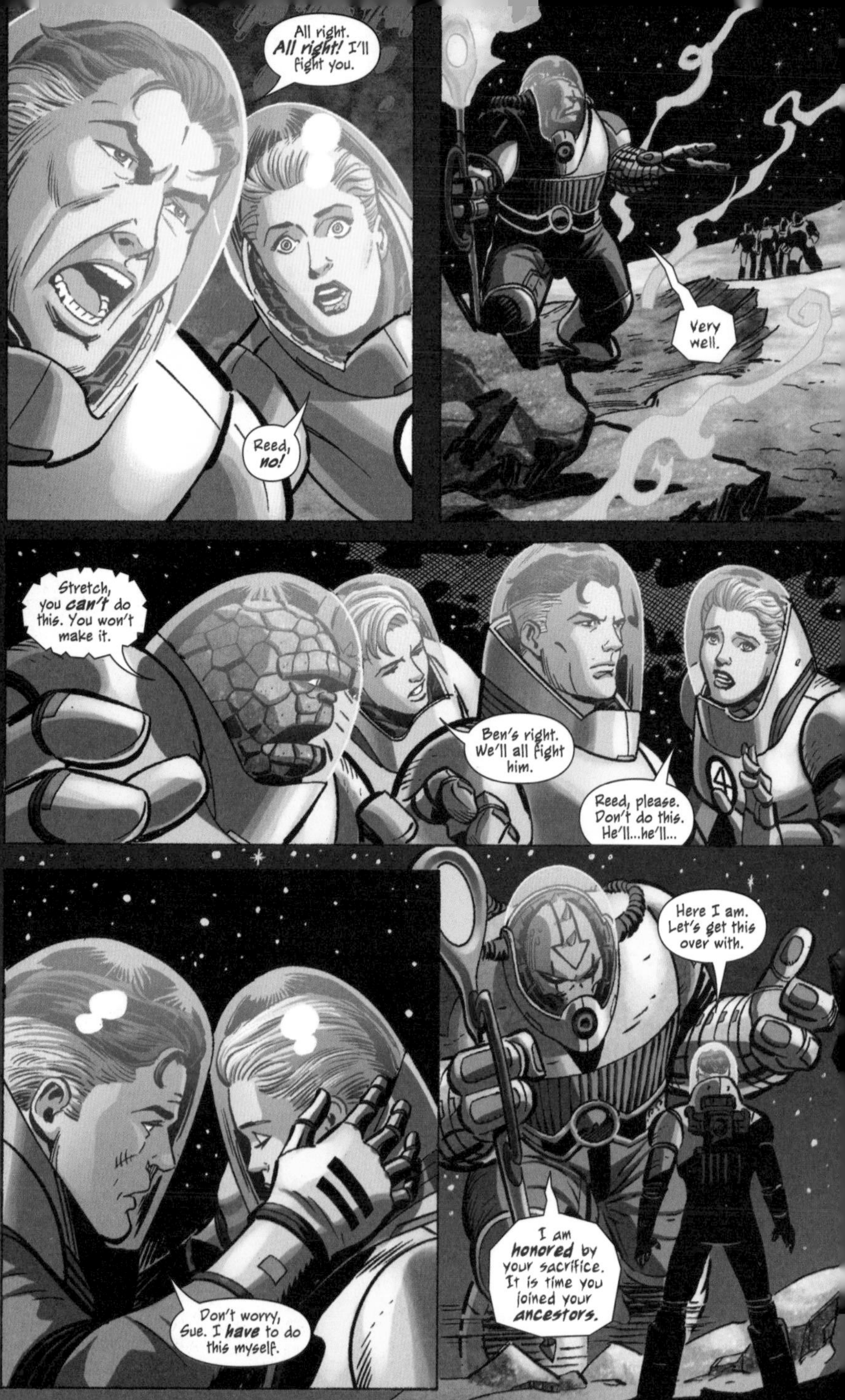
All right. All right! I'll fight you.
Reed, no!
Very well.
Stretch, you can't do this. You won't make it.
Ben's right. We'll all fight him.
Reed, please. Don't do this. He'll...he'll...
Don't worry, Sue. I have to do this myself.
Here I am. Let's get this over with.
I am honored by your sacrifice. It is time you joined your ancestors.

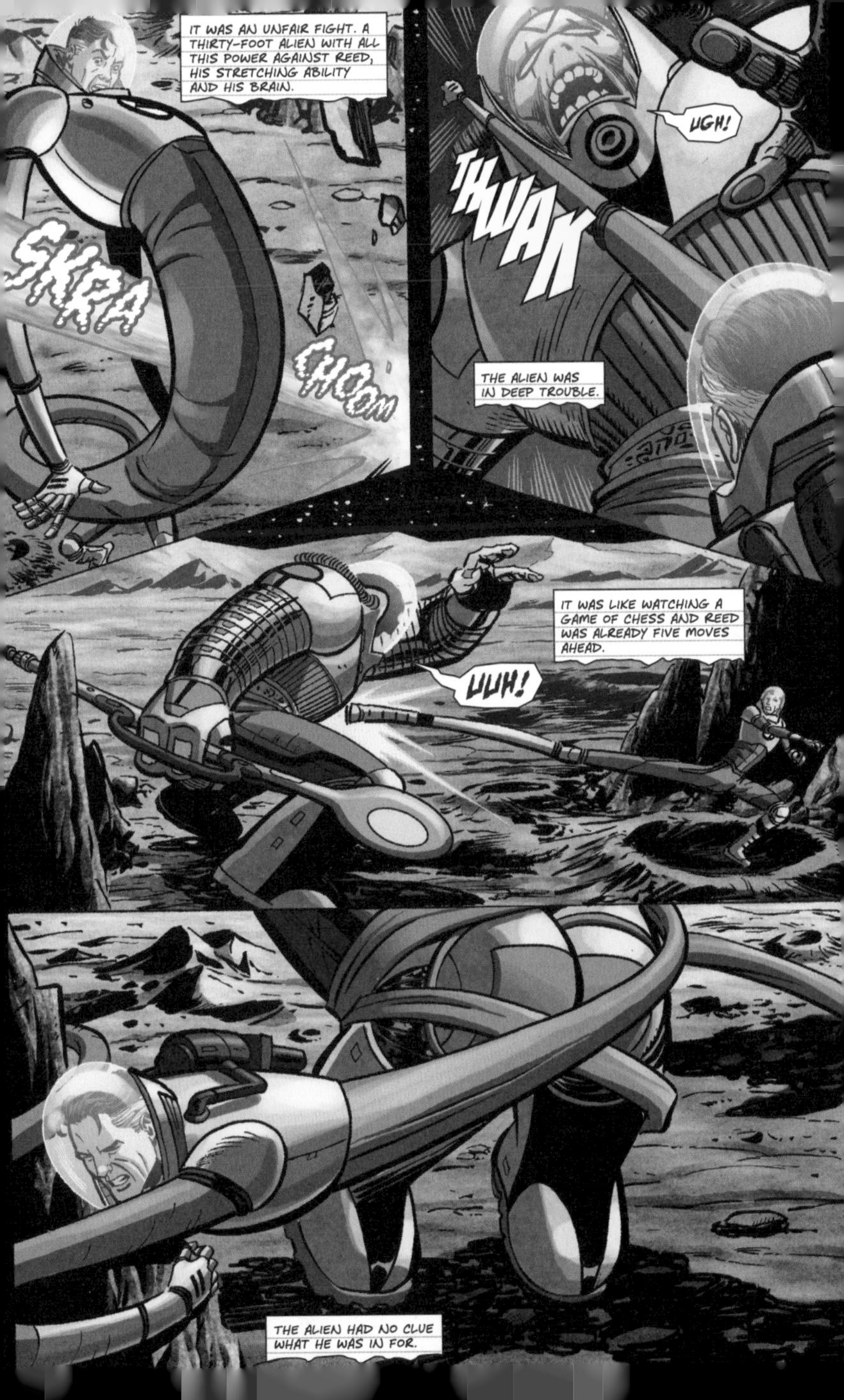
IT WAS AN UNFAIR FIGHT. A THIRTY-FOOT ALIEN WITH ALL THIS POWER AGAINST REED, HIS STRETCHING ABILITY AND HIS BRAIN.
SKRA
CHOOM
UGH!
THWAK
THE ALIEN WAS IN DEEP TROUBLE.
IT WAS LIKE WATCHING A GAME OF CHESS AND REED WAS ALREADY FIVE MOVES AHEAD.
UUH!
THE ALIEN HAD NO CLUE WHAT HE WAS IN FOR.

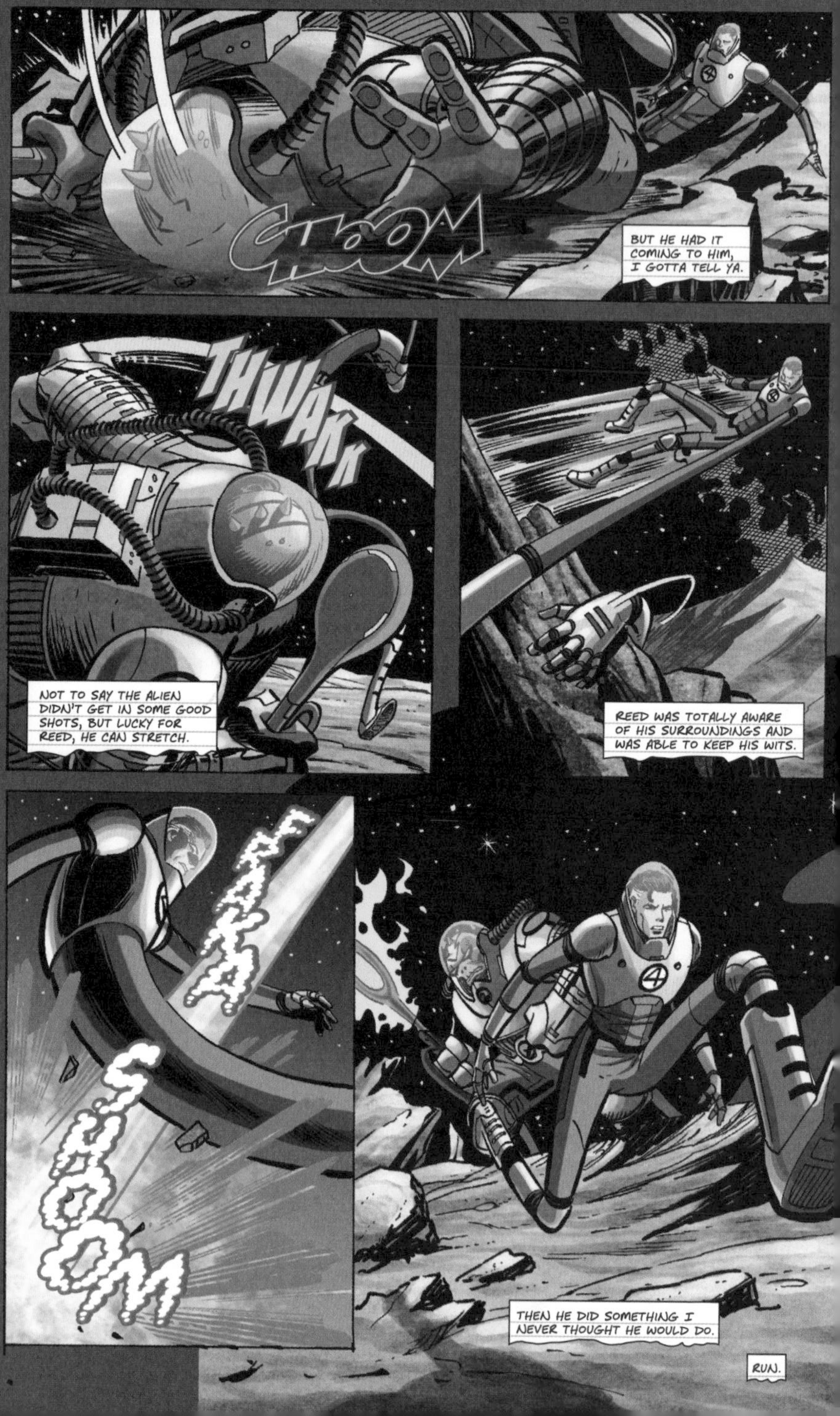
CHOOM
BUT HE HAD IT COMING TO HIM, I GOTTA TELL YA.
THWAKK
NOT TO SAY THE ALIEN DIDN'T GET IN SOME GOOD SHOTS, BUT LUCKY FOR REED, HE CAN STRETCH.
REED WAS TOTALLY AWARE OF HIS SURROUNDINGS AND WAS ABLE TO KEEP HIS WITS.
THEN HE DID SOMETHING I NEVER THOUGHT HE WOULD DO.
RUN.

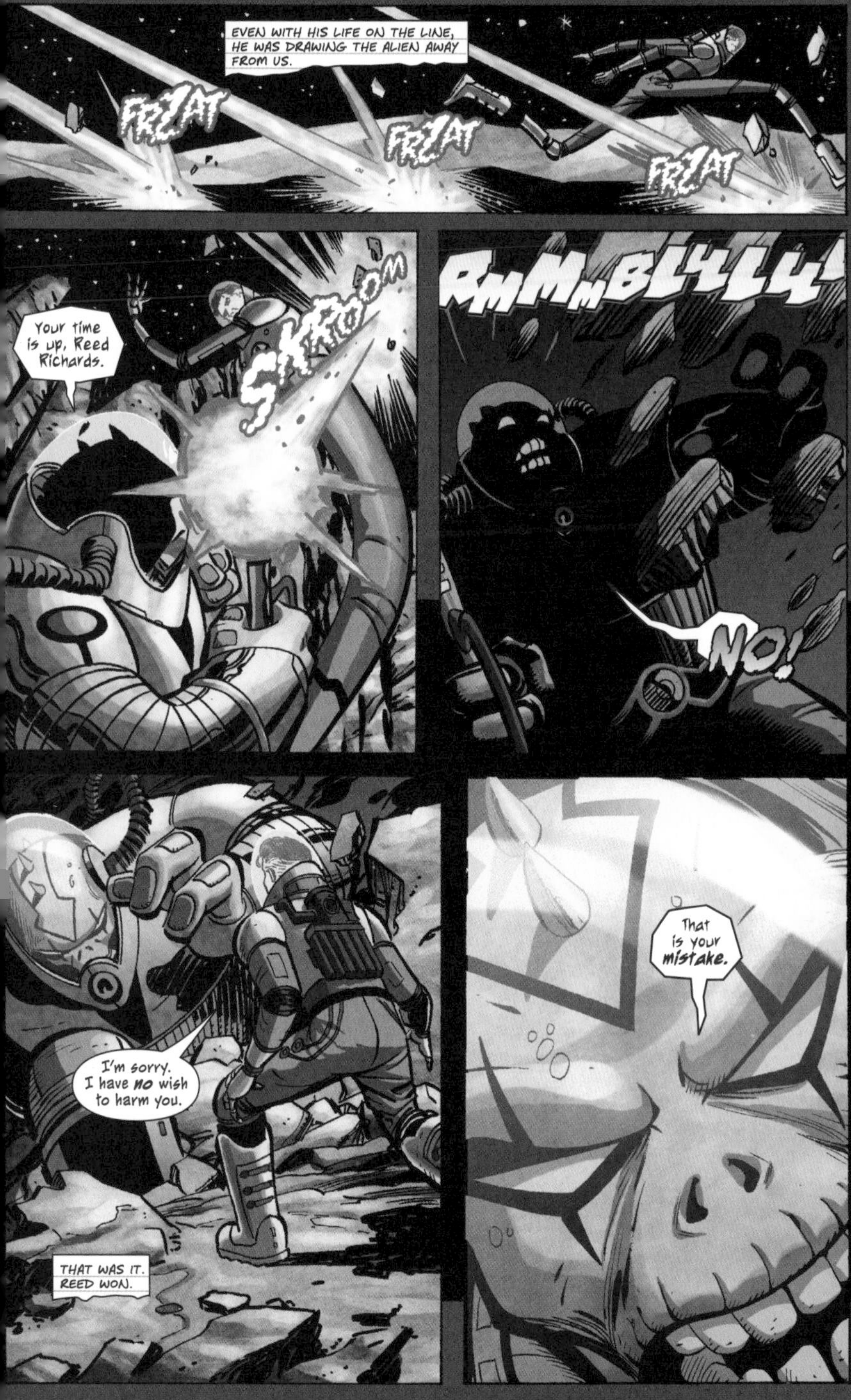
EVEN WITH HIS LIFE ON THE LINE, HE WAS DRAWING THE ALIEN AWAY FROM US.
FRZAT
FRZAT
FRZAT
Your time is up, Reed Richards.
SKROOM
RMMMBLLLL!
NO!
I'm sorry. I have **no** wish to harm you.
THAT WAS IT. REED WON.
That is your **mistake.**

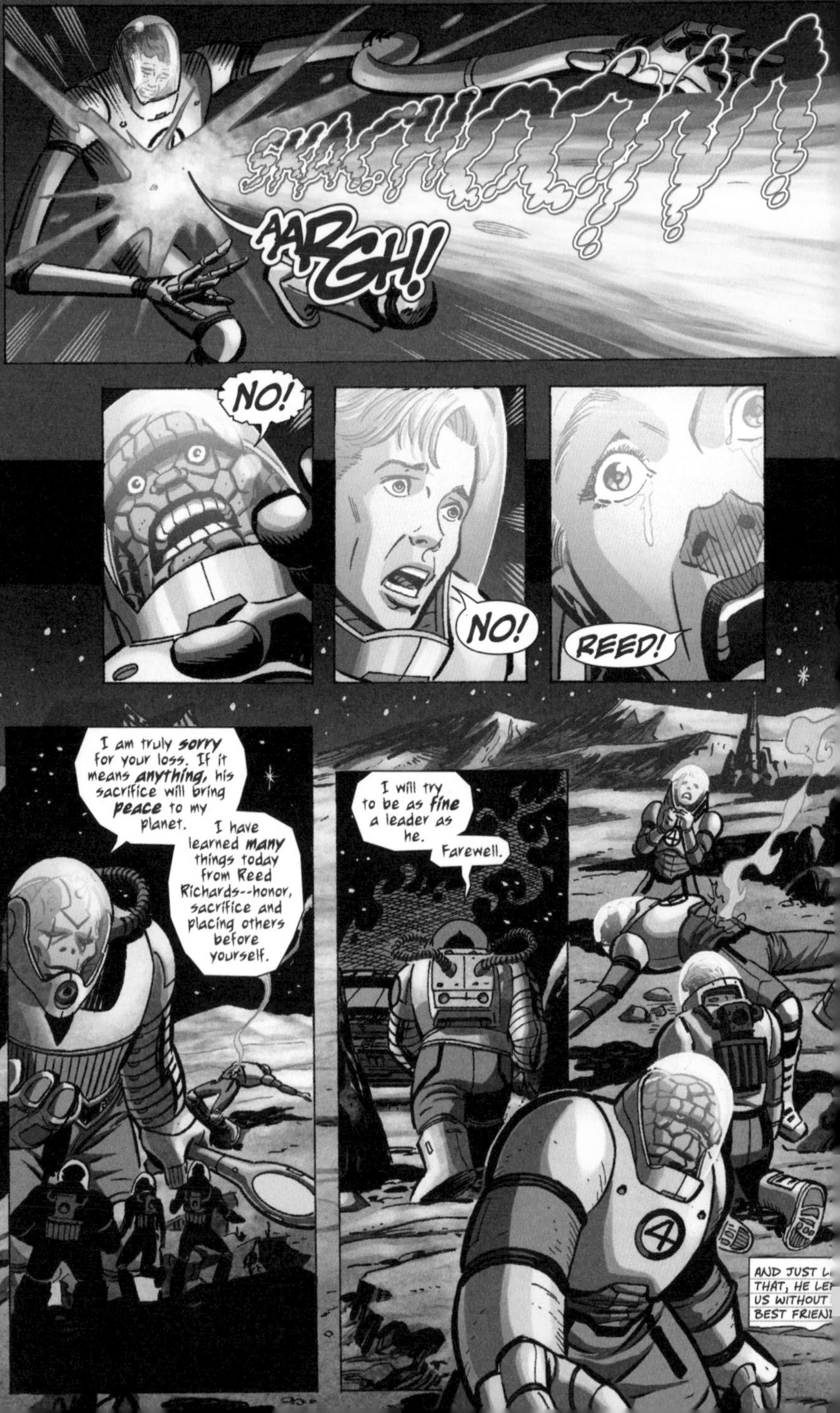
AARGH!
NO!
NO!
REED!
I am truly sorry for your loss. If it means anything, his sacrifice will bring peace to my planet.
I have learned many things today from Reed Richards--honor, sacrifice and placing others before yourself.
I will try to be as fine a leader as he.
Farewell.
AND JUST L
THAT, HE LE
US WITHOUT
BEST FRIEN

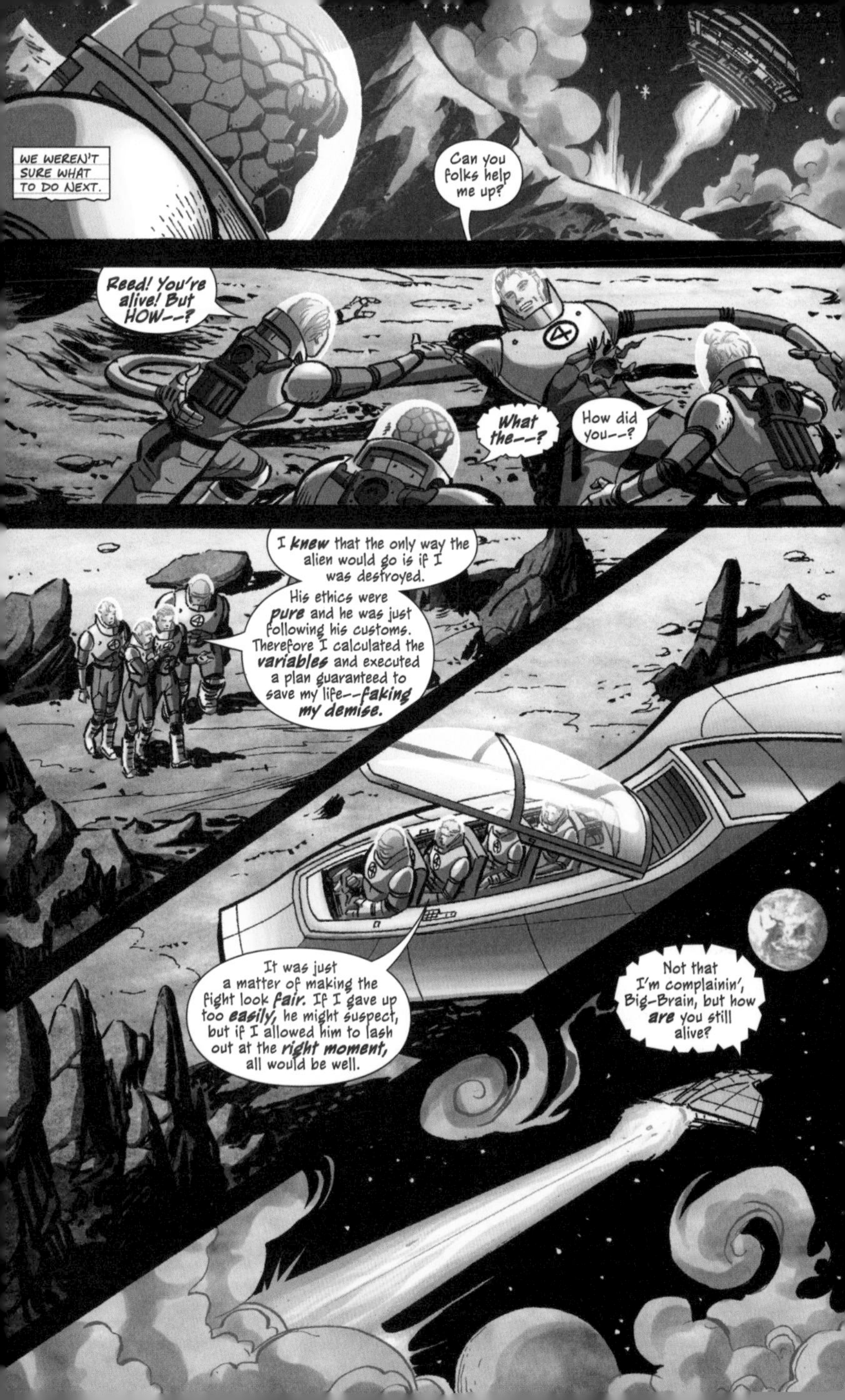

WE WEREN'T SURE WHAT TO DO NEXT.
Can you folks help me up?
Reed! You're alive! But HOW--?
What the--?
How did you--?
I knew that the only way the alien would go is if I was destroyed.
His ethics were pure and he was just following his customs. Therefore I calculated the variables and executed a plan guaranteed to save my life--faking my demise.
It was just a matter of making the fight look fair. If I gave up too easily, he might suspect, but if I allowed him to lash out at the right moment, all would be well.
Not that I'm complainin', Big-Brain, but how are you still alive?

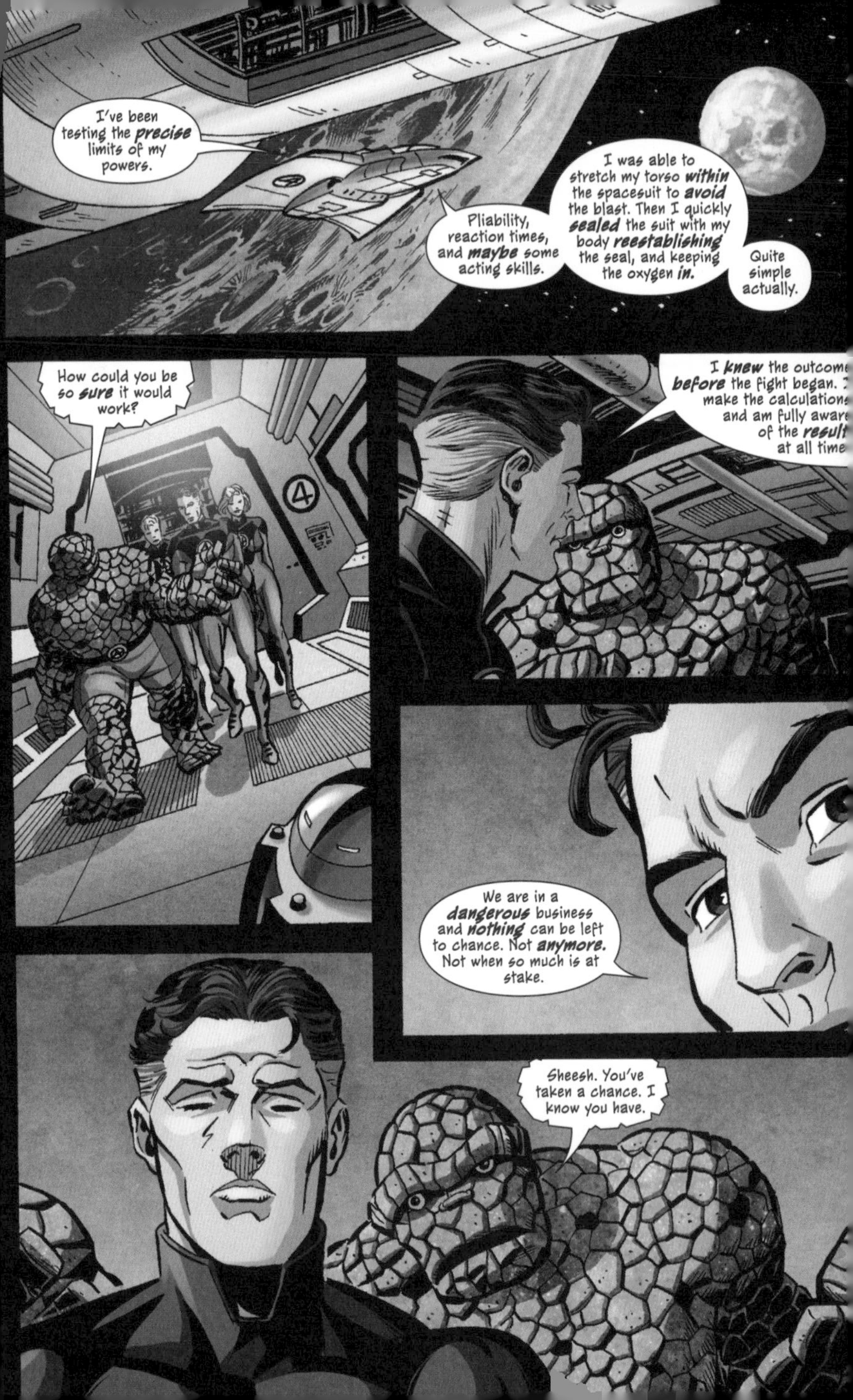

I've been testing the precise limits of my powers.
Pliability, reaction times, and maybe some acting skills.
I was able to stretch my torso within the spacesuit to avoid the blast. Then I quickly sealed the suit with my body reestablishing the seal, and keeping the oxygen in.
Quite simple actually.
How could you be so sure it would work?
I knew the outcome before the fight began.
make the calculation
and am fully aware
of the result
at all time
We are in a dangerous business and nothing can be left to chance. Not anymore. Not when so much is at stake.
Sheesh. You've taken a chance. I know you have.

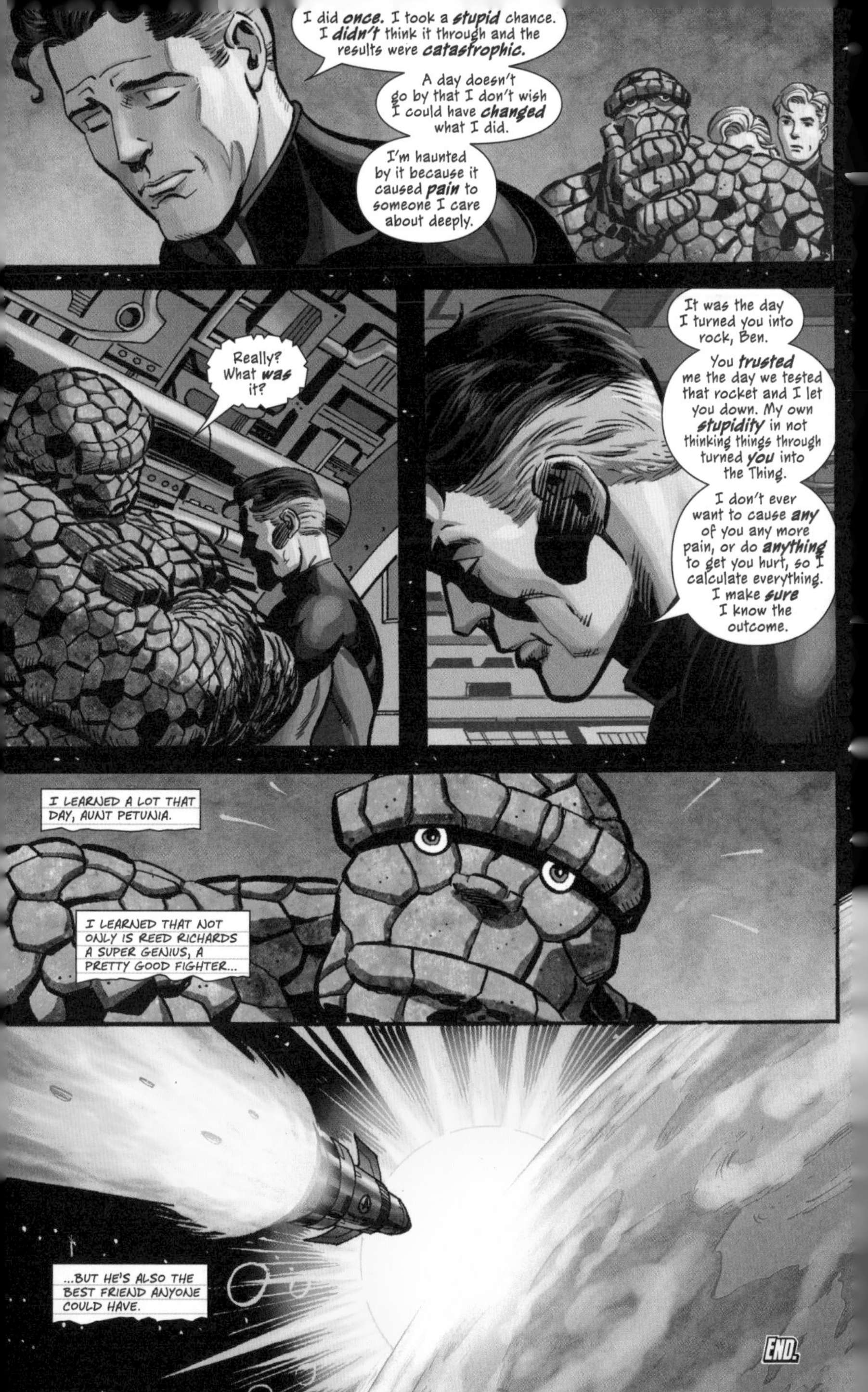
I did *once.* I took a *stupid* chance. I *didn't* think it through and the results were *catastrophic.*
A day doesn't go by that I don't wish I could have *changed* what I did.
I'm haunted by it because it caused *pain* to someone I care about deeply.
Really? What *was* it?
It was the day I turned you into rock, Ben.
You *trusted* me the day we tested that rocket and I let you down. My own *stupidity* in not thinking things through turned *you* into the Thing.
I don't ever want to cause *any* of you any more pain, or do *anything* to get you hurt, so I calculate everything. I make *sure* I know the outcome.
I LEARNED A LOT THAT DAY, AUNT PETUNIA.
I LEARNED THAT NOT ONLY IS REED RICHARDS A SUPER GENIUS, A PRETTY GOOD FIGHTER...
...BUT HE'S ALSO THE BEST FRIEND ANYONE COULD HAVE.
END.

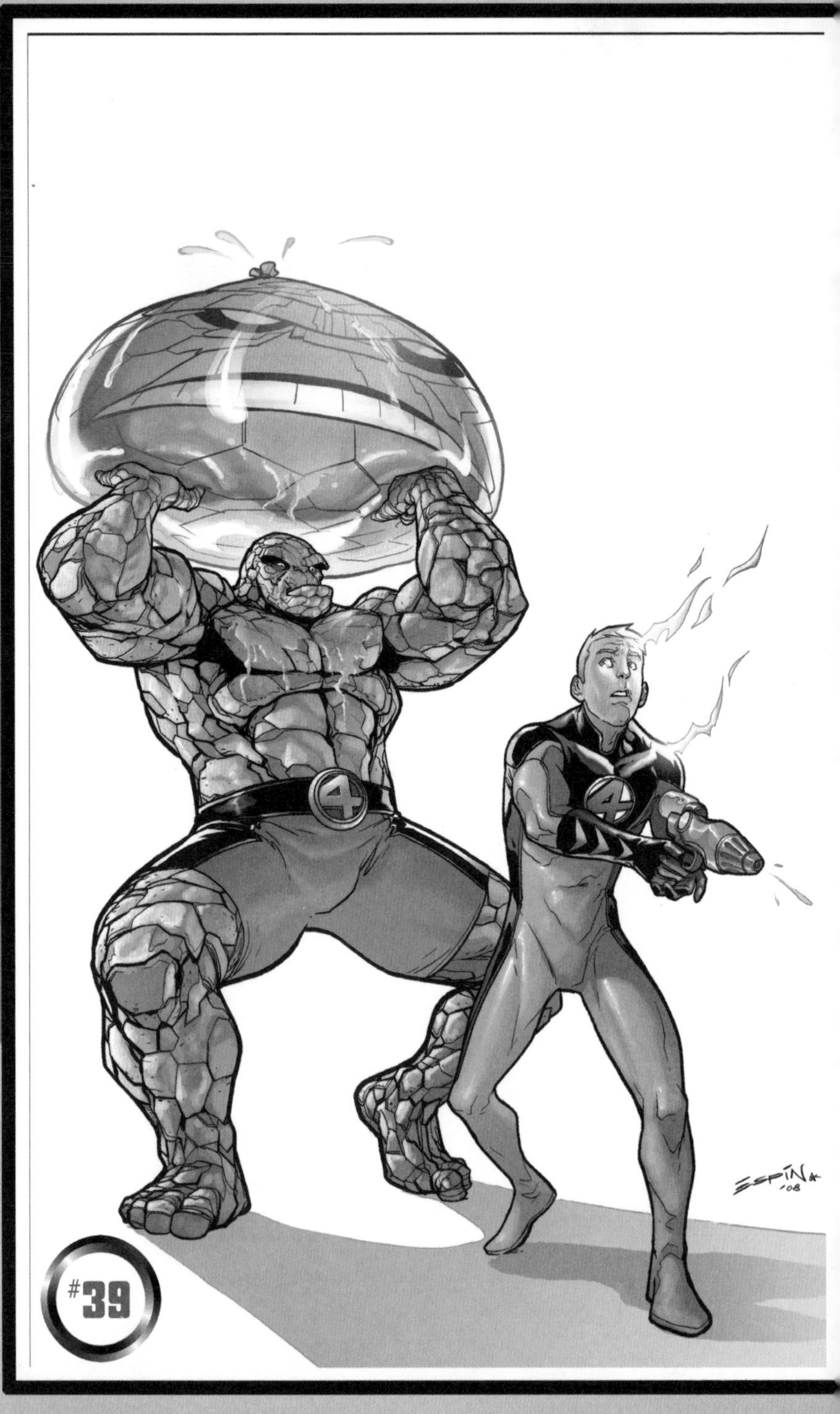

#39

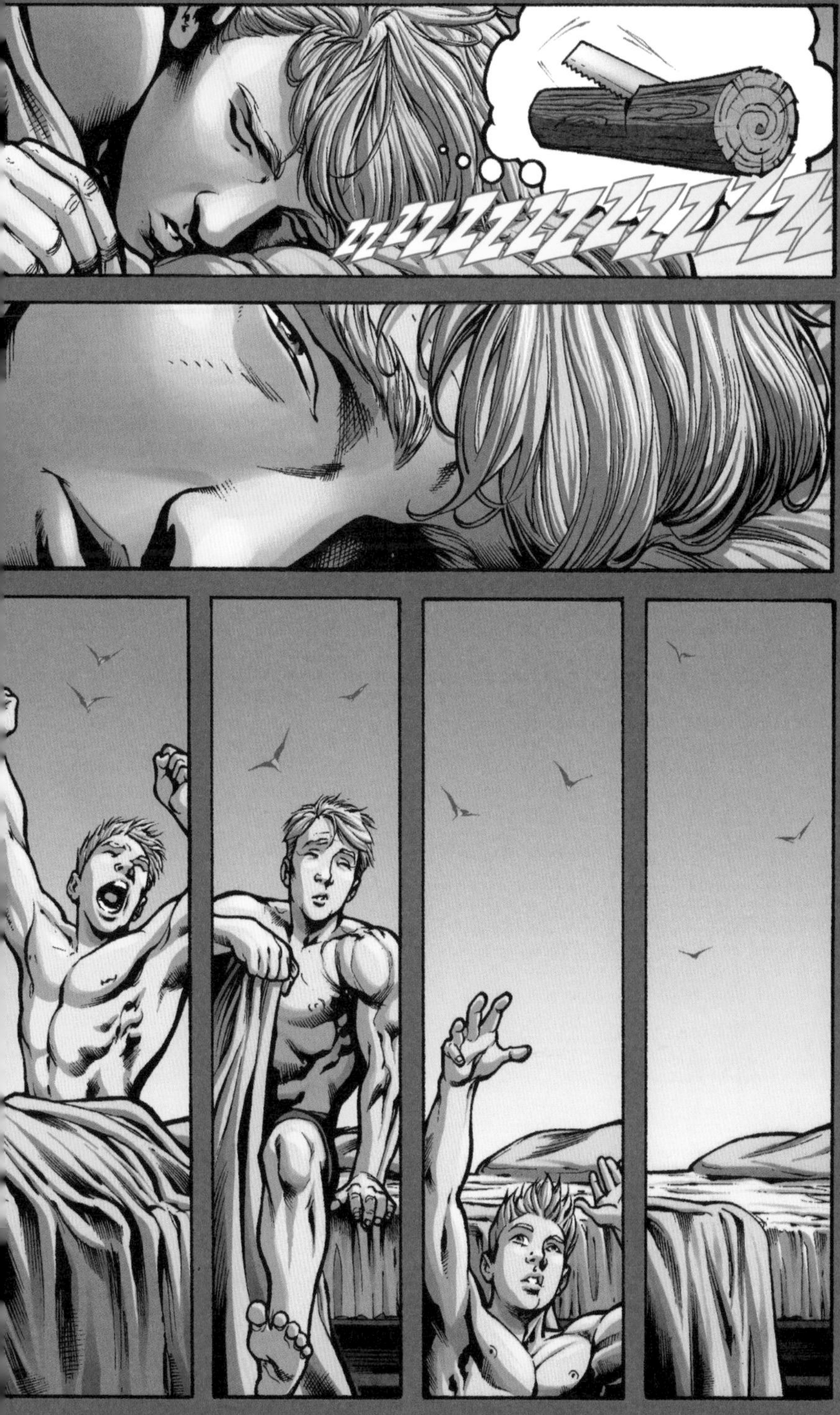
ZZZZZZZZZZZZZZ

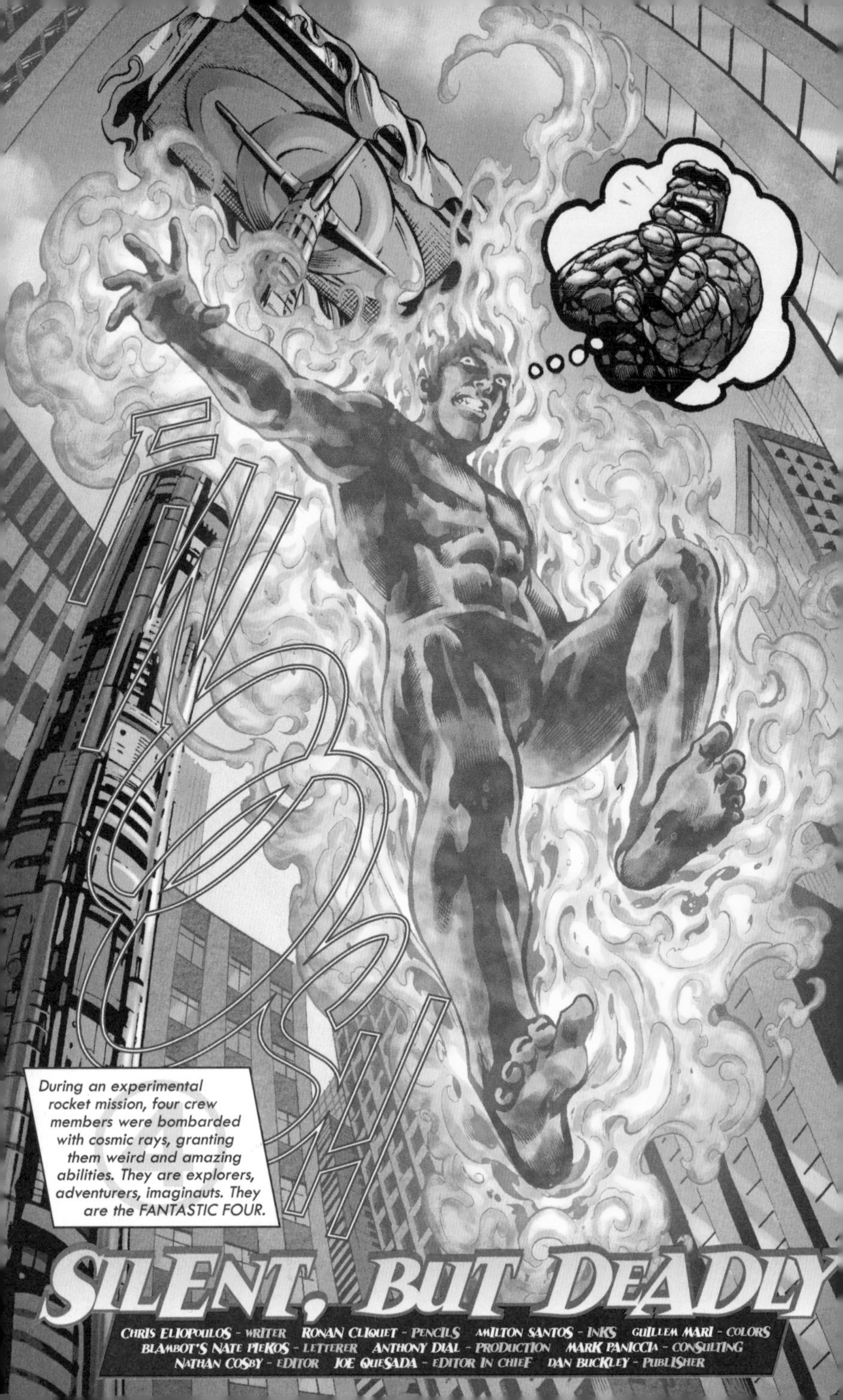

FWOOOSH
During an experimental rocket mission, four crew members were bombarded with cosmic rays, granting them weird and amazing abilities. They are explorers, adventurers, imaginauts. They are the FANTASTIC FOUR.
SILENT, BUT DEADLY
CHRIS ELIOPOULOS - WRITER RONAN CLIQUET - PENCILS AMILTON SANTOS - INKS GUILLEM MARI - COLORS
BLAMBOT'S NATE PIEKOS - LETTERER ANTHONY DIAL - PRODUCTION MARK PANICCIA - CONSULTING
NATHAN COSBY - EDITOR JOE QUESADA - EDITOR IN CHIEF DAN BUCKLEY - PUBLISHER

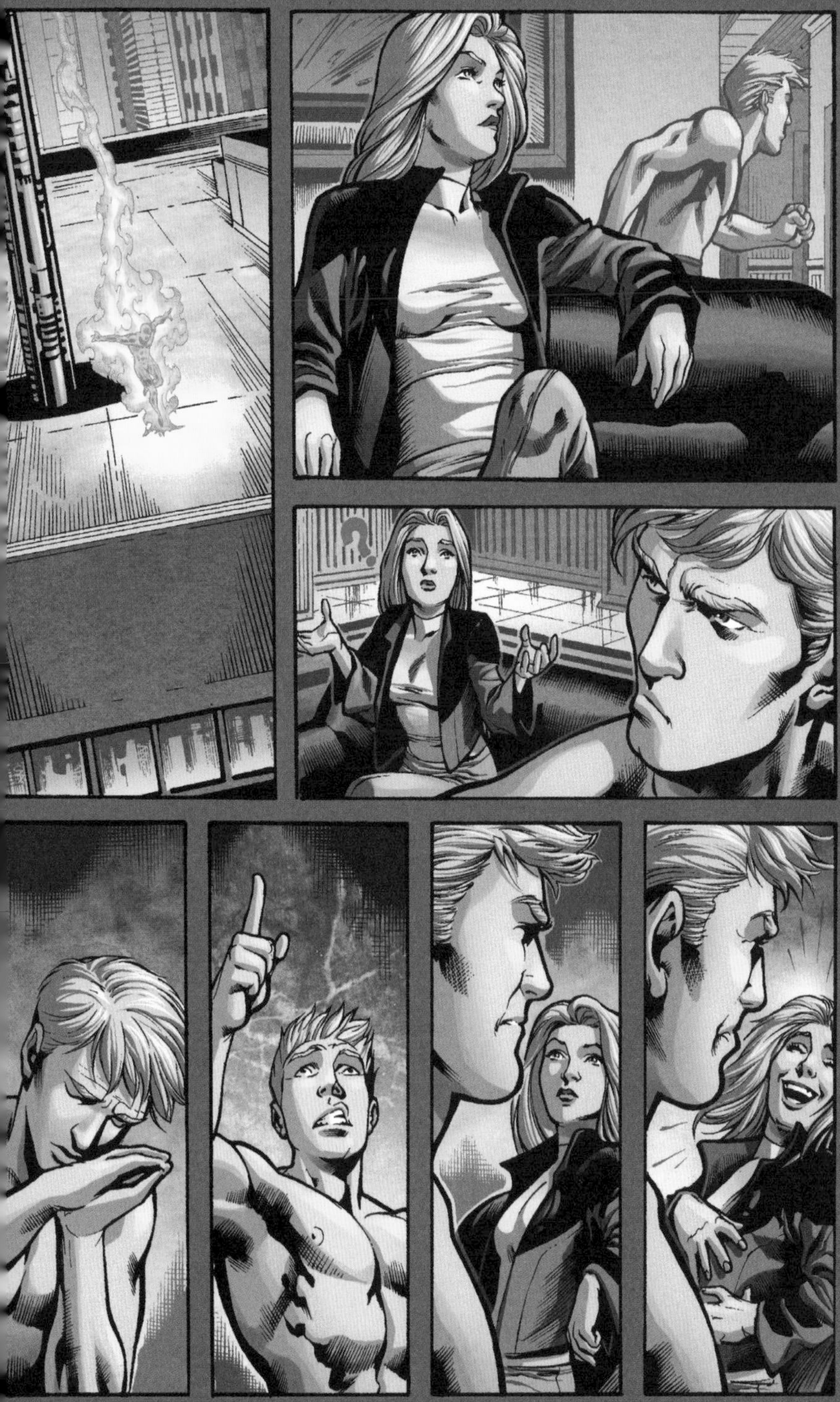

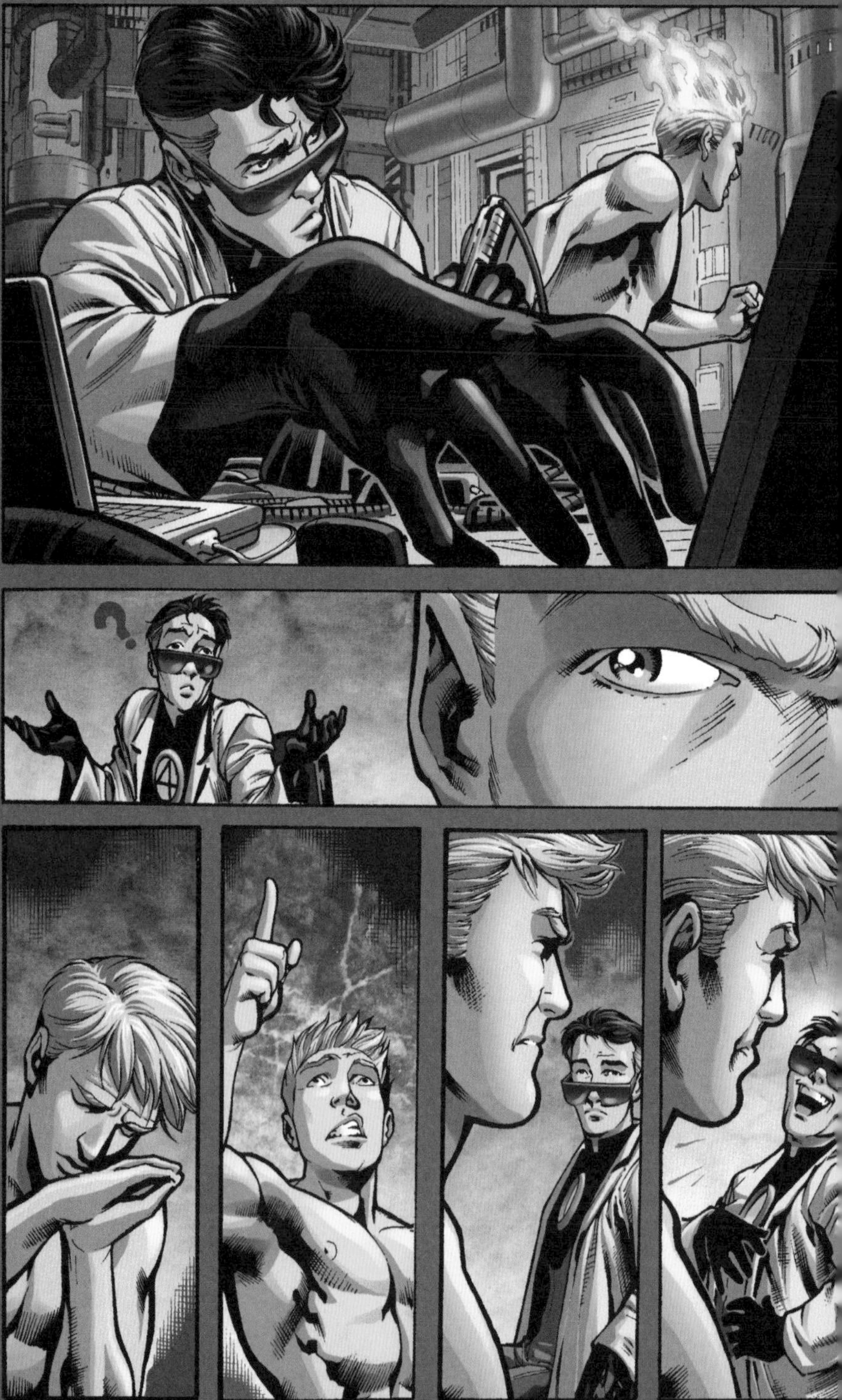
?

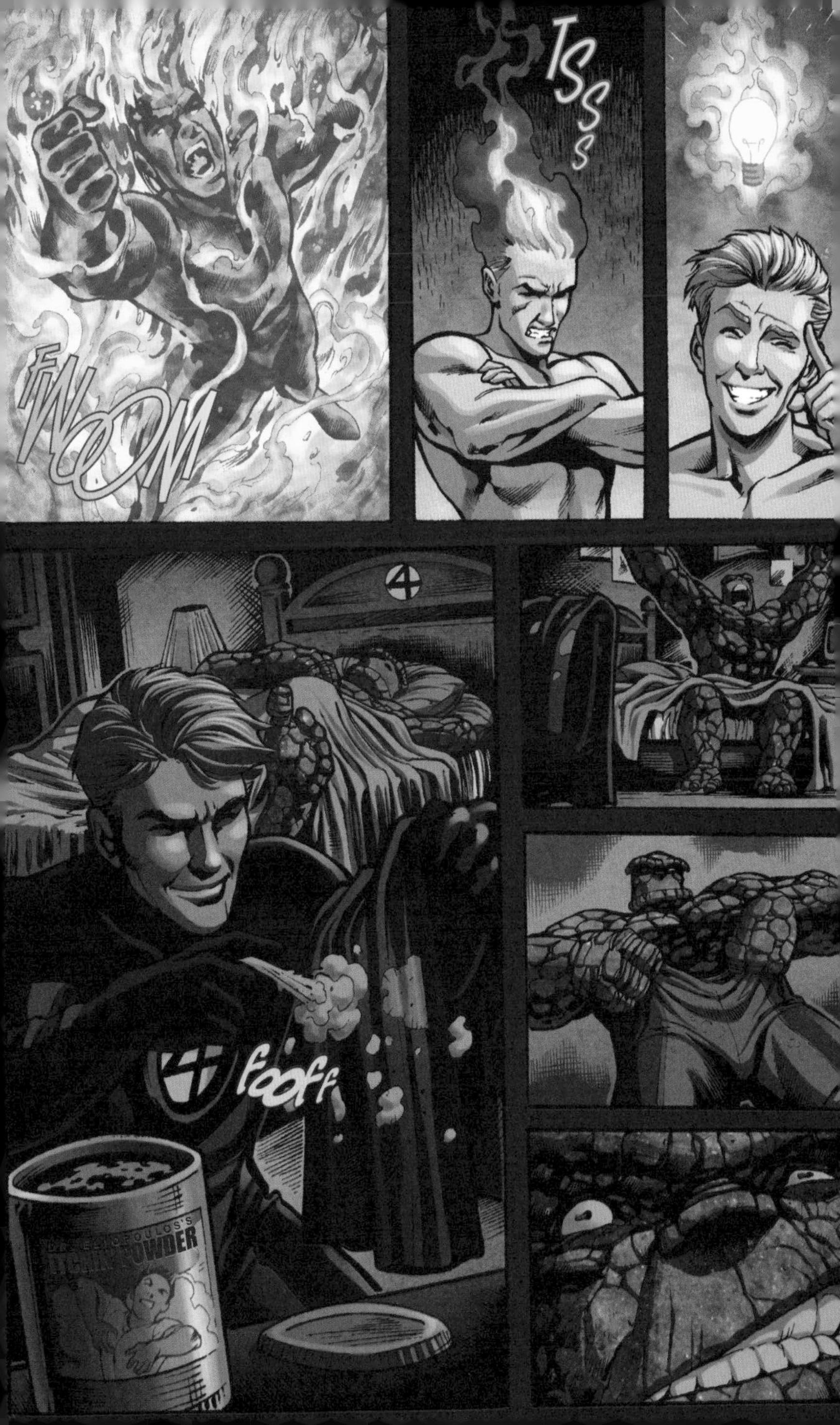
FWOOM
TSSSS
fooff

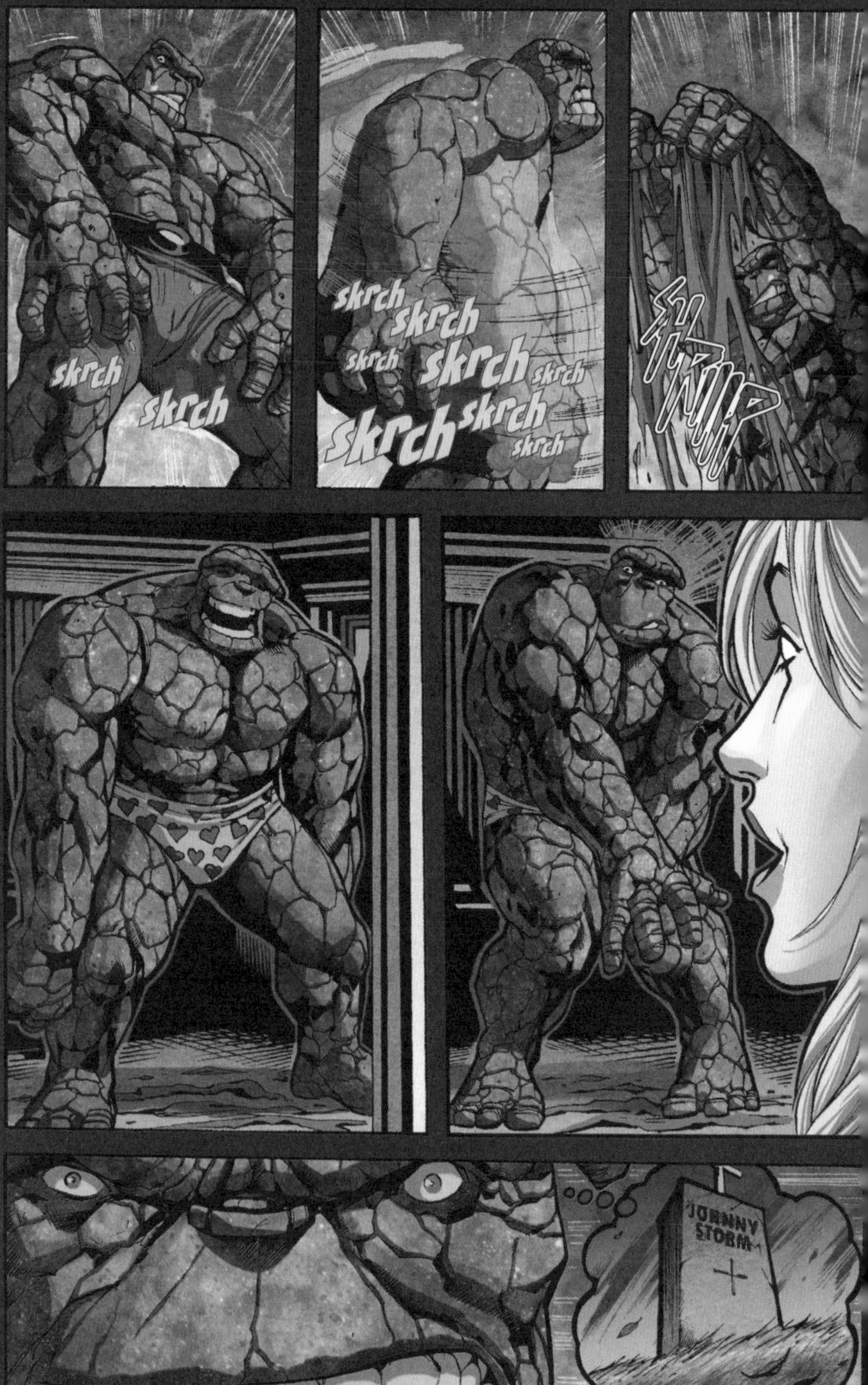
skrch
skrch
skrch
skrch
skrch
skrch
skrch
skrch
skrch
skrch
JOHNNY
STORM

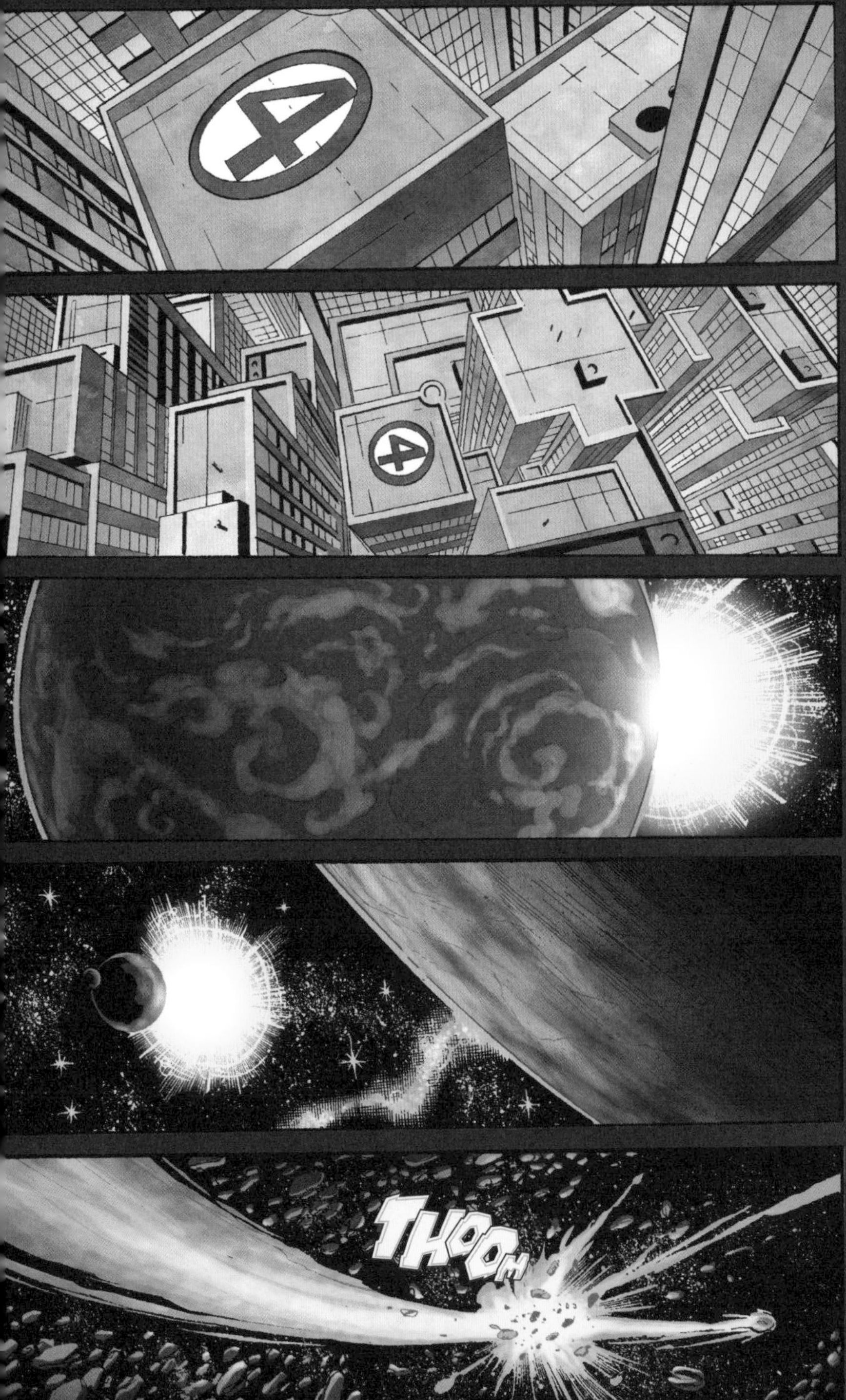
THOOOM

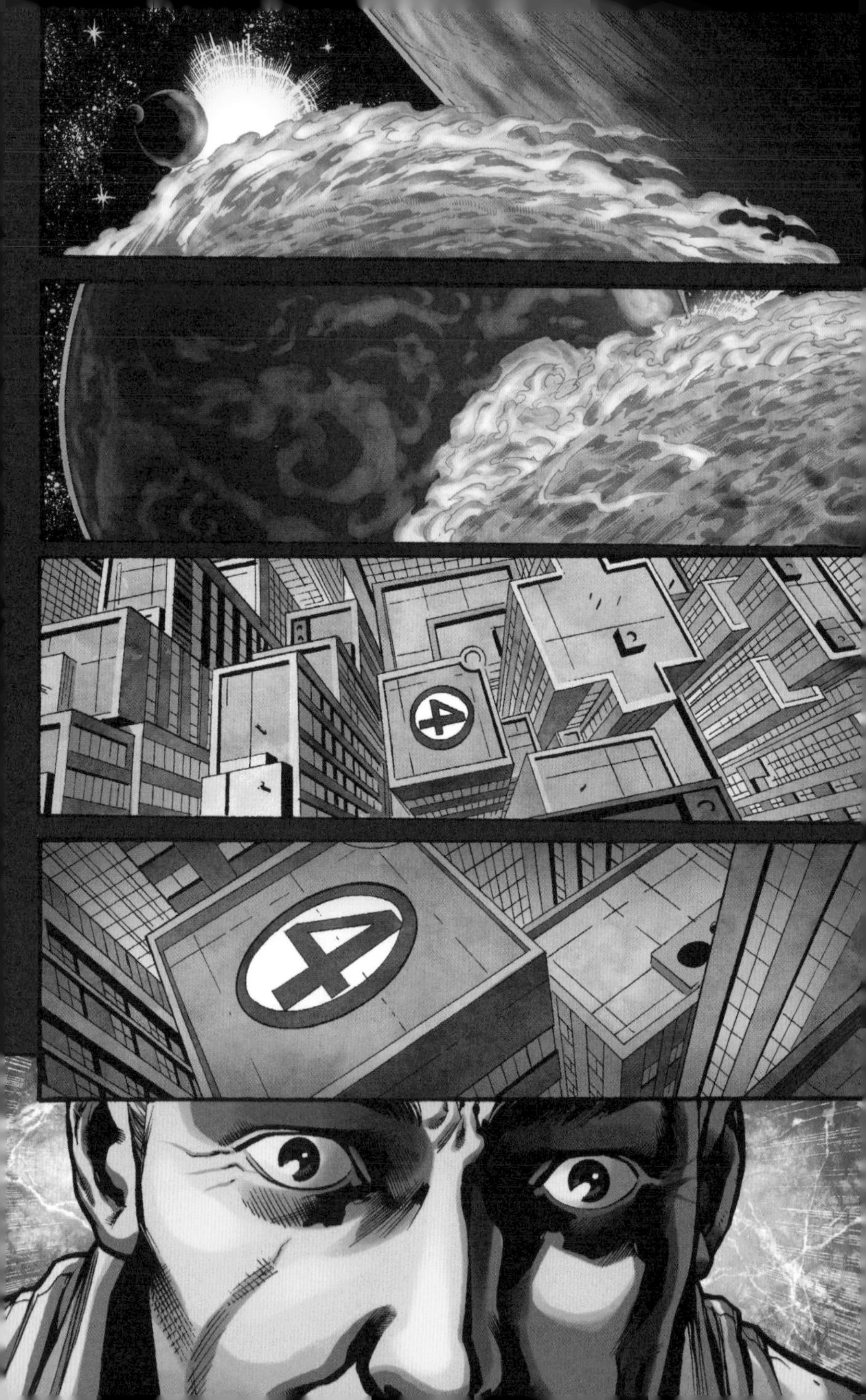

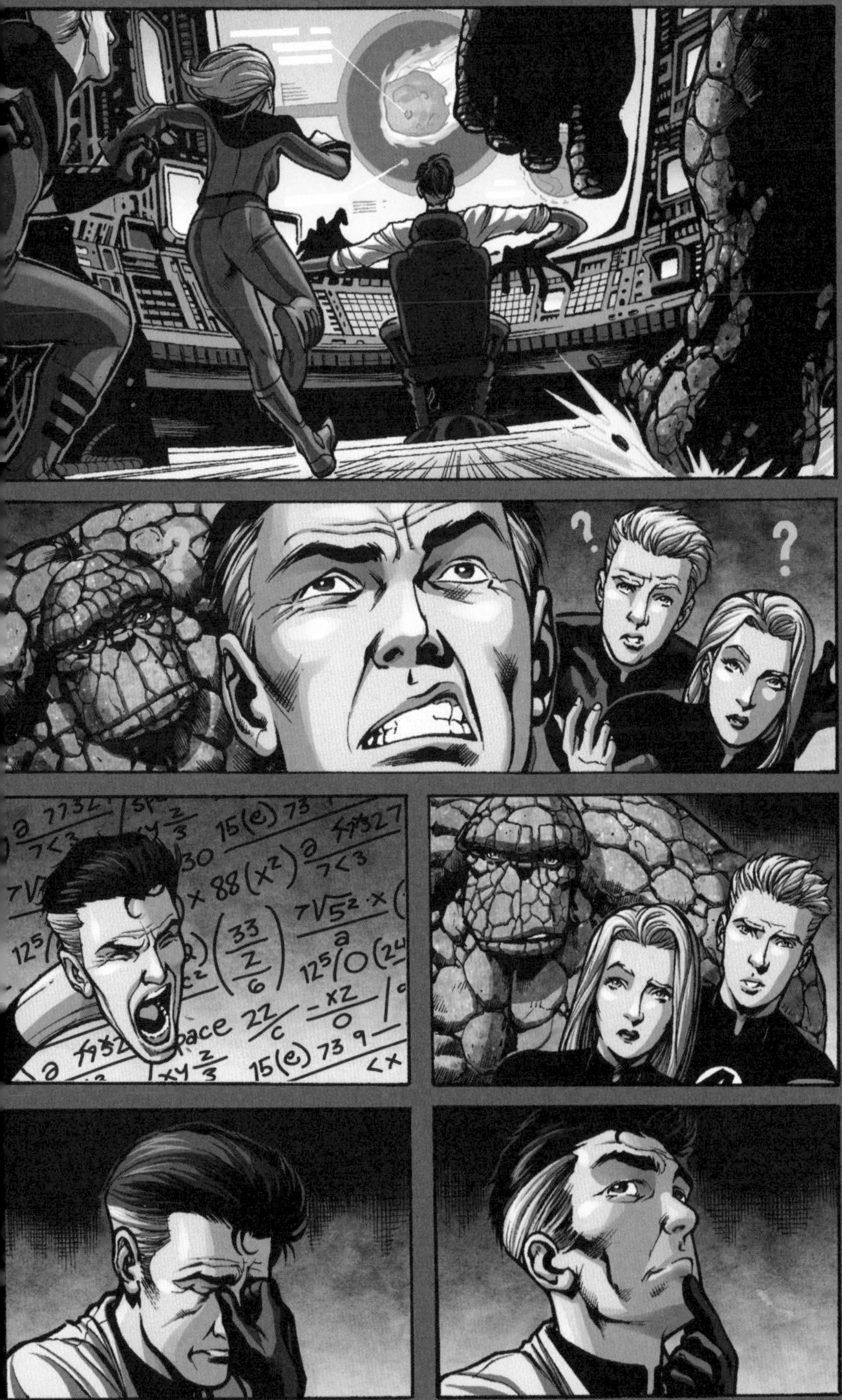

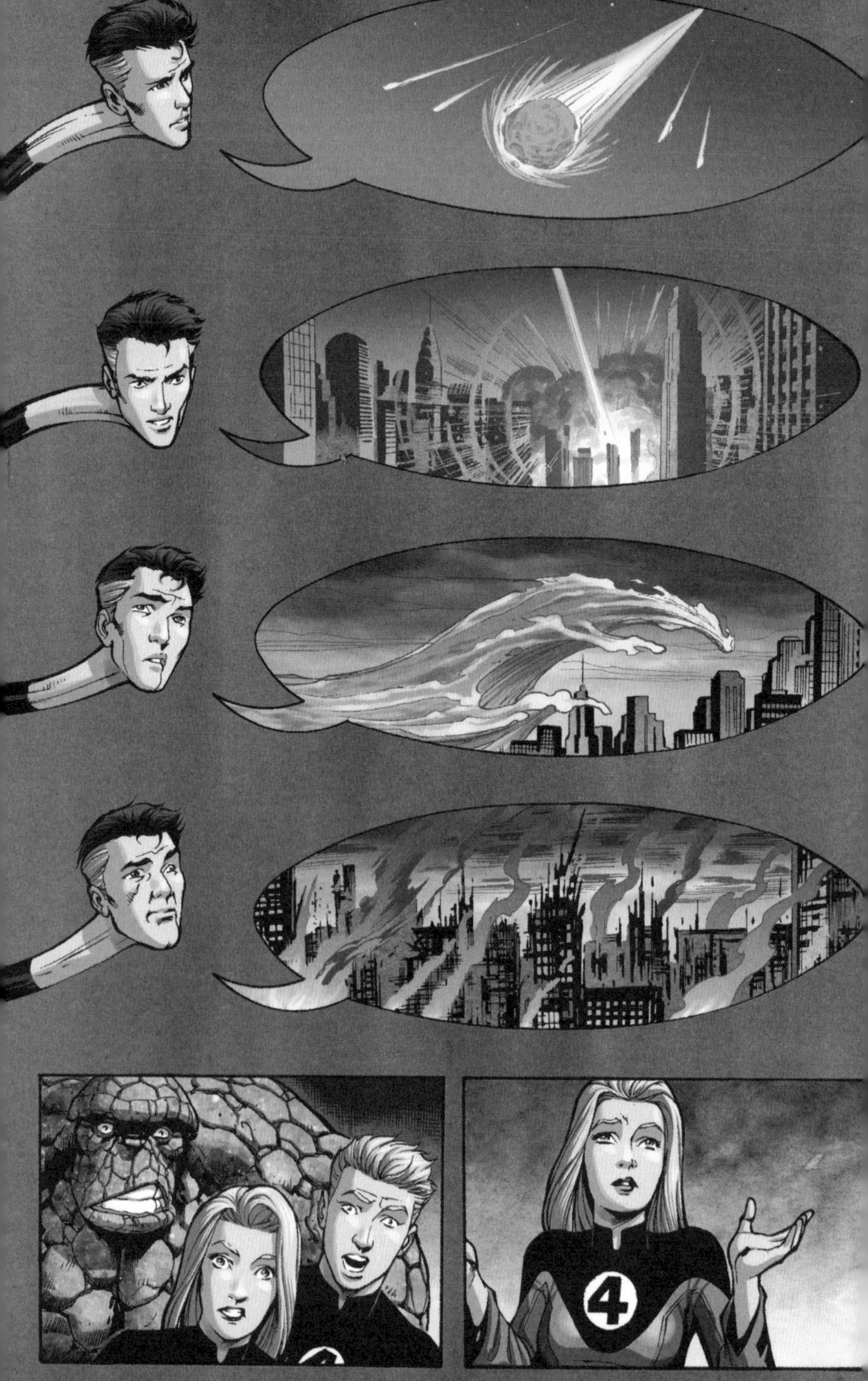

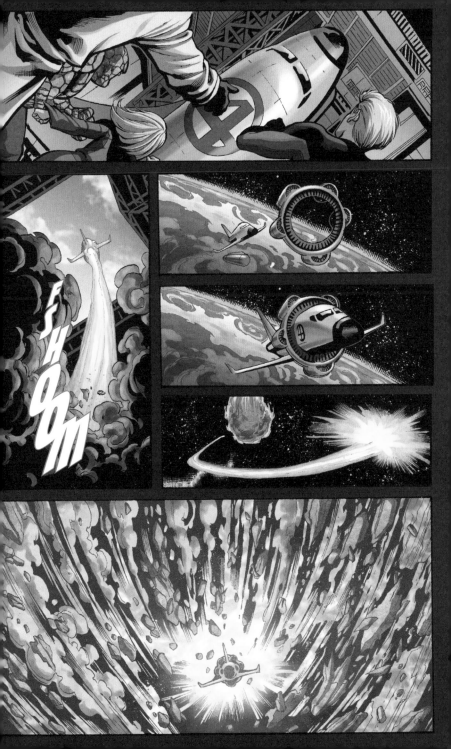

FSHOOM

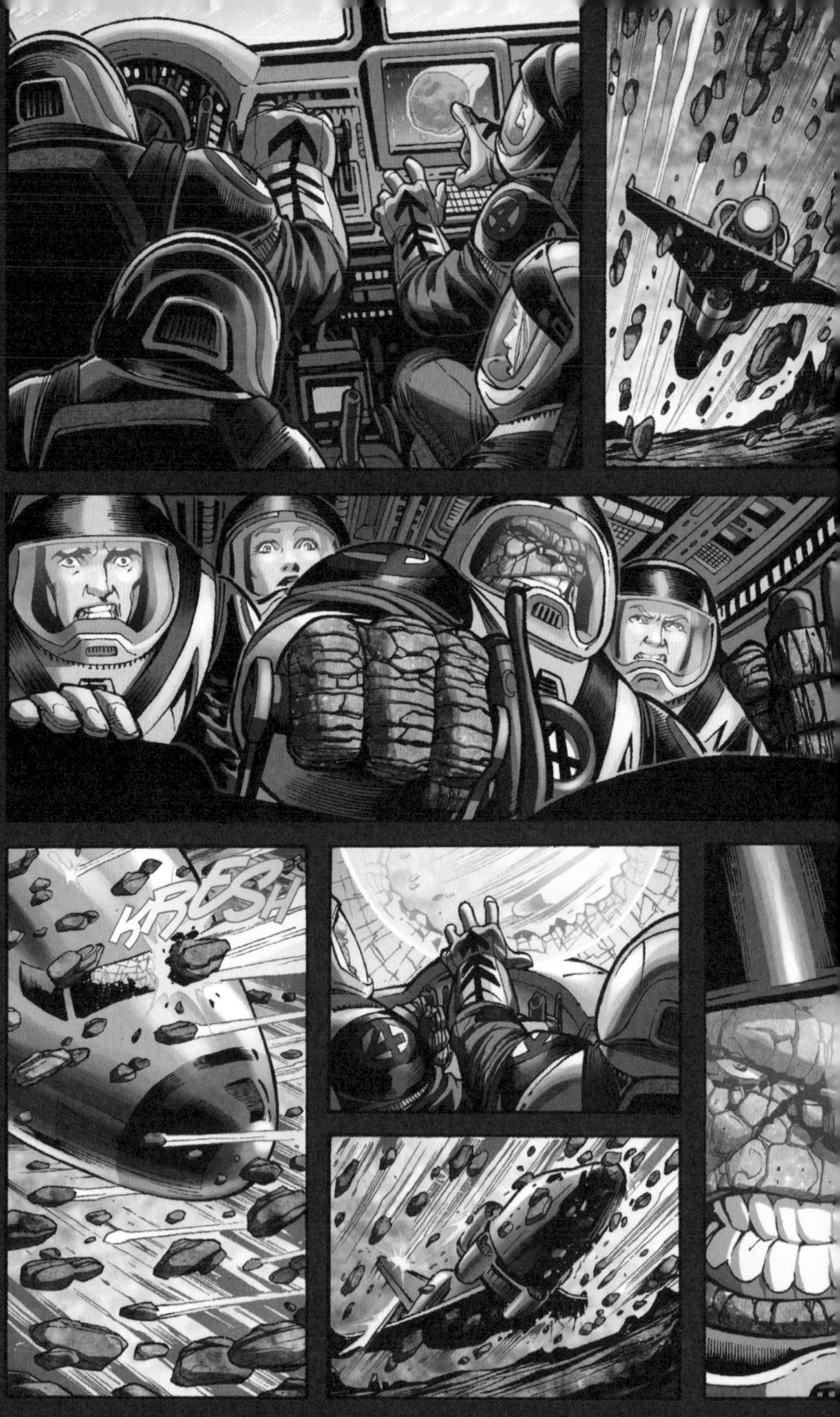
KRESH

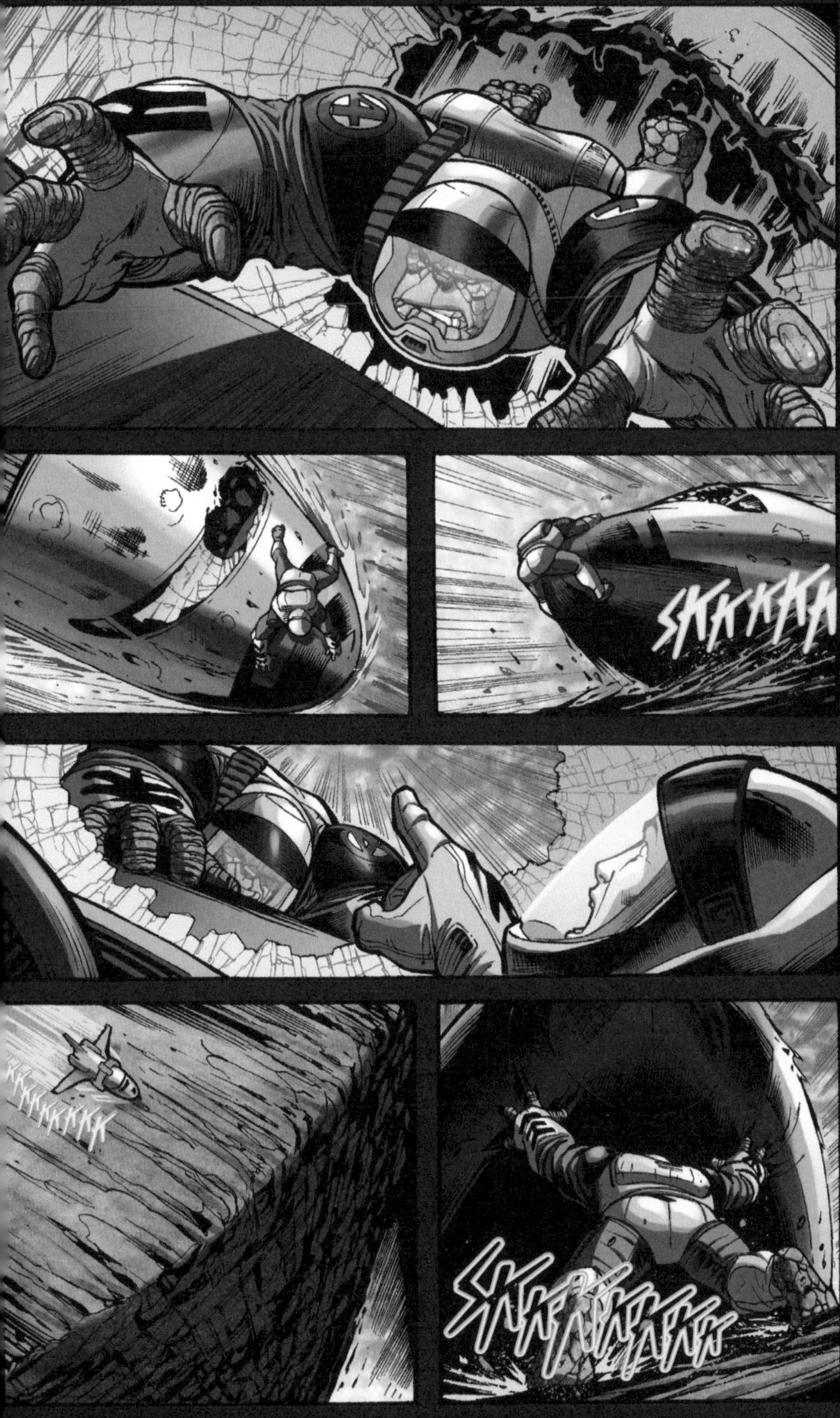
SKKKKK

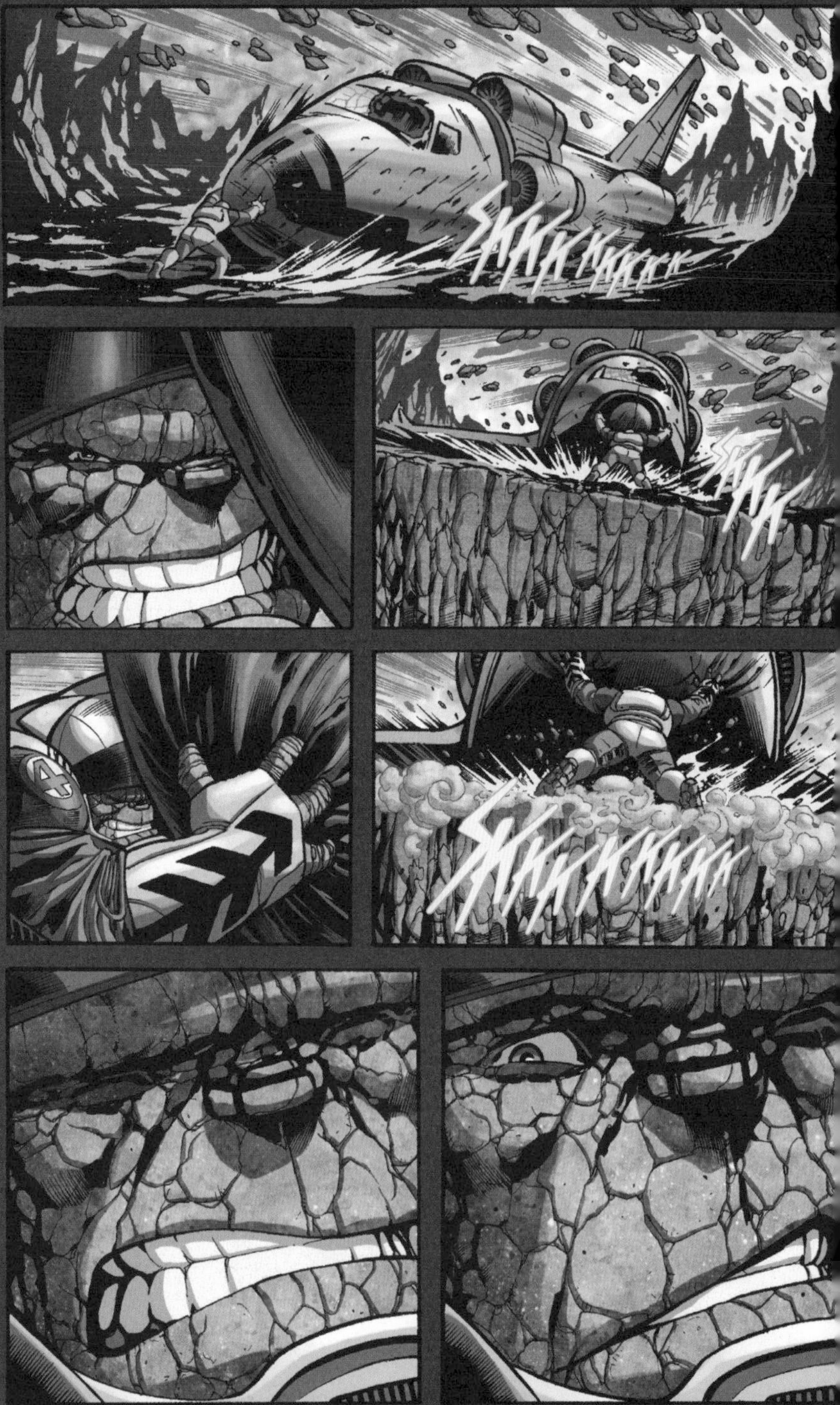

SKKKKKKKKKK
SKKK
SKKKKKKKKKK

SKKKKK

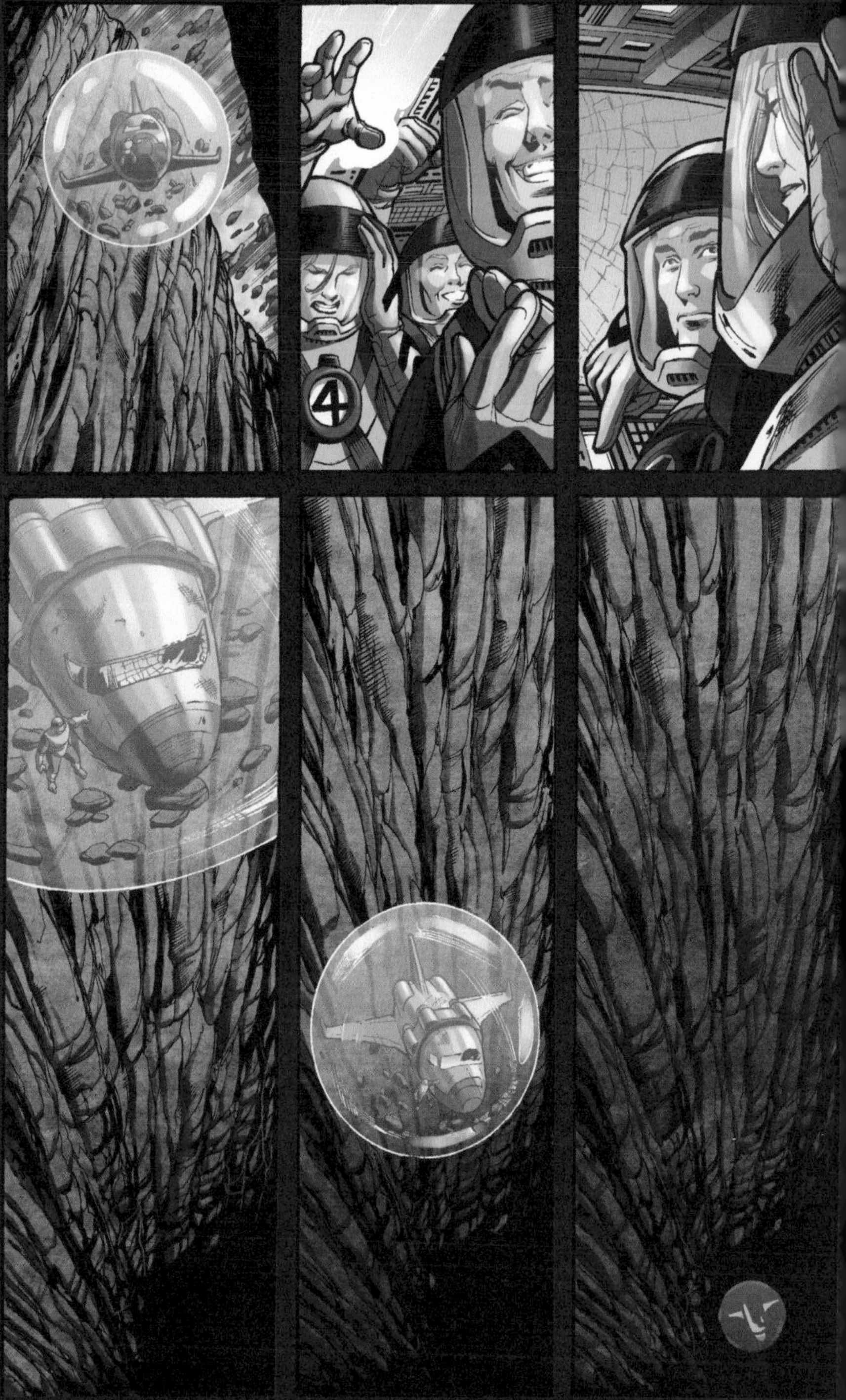

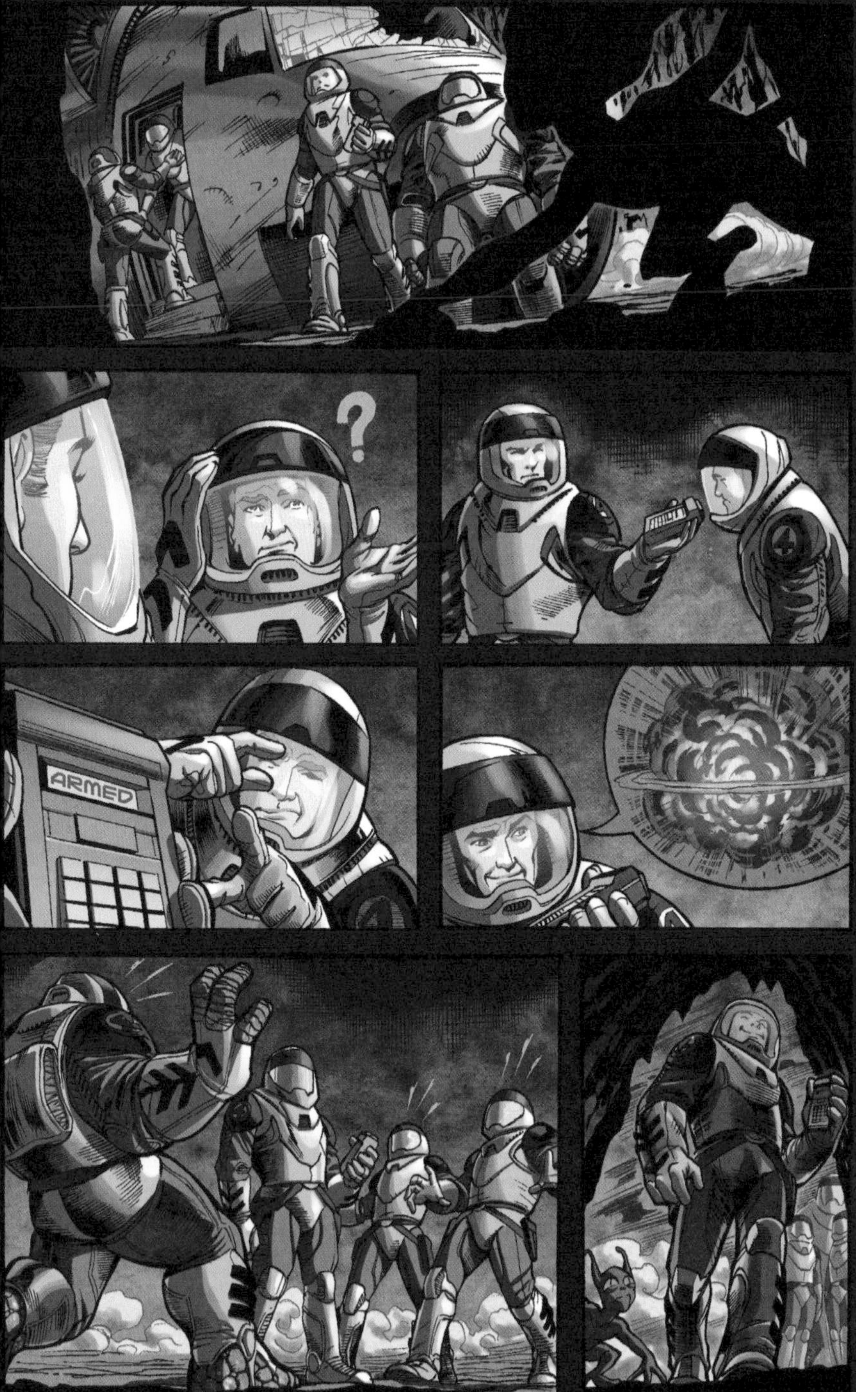
?
ARMED

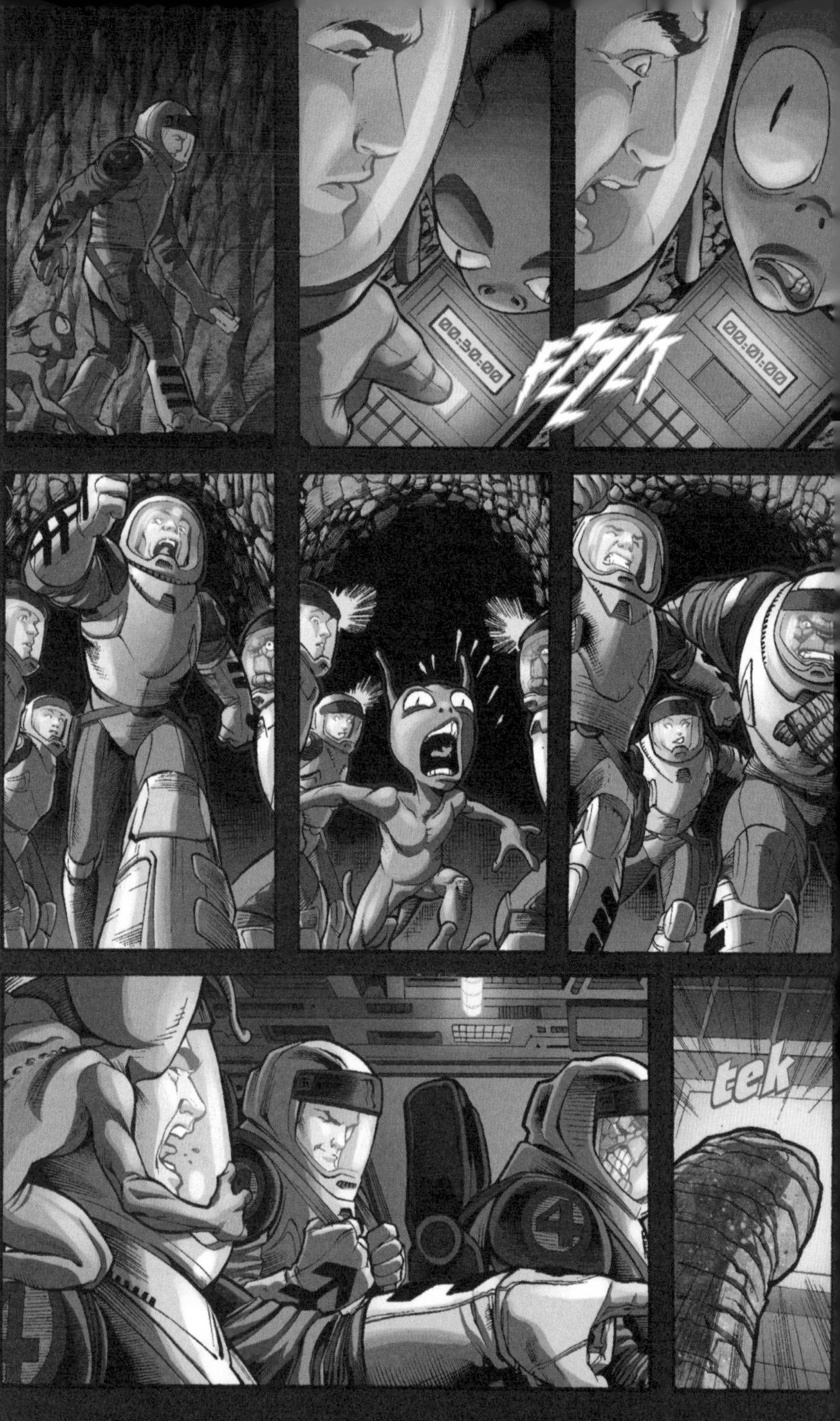
00:30:00
FZZZT
00:01:00
tek

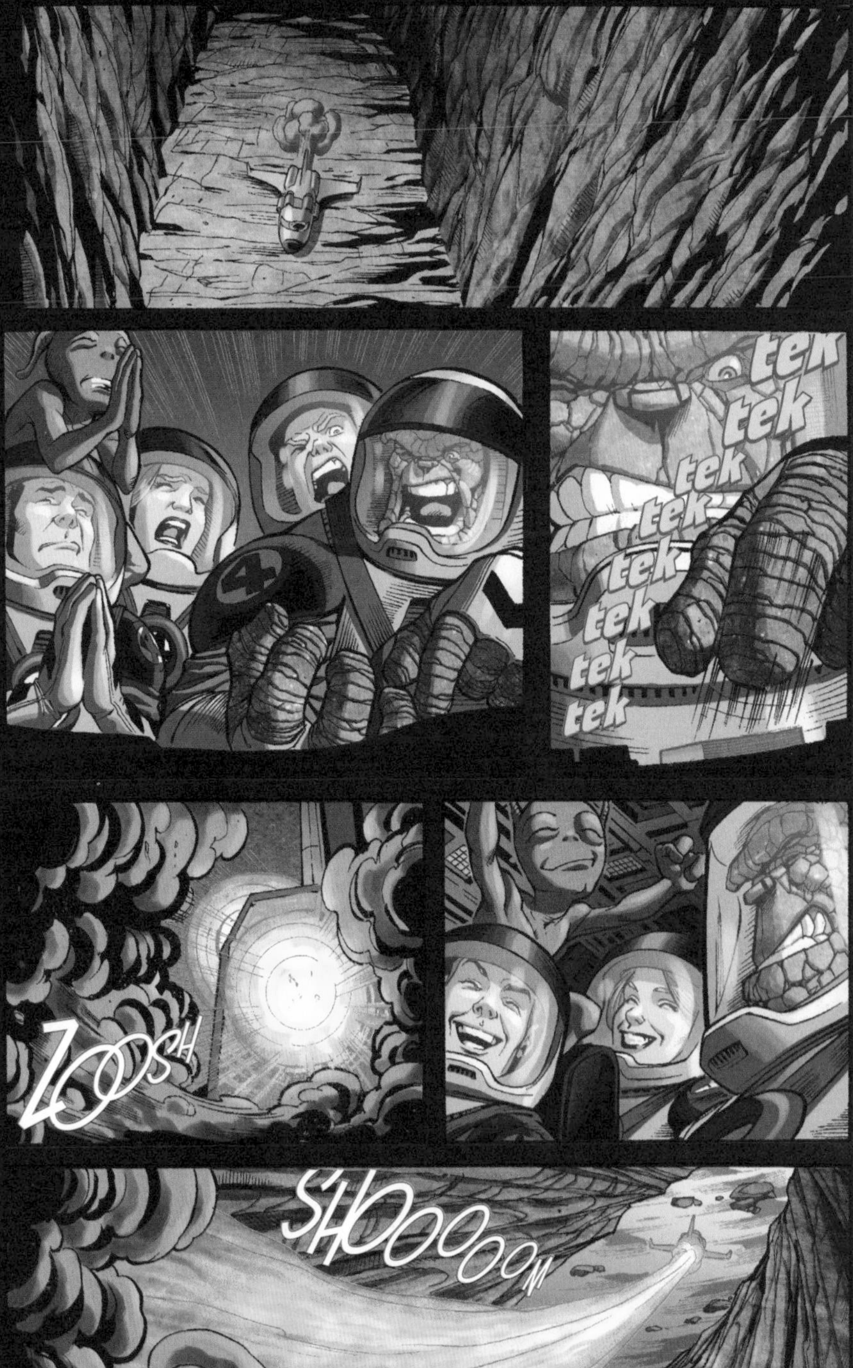

tek
tek
tek
tek
tek
tek
tek
tek
tek
ZOOSH
SHOOOOOM

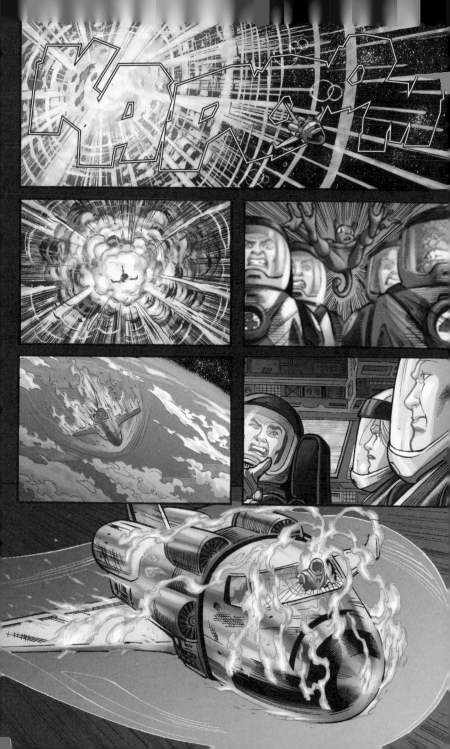

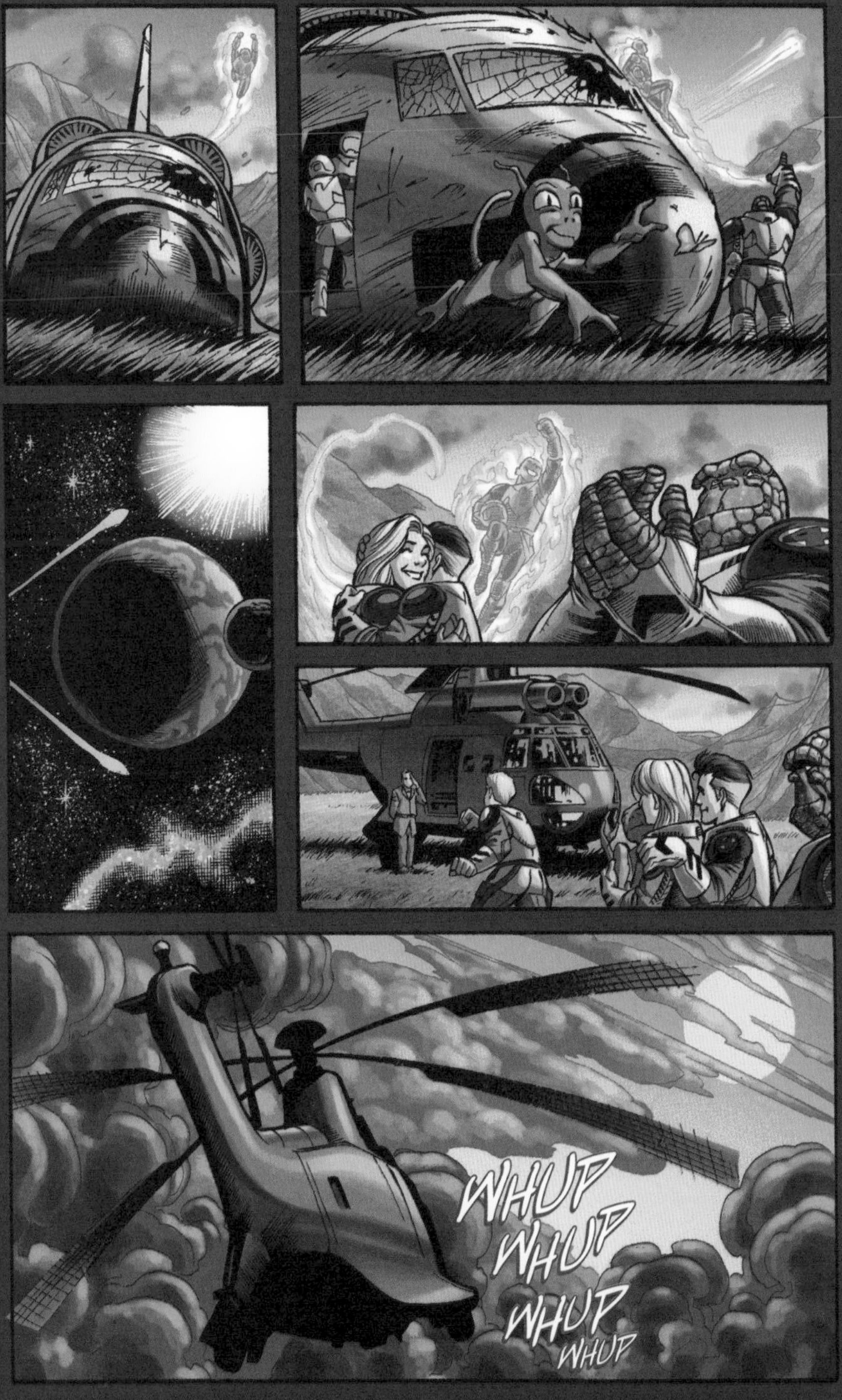

WHUP
WHUP
WHUP
WHUP

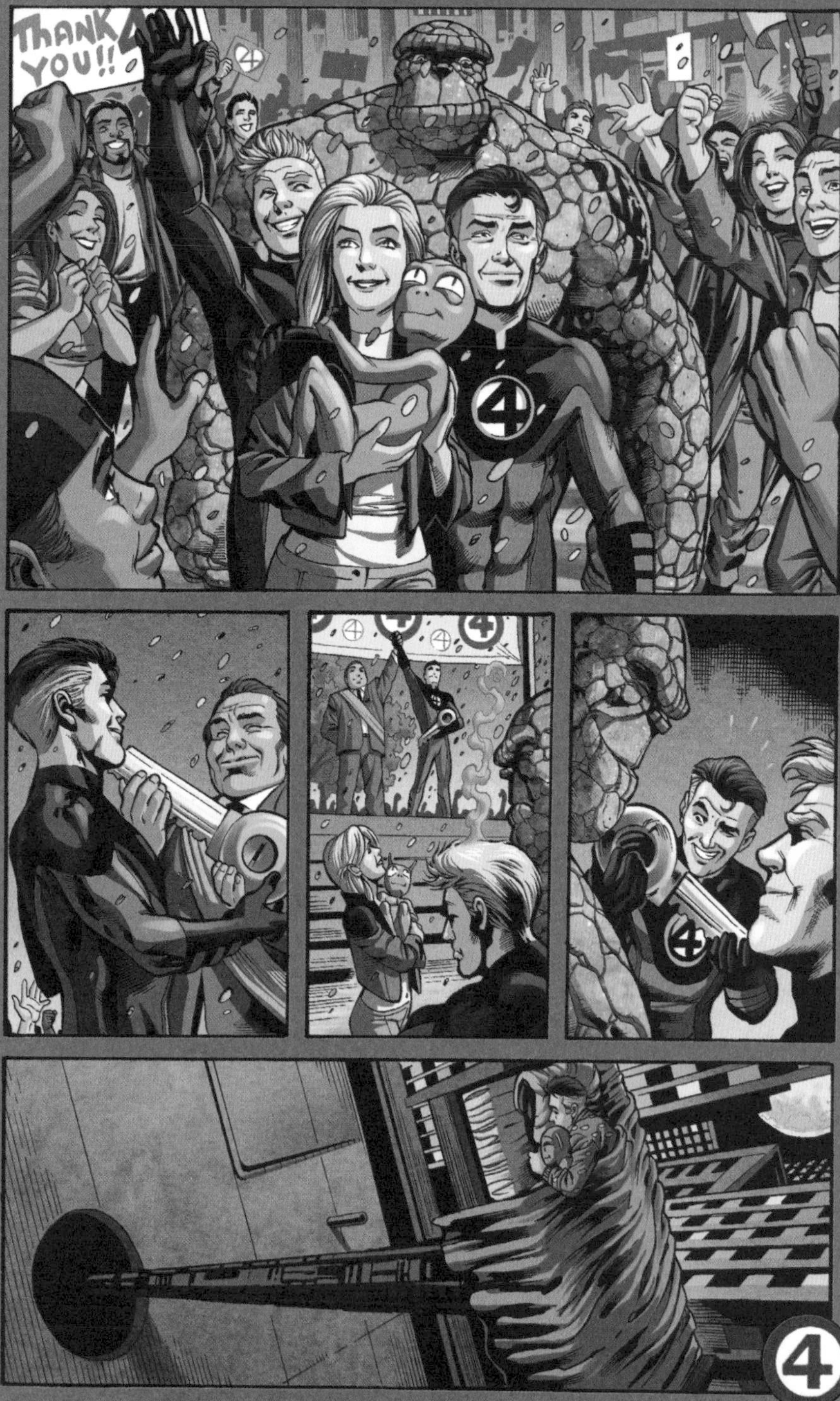
THANK YOU!!

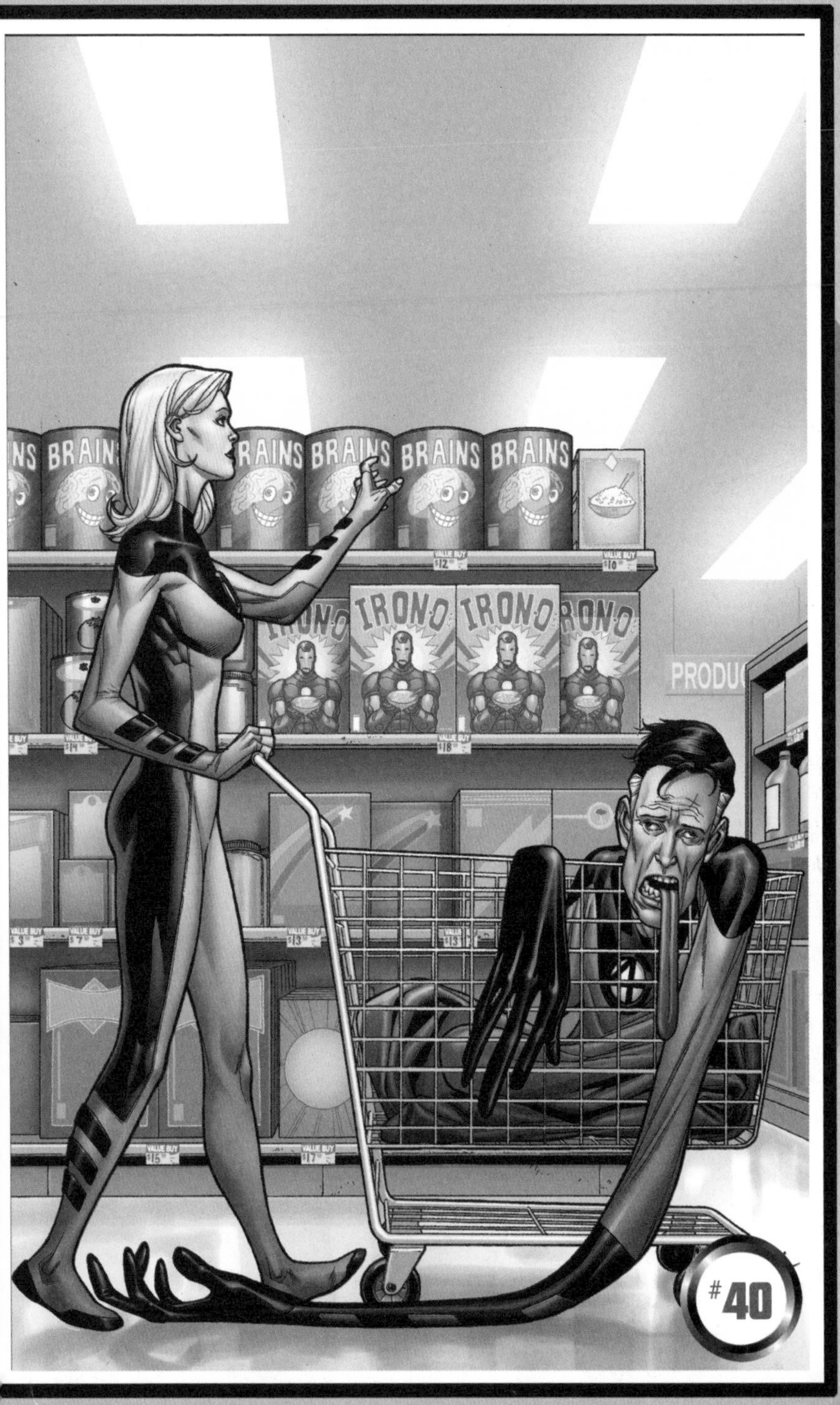

BRAINS
IRON-O
PRODUC
VALUE BUY
#40

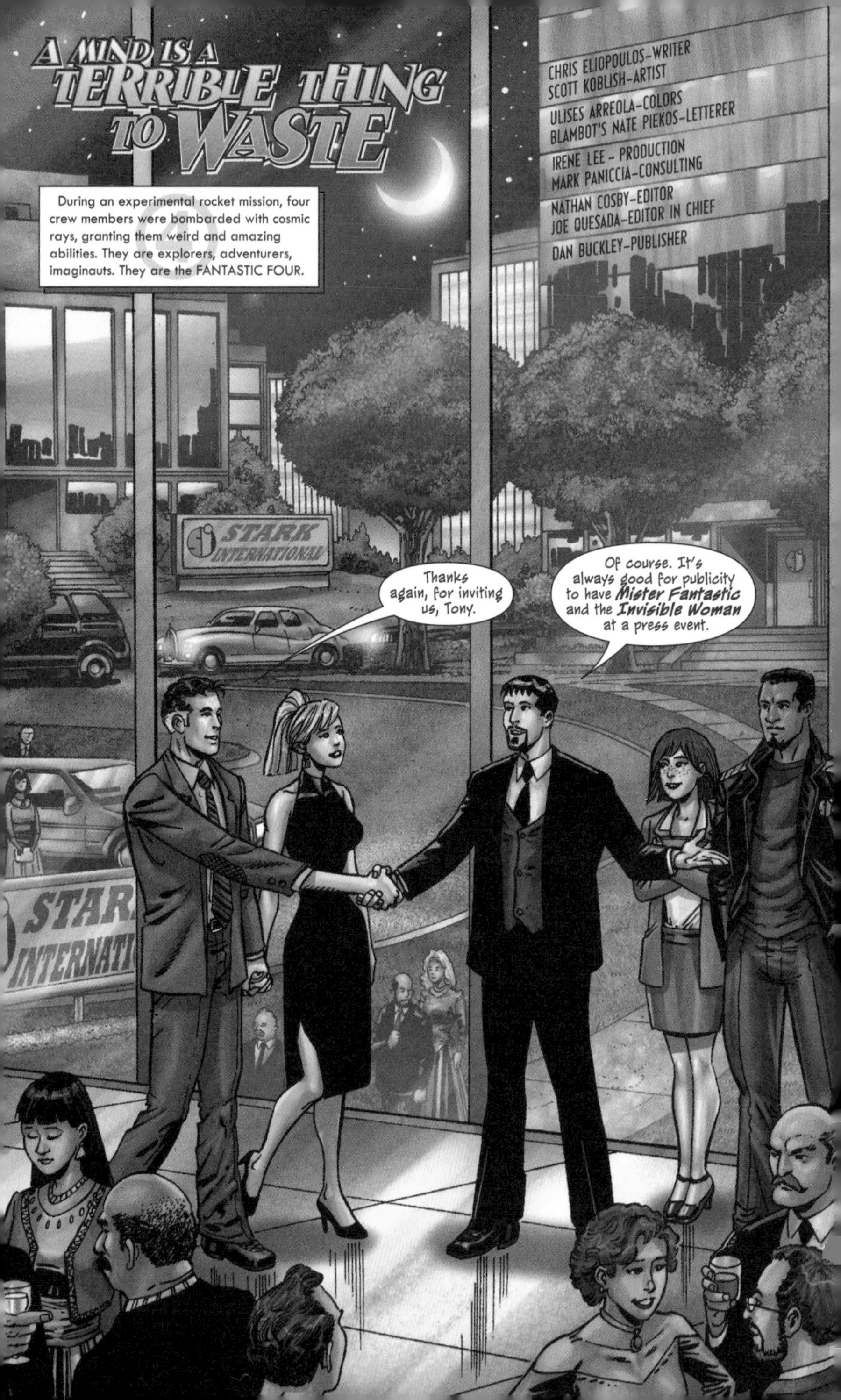

A MIND IS A TERRIBLE THING TO WASTE
CHRIS ELIOPOULOS-WRITER
SCOTT KOBLISH-ARTIST
ULISES ARREOLA-COLORS
BLAMBOT'S NATE PIEKOS-LETTERER
IRENE LEE - PRODUCTION
MARK PANICCIA-CONSULTING
NATHAN COSBY-EDITOR
JOE QUESADA-EDITOR IN CHIEF
DAN BUCKLEY-PUBLISHER
During an experimental rocket mission, four crew members were bombarded with cosmic rays, granting them weird and amazing abilities. They are explorers, adventurers, imaginauts. They are the FANTASTIC FOUR.
STARK INTERNATIONAL
Thanks again, for inviting us, Tony.
Of course. It's always good for publicity to have *Mister Fantastic* and the *Invisible Woman* at a press event.
STARK INTERNATI

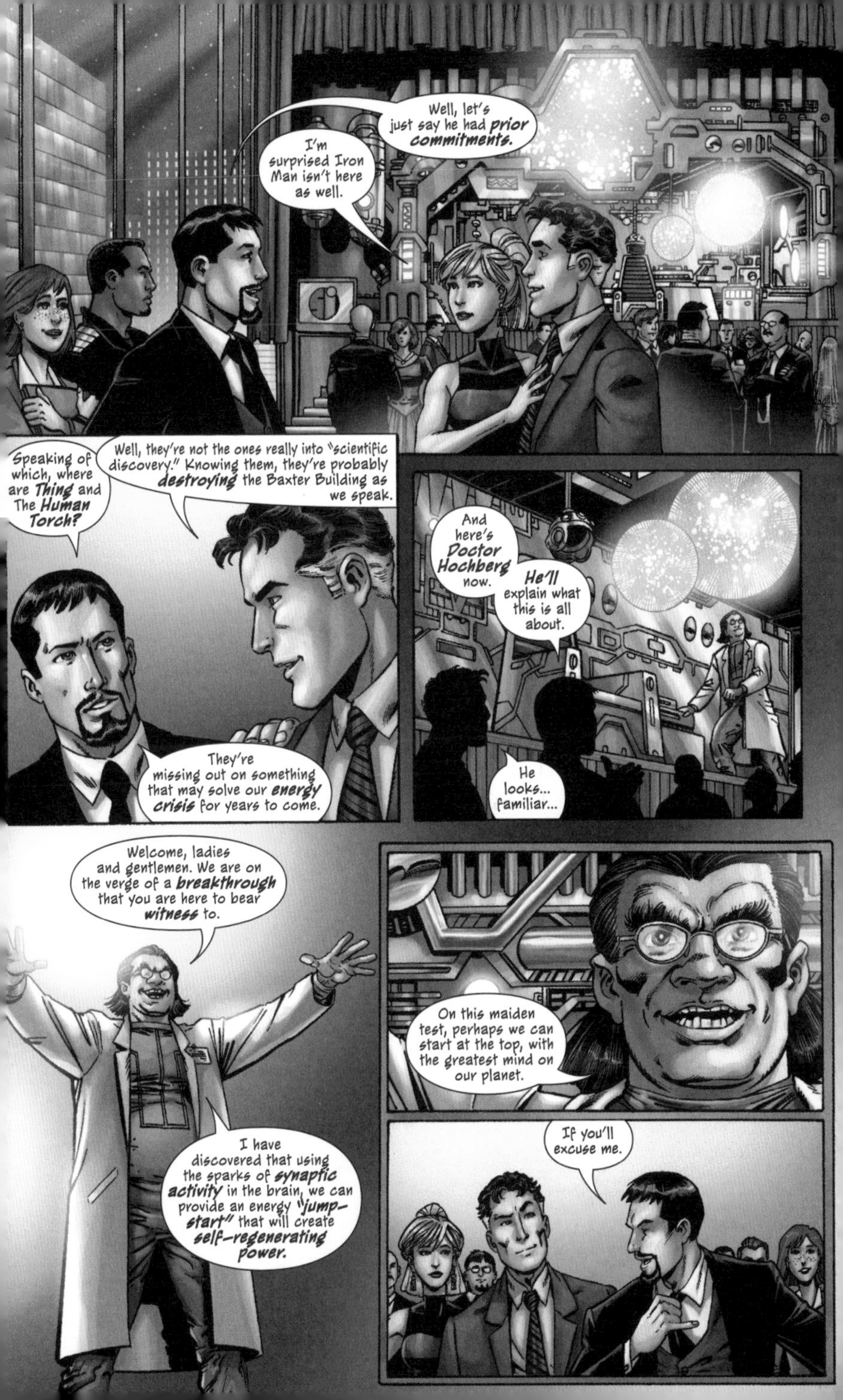
I'm surprised Iron Man isn't here as well.
Well, let's just say he had prior commitments.
Speaking of which, where are Thing and The Human Torch?
Well, they're not the ones really into "scientific discovery." Knowing them, they're probably destroying the Baxter Building as we speak.
They're missing out on something that may solve our energy crisis for years to come.
And here's Doctor Hochberg now.
He'll explain what this is all about.
He looks... familiar...
Welcome, ladies and gentlemen. We are on the verge of a breakthrough that you are here to bear witness to.
I have discovered that using the sparks of synaptic activity in the brain, we can provide an energy "jump-start" that will create self-regenerating power.
On this maiden test, perhaps we can start at the top, with the greatest mind on our planet.
If you'll excuse me.

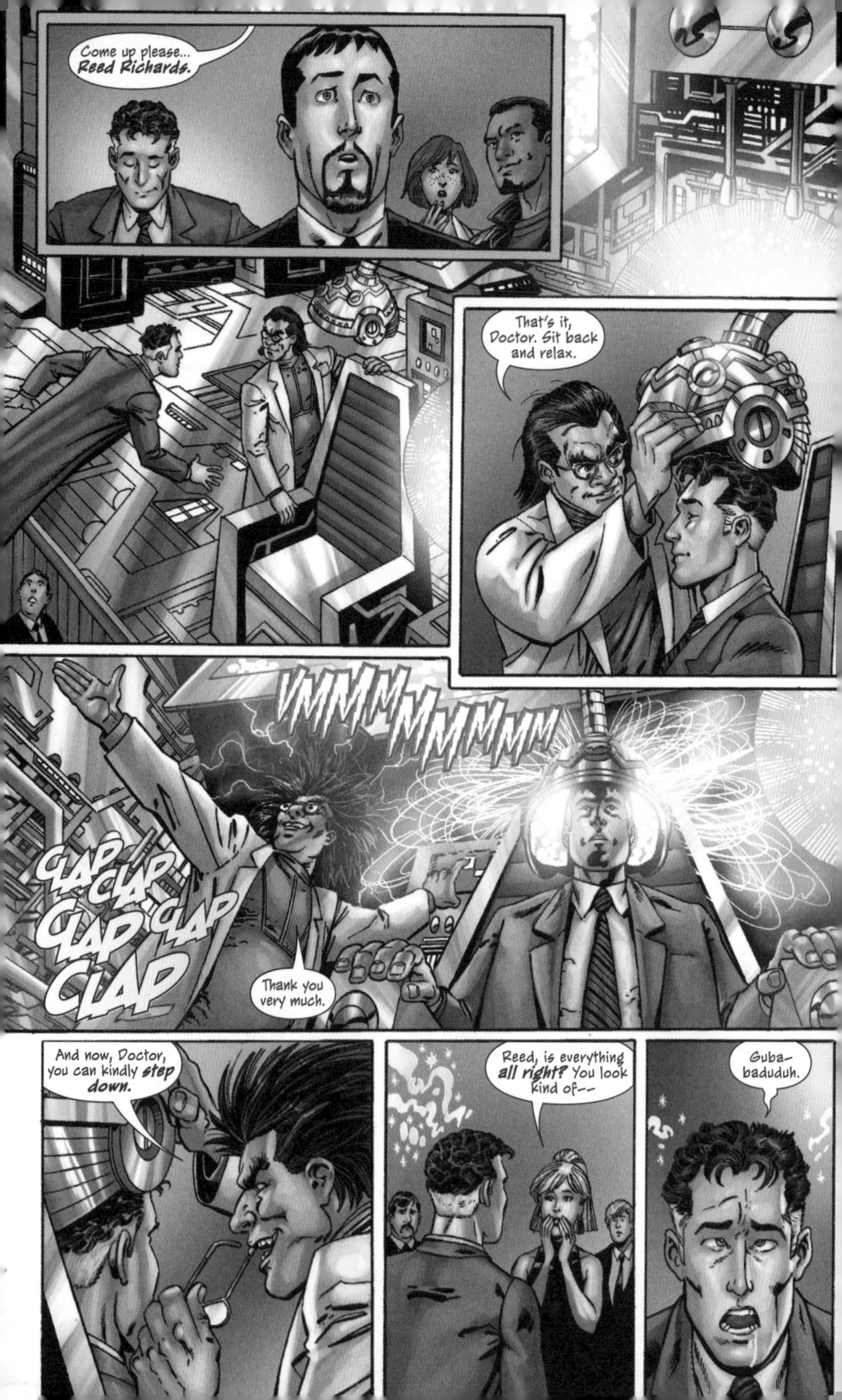

Come up please... **Reed Richards.**
That's it, Doctor. Sit back and relax.
VMMMMMMMMM
CLAP CLAP CLAP CLAP CLAP
Thank you very much.
And now, Doctor, you can kindly ***step down.***
Reed, is everything ***all right?*** You look kind of--
Guba-baduduh.

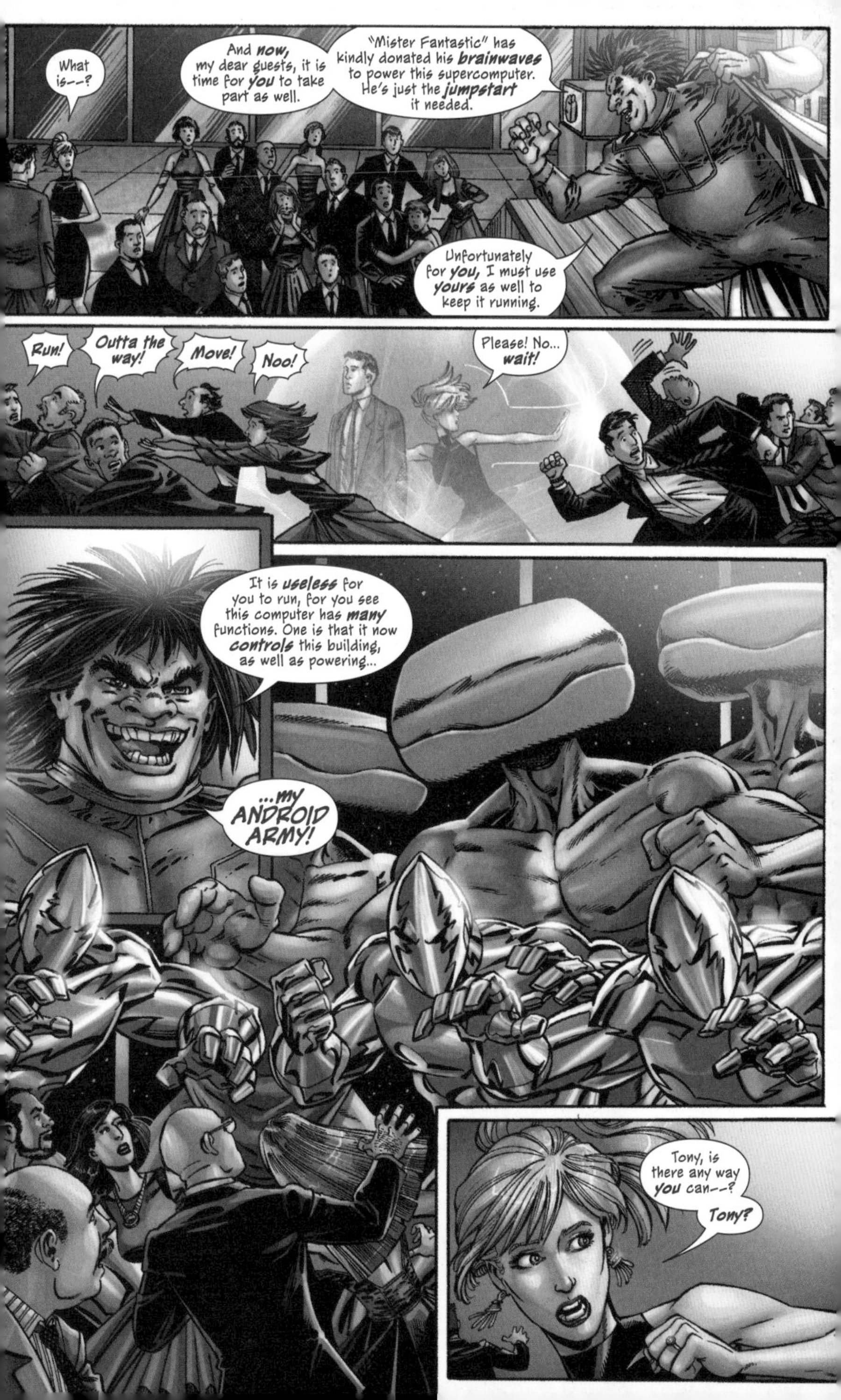
What is--?
And now, my dear guests, it is time for you to take part as well.
"Mister Fantastic" has kindly donated his brainwaves to power this supercomputer. He's just the jumpstart it needed.
Unfortunately for you, I must use yours as well to keep it running.
Run!
Outta the way!
Move!
Noo!
Please! No... wait!
It is useless for you to run, for you see this computer has many functions. One is that it now controls this building, as well as powering...
...my ANDROID ARMY!
Tony, is there any way you can--?
Tony?

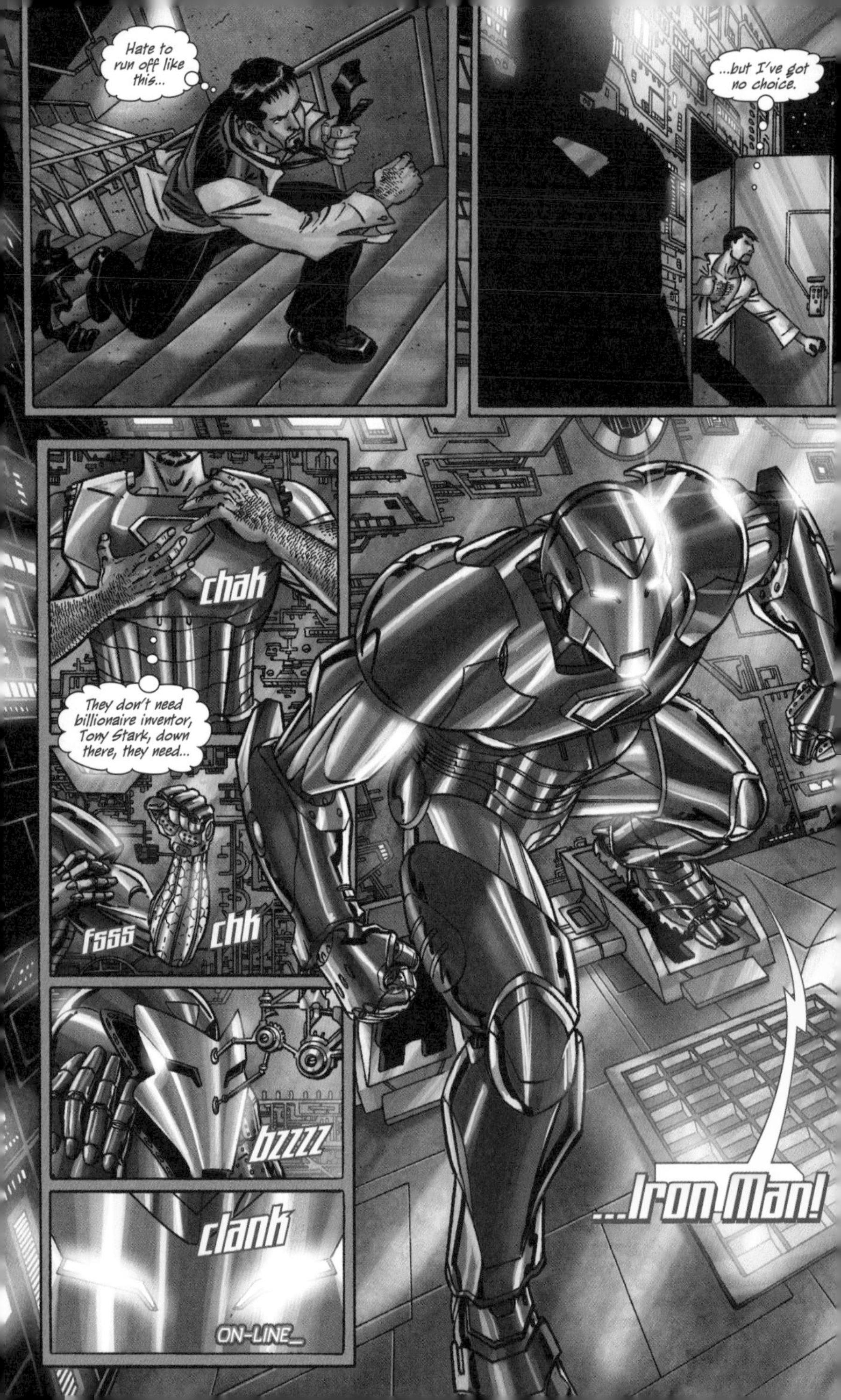

Hate to run off like this...
...but I've got no choice.
chak
They don't need billionaire inventor, Tony Stark, down there, they need...
fsss
chk
bzzzz
clank
ON-LINE_
...Iron Man!

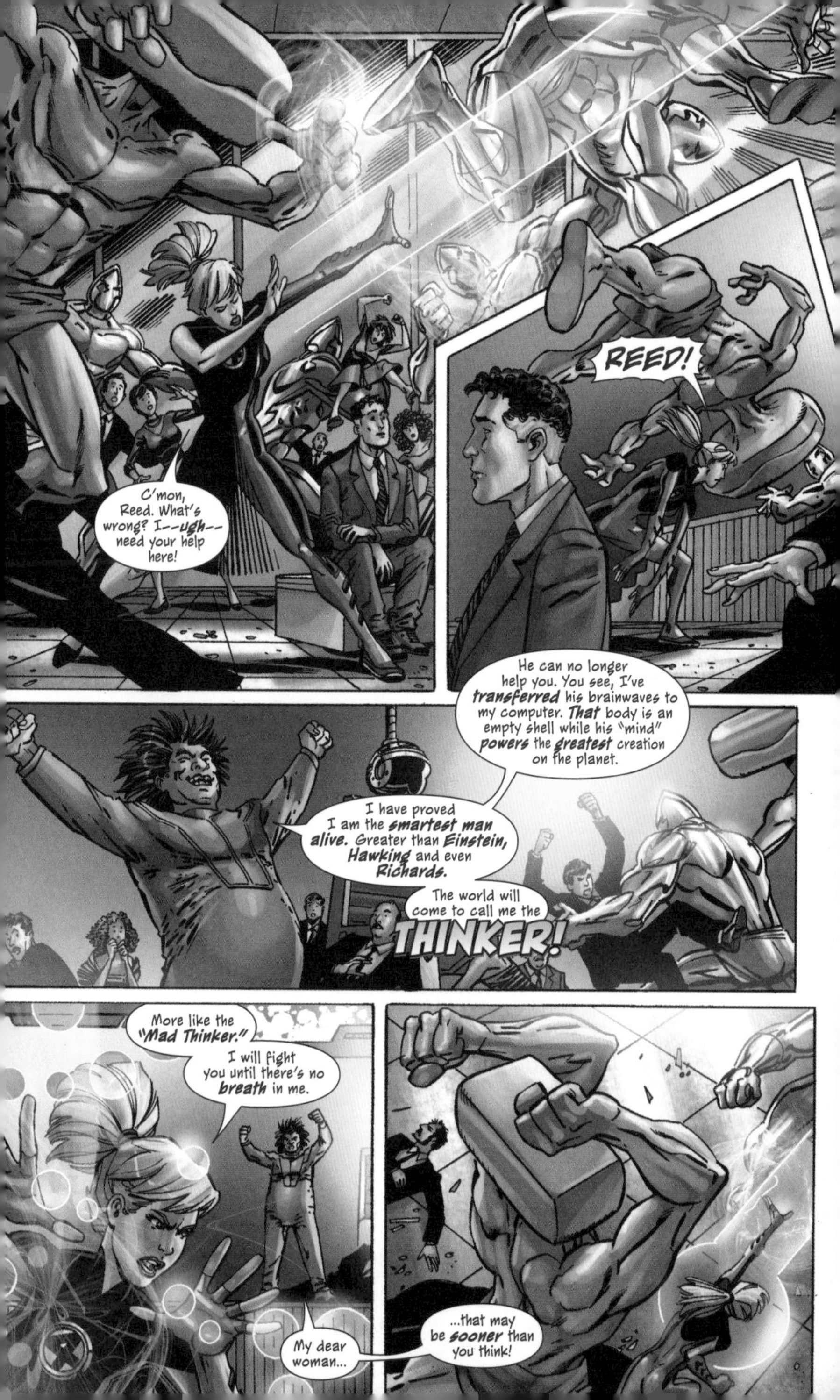

C'mon, Reed. What's wrong? I--ugh--need your help here!
REED!
He can no longer help you. You see, I've transferred his brainwaves to my computer. That body is an empty shell while his "mind" powers the greatest creation on the planet.
I have proved I am the smartest man alive. Greater than Einstein, Hawking and even Richards.
The world will come to call me the
THINKER!
More like the "Mad Thinker."
I will fight you until there's no breath in me.
My dear woman...
...that may be sooner than you think!

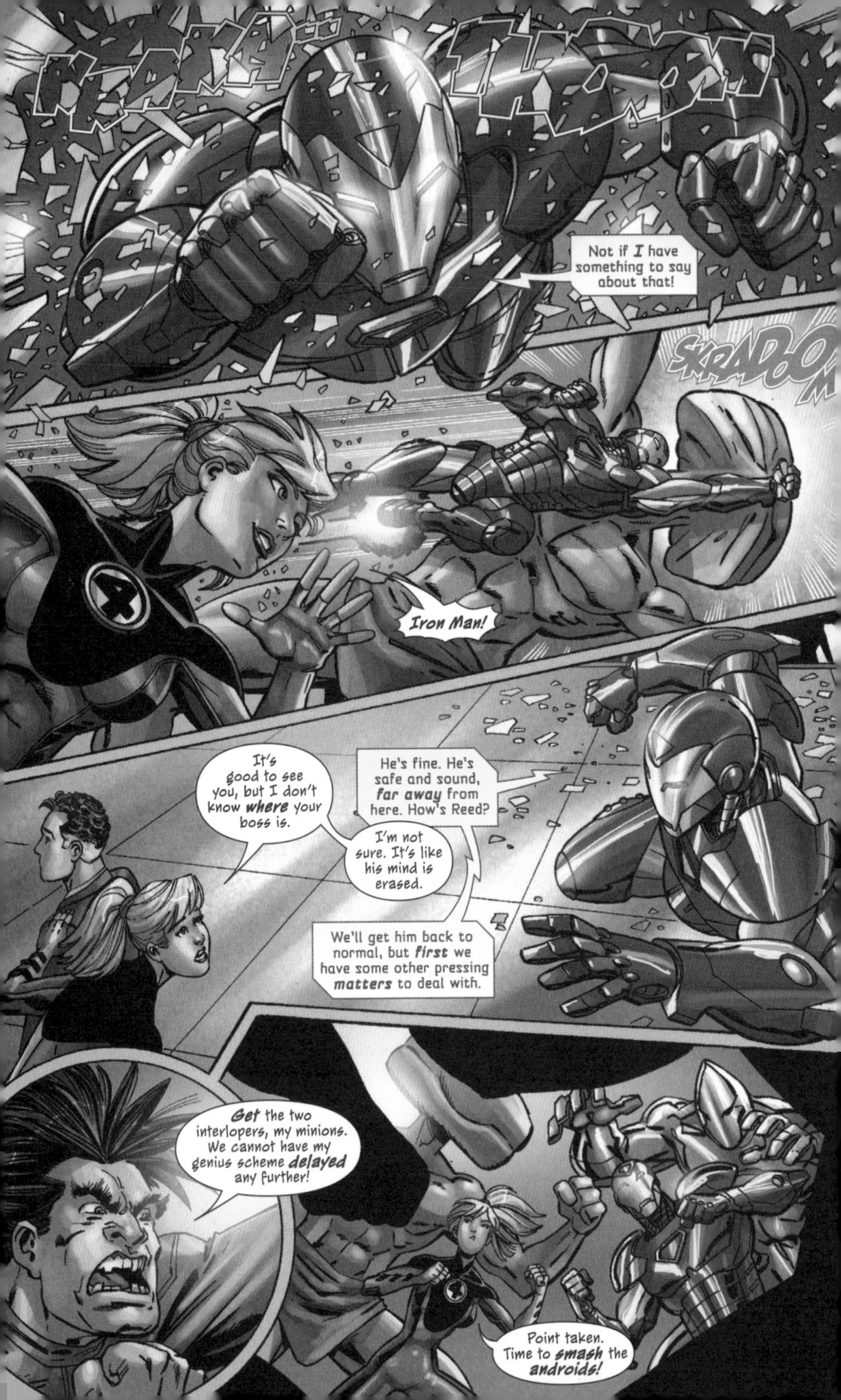
Not if *I* have something to say about that!
SKRADOOM
Iron Man!
It's good to see you, but I don't know *where* your boss is.
He's fine. He's safe and sound, *far away* from here. How's Reed?
I'm not sure. It's like his mind is erased.
We'll get him back to normal, but *first* we have some other pressing *matters* to deal with.
Get the two interlopers, my minions. We cannot have my genius scheme *delayed* any further!
Point taken. Time to *smash* the *androids!*

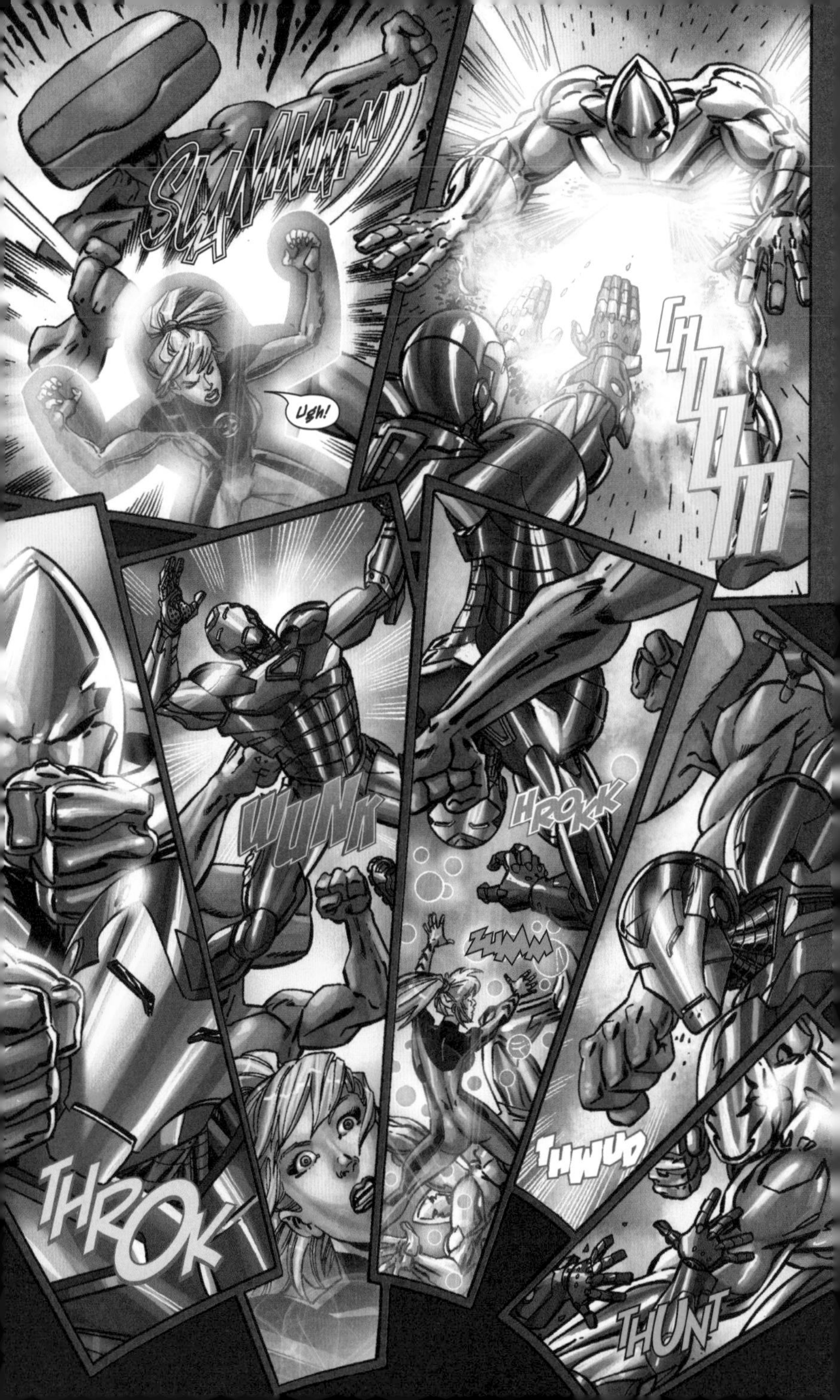
SLAMMMMMM
Ugh!
CHOOM
THROK
WUNK
HROKK
ZUMM
THWUD
THUNT

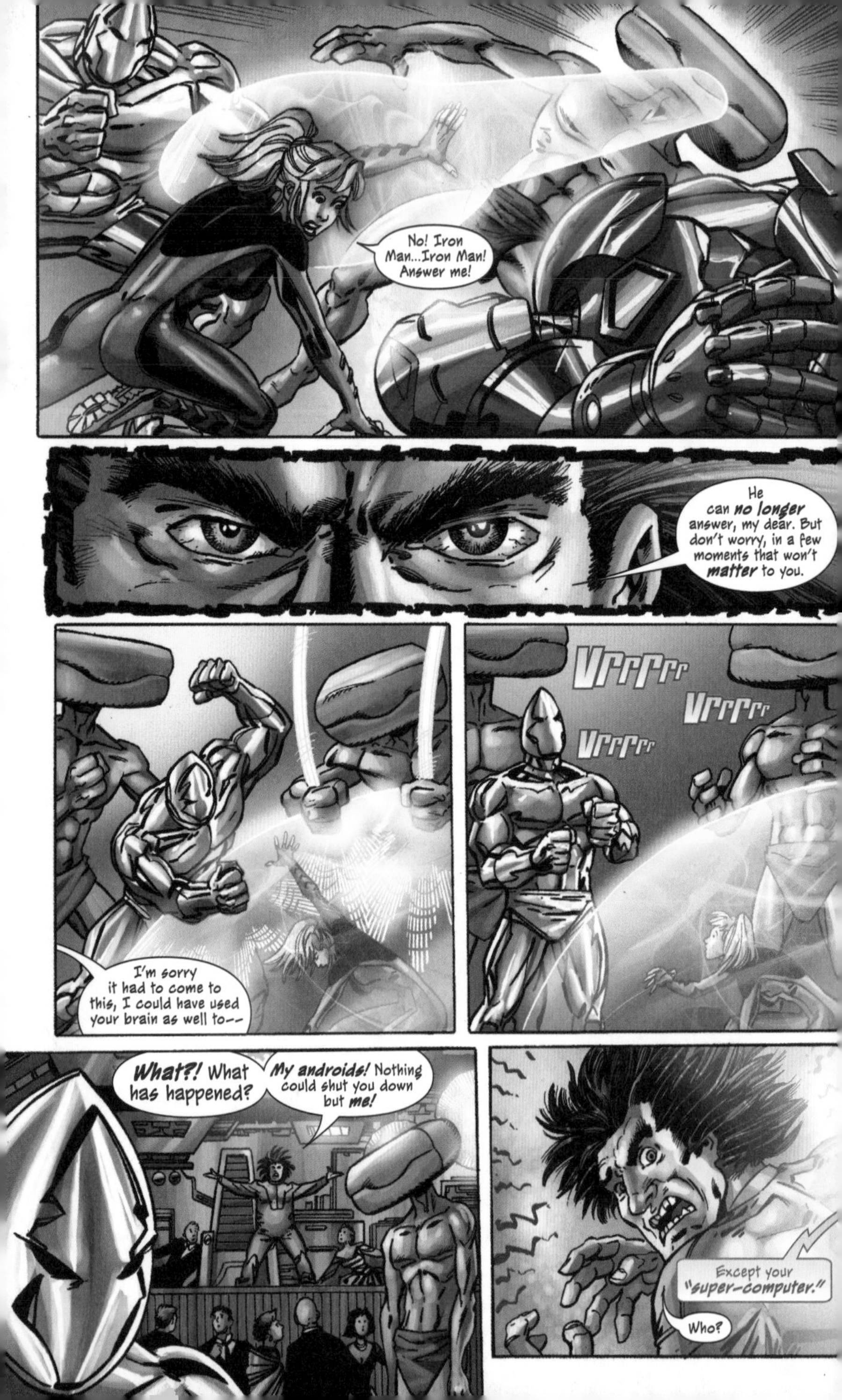
No! Iron Man...Iron Man! Answer me!
He can *no longer* answer, my dear. But don't worry, in a few moments that won't *matter* to you.
I'm sorry it had to come to this, I could have used your brain as well to--
VRRRRR
VRRRRR
VRRRRR
What?! What has happened?
My androids! Nothing could shut you down but *me!*
Except your "*super-computer.*"
Who?

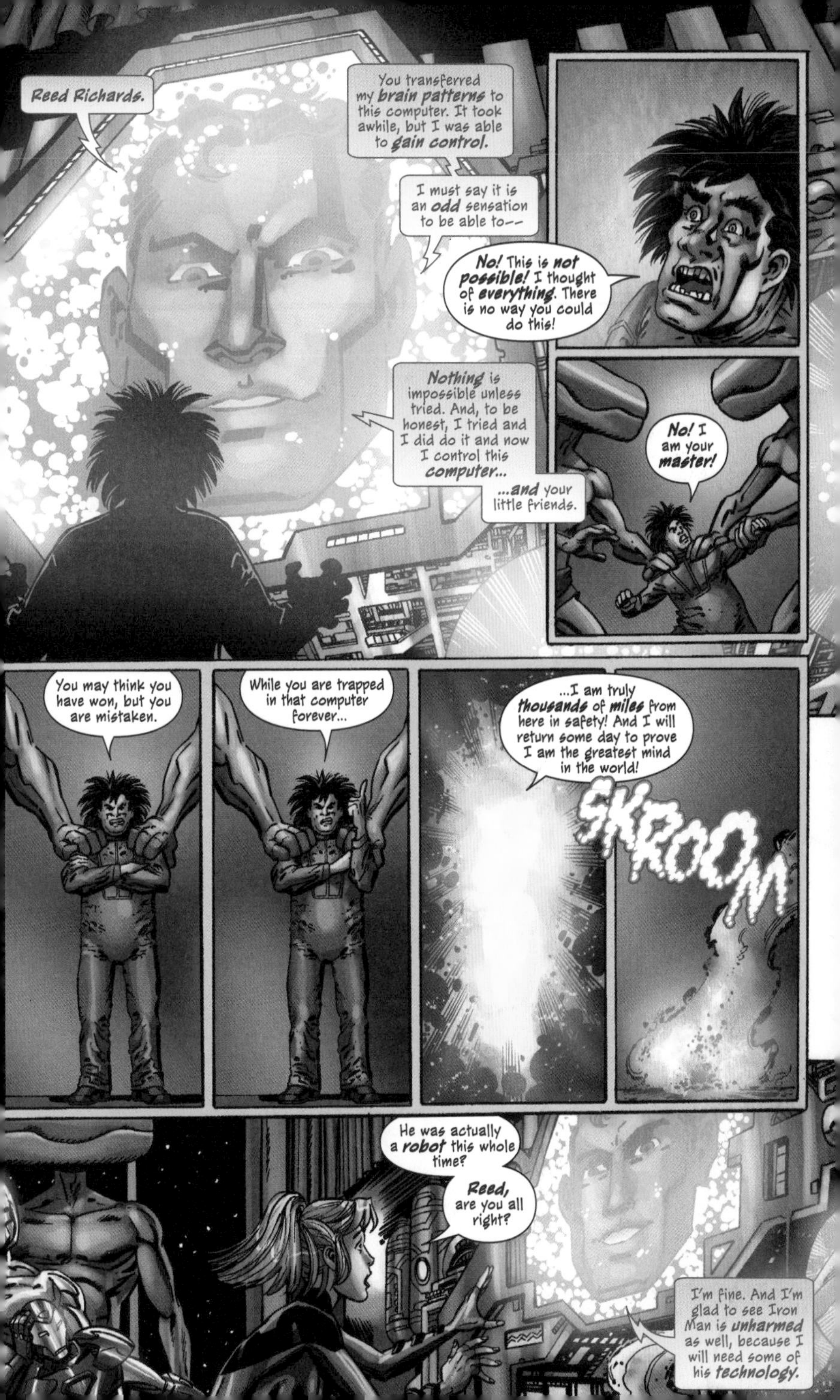

Reed Richards.
You transferred my brain patterns to this computer. It took awhile, but I was able to gain control.
I must say it is an odd sensation to be able to--
No! This is not possible! I thought of everything. There is no way you could do this!
Nothing is impossible unless tried. And, to be honest, I tried and I did do it and now I control this computer...
...and your little friends.
No! I am your master!
You may think you have won, but you are mistaken.
While you are trapped in that computer forever...
...I am truly thousands of miles from here in safety! And I will return some day to prove I am the greatest mind in the world!
SKROOM
He was actually a robot this whole time?
Reed, are you all right?
I'm fine. And I'm glad to see Iron Man is unharmed as well, because I will need some of his technology.

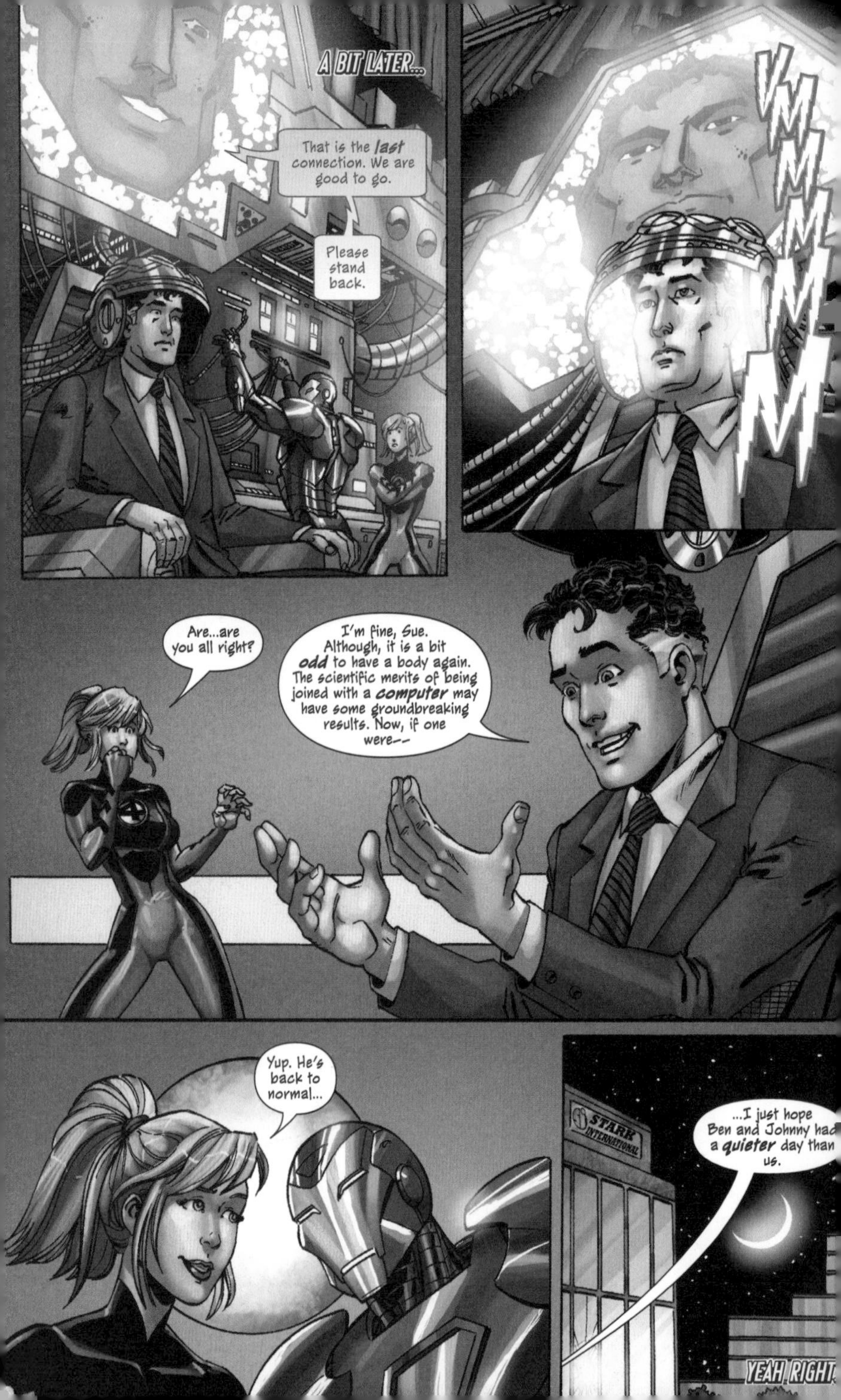
A BIT LATER...
That is the *last* connection. We are good to go.
Please stand back.
VMMMMMM
Are...are you all right?
I'm fine, Sue. Although, it is a bit *odd* to have a body again. The scientific merits of being joined with a *computer* may have some groundbreaking results. Now, if one were--
Yup. He's back to normal...
STARK INTERNATIONAL
...I just hope Ben and Johnny had a *quieter* day than us.
YEAH RIGHT.

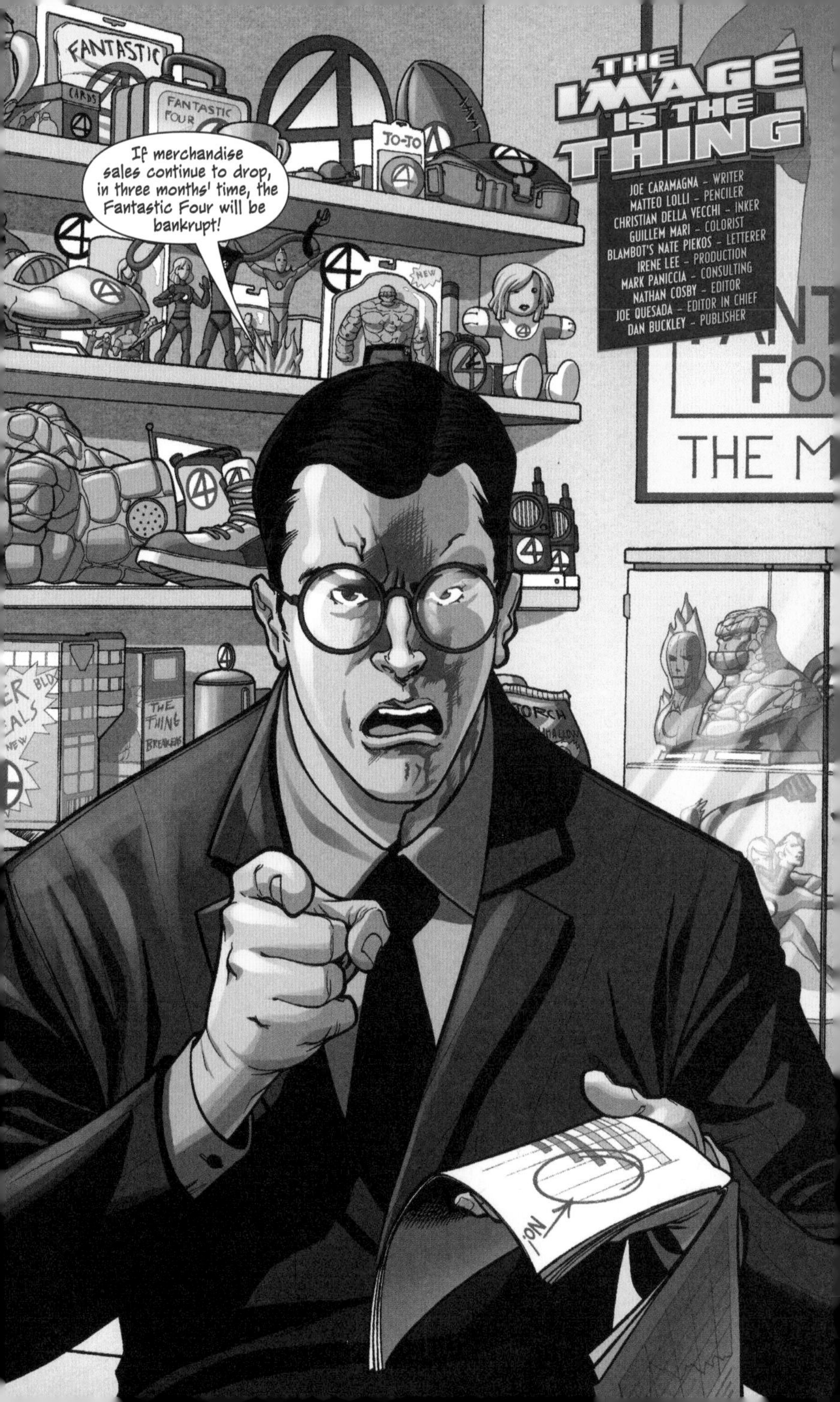
If merchandise sales continue to drop, in three months' time, the Fantastic Four will be bankrupt!
THE IMAGE IS THE THING
JOE CARAMAGNA - WRITER
MATTEO LOLLI - PENCILER
CHRISTIAN DELLA VECCHI - INKER
GUILLEM MARI - COLORIST
BLAMBOT'S NATE PIEKOS - LETTERER
IRENE LEE - PRODUCTION
MARK PANICCIA - CONSULTING
NATHAN COSBY - EDITOR
JOE QUESADA - EDITOR IN CHIEF
DAN BUCKLEY - PUBLISHER
FANTASTIC
FANTASTIC FOUR
JO-JO
NEW
THE THING
THE M
No!

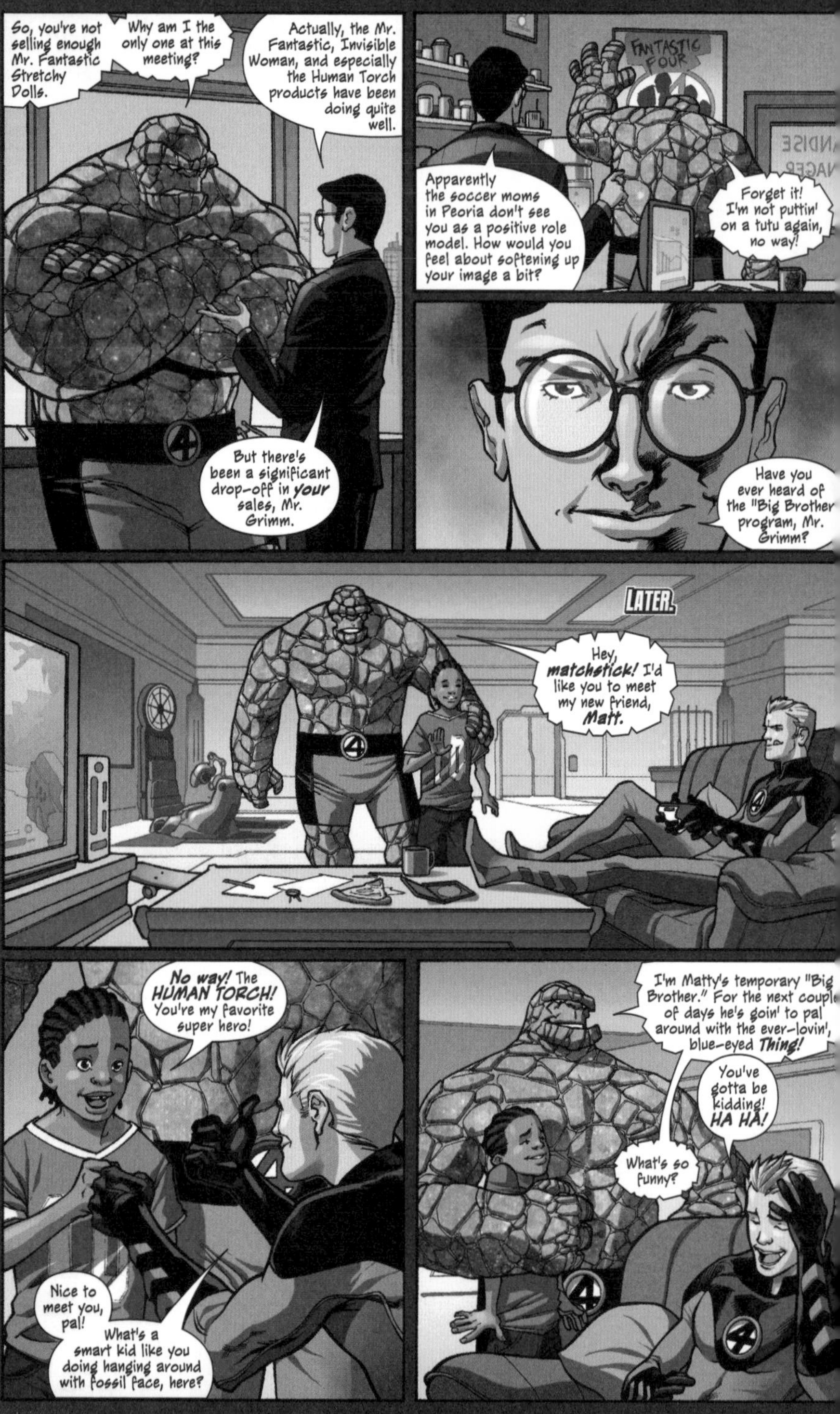

So, you're not selling enough Mr. Fantastic Stretchy Dolls.
Why am I the only one at this meeting?
Actually, the Mr. Fantastic, Invisible Woman, and especially the Human Torch products have been doing quite well.
But there's been a significant drop-off in *your* sales, Mr. Grimm.
FANTASTIC FOUR
Apparently the soccer moms in Peoria don't see you as a positive role model. How would you feel about softening up your image a bit?
Forget it! I'm not puttin' on a tutu again, no way!
Have you ever heard of the "Big Brother program, Mr. Grimm?
LATER.
Hey, *matchstick!* I'd like you to meet my new friend, *Matt.*
No way! The *HUMAN TORCH!* You're my favorite super hero!
Nice to meet you, pal!
What's a smart kid like you doing hanging around with fossil face, here?
I'm Matty's temporary "Big Brother." For the next coupl of days he's goin' to pal around with the ever-lovin', blue-eyed *Thing!*
You've gotta be kidding! *HA HA!*
What's so funny?

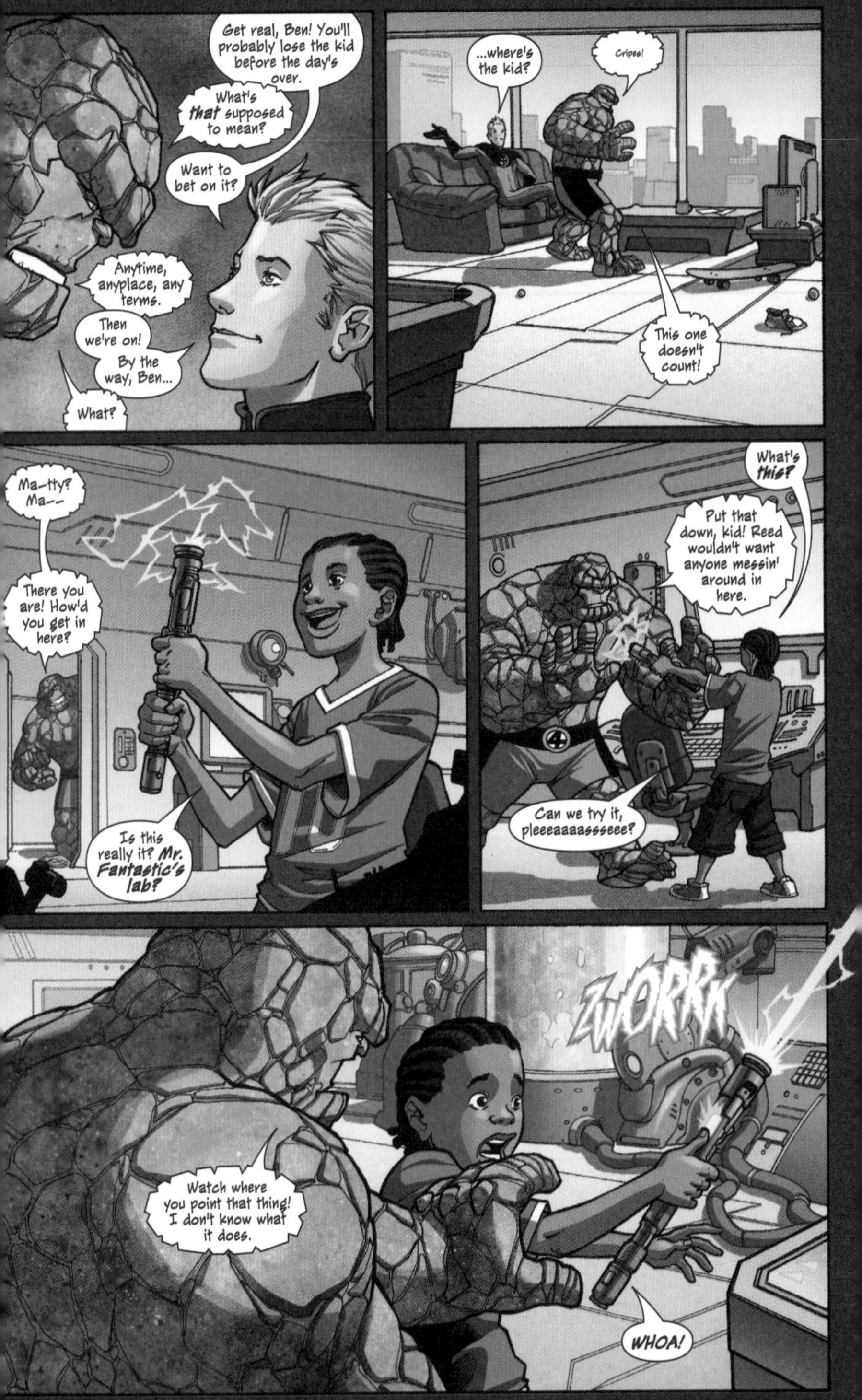
Get real, Ben! You'll probably lose the kid before the day's over.
What's that supposed to mean?
Want to bet on it?
Anytime, anyplace, any terms.
Then we're on!
By the way, Ben...
What?
...where's the kid?
Cripes!
This one doesn't count!
Ma-tty? Ma--
There you are! How'd you get in here?
Is this really it? Mr. Fantastic's lab?
What's this?
Put that down, kid! Reed wouldn't want anyone messin' around in here.
Can we try it, pleeeaaaaassseee?
ZWORRK
Watch where you point that thing! I don't know what it does.
WHOA!

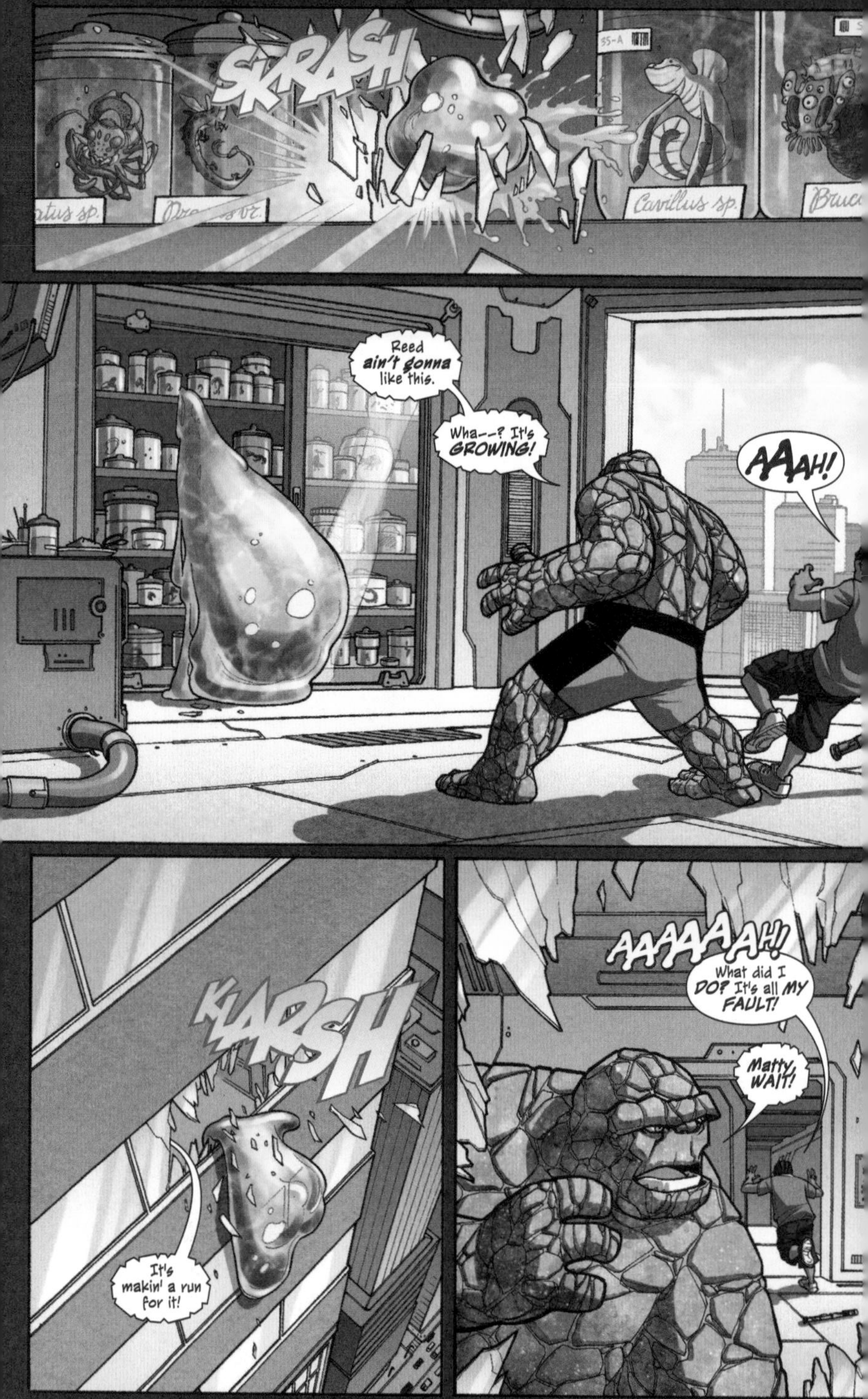
SKRASH
Cavillus sp.
Reed ain't gonna like this.
Wha--? It's GROWING!
AAAH!
KLARSH
It's makin' a run for it!
AAAAAAH!
What did I DO? It's all MY FAULT!
Matty, WAIT!

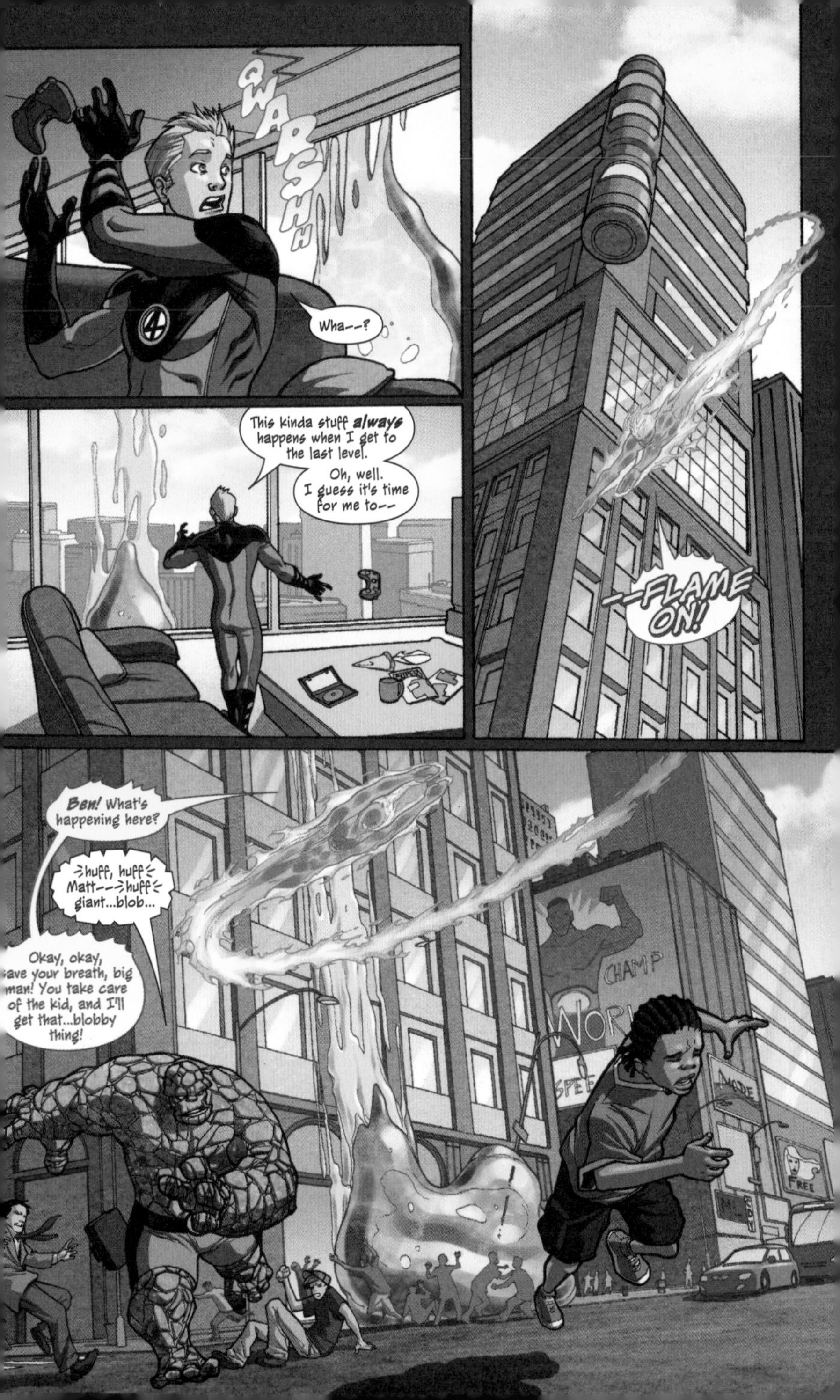

QWARSHH
Wha--?
This kinda stuff *always* happens when I get to the last level.
Oh, well. I guess it's time for me to--
--FLAME ON!
Ben! What's happening here?
huff, huff Matt-- huff giant...blob...
Okay, okay, save your breath, big man! You take care of the kid, and I'll get that...blobby thing!
CHAMP
FREE

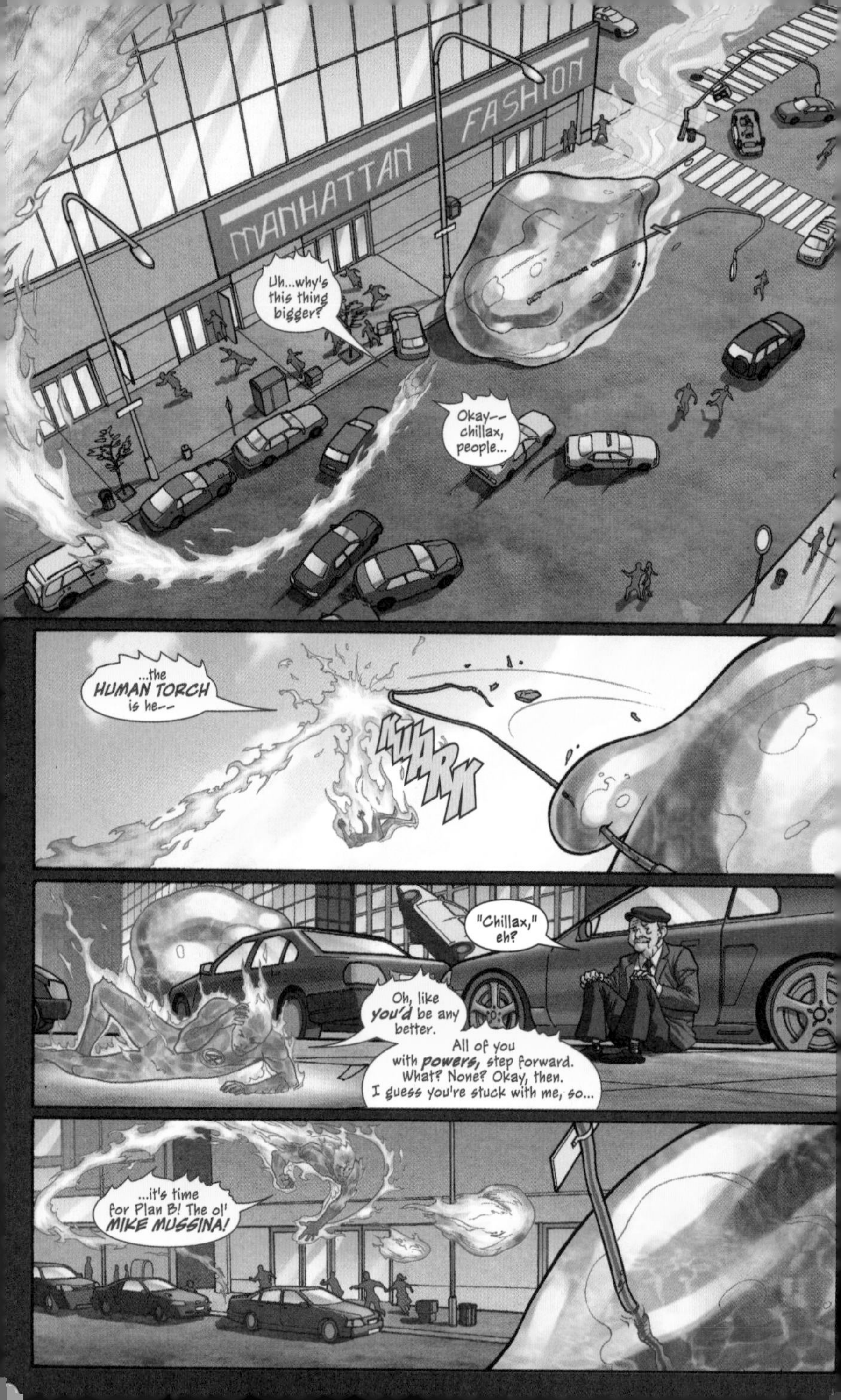

MANHATTAN FASHION
Uh...why's this thing bigger?
Okay-- chillax, people...
...the HUMAN TORCH is he--
KWARK
"Chillax," eh?
Oh, like you'd be any better.
All of you with powers, step forward. What? None? Okay, then. I guess you're stuck with me, so...
...it's time for Plan B! The ol' MIKE MUSSINA!

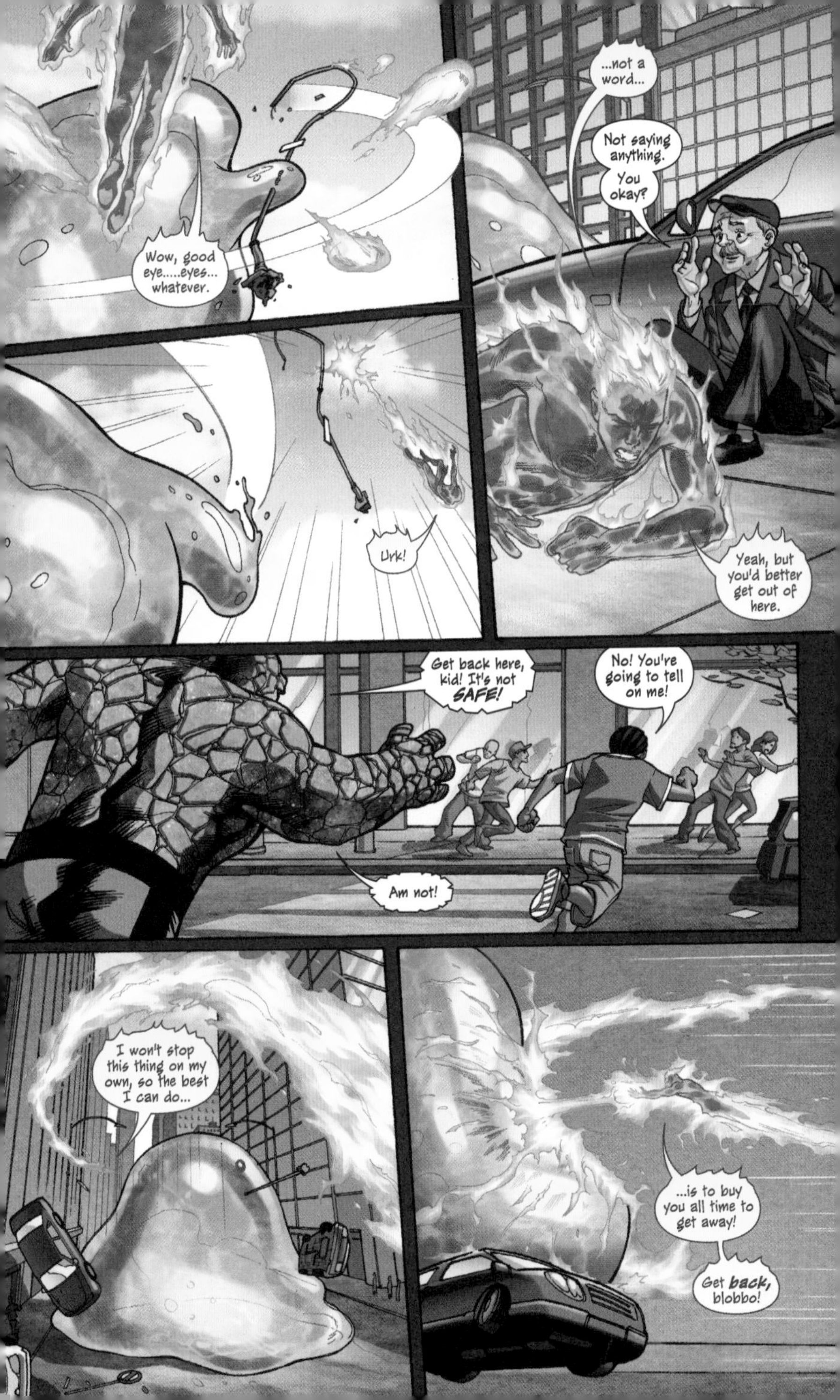
Wow, good eye.....eyes... whatever.
...not a word...
Not saying anything. You okay?
Urk!
Yeah, but you'd better get out of here.
Get back here, kid! It's not SAFE!
No! You're going to tell on me!
Am not!
I won't stop this thing on my own, so the best I can do...
...is to buy you all time to get away!
Get back, blobbo!

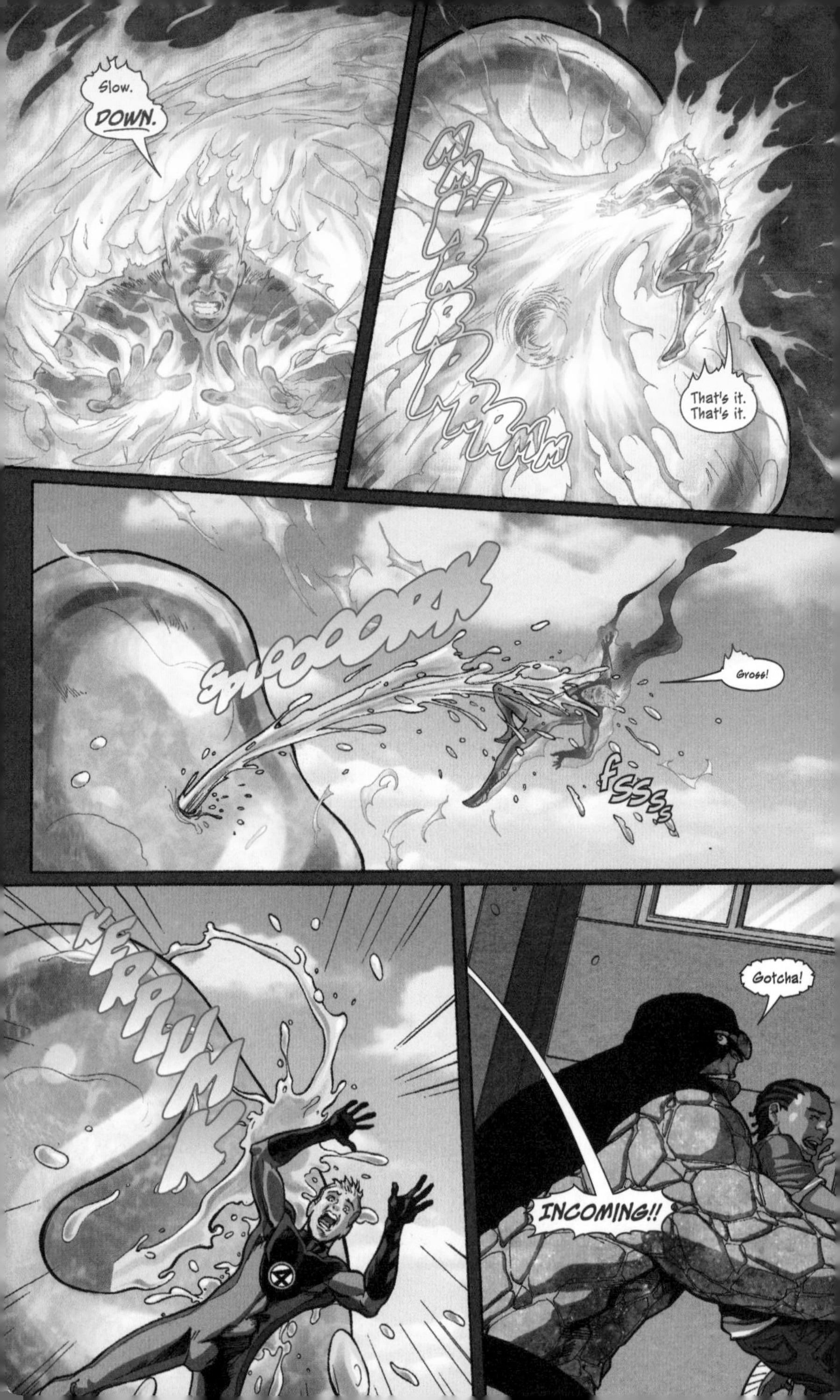

Slow.
DOWN.
That's it.
That's it.
SPLOOOORRH
Gross!
fSSSs
KERPLUNK
Gotcha!
INCOMING!!

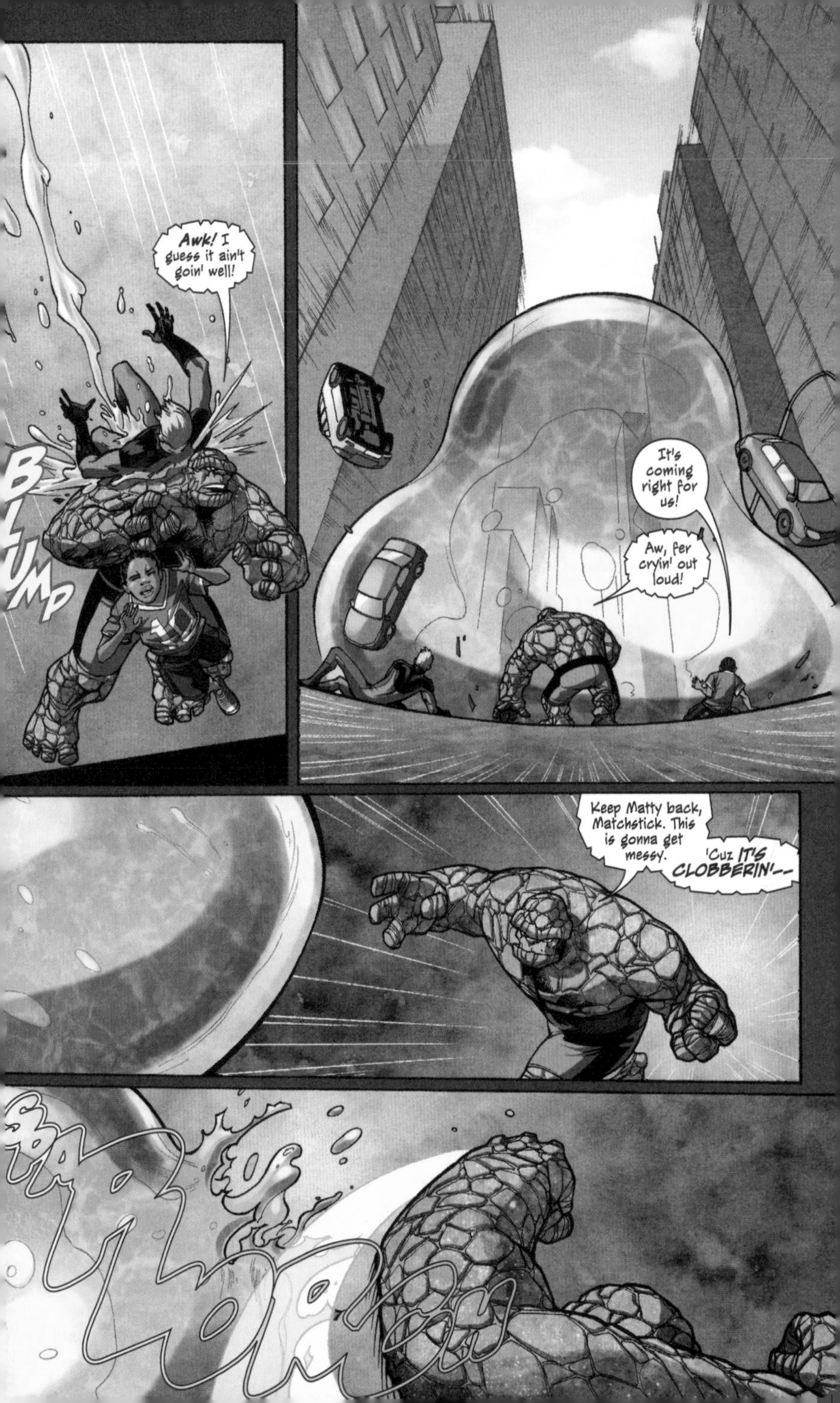

Awk! I guess it ain't goin' well!
BLUMP
It's coming right for us!
Aw, fer cryin' out loud!
Keep Matty back, Matchstick. This is gonna get messy.
'Cuz IT'S CLOBBERIN'--

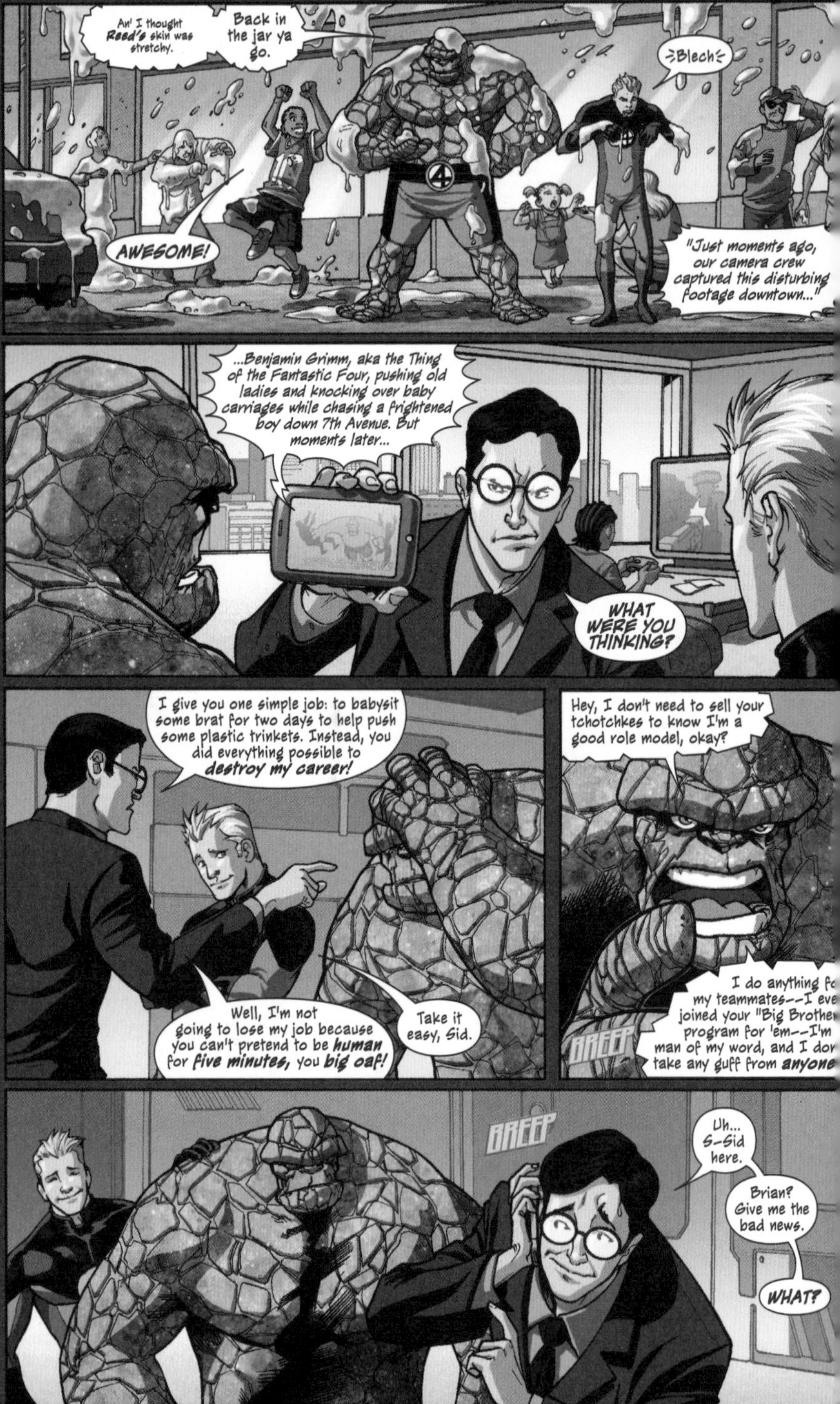
Ah! I thought Reed's skin was stretchy.
Back in the jar ya go.
=Blech=
AWESOME!
"Just moments ago, our camera crew captured this disturbing footage downtown..."
...Benjamin Grimm, aka the Thing of the Fantastic Four, pushing old ladies and knocking over baby carriages while chasing a frightened boy down 7th Avenue. But moments later...
WHAT WERE YOU THINKING?
I give you one simple job: to babysit some brat for two days to help push some plastic trinkets. Instead, you did everything possible to destroy my career!
Well, I'm not going to lose my job because you can't pretend to be human for five minutes, you big oaf!
Take it easy, Sid.
Hey, I don't need to sell your tchotchkes to know I'm a good role model, okay?
BREEP
BREEP
Uh... S-Sid here.
Brian? Give me the bad news.
WHAT?

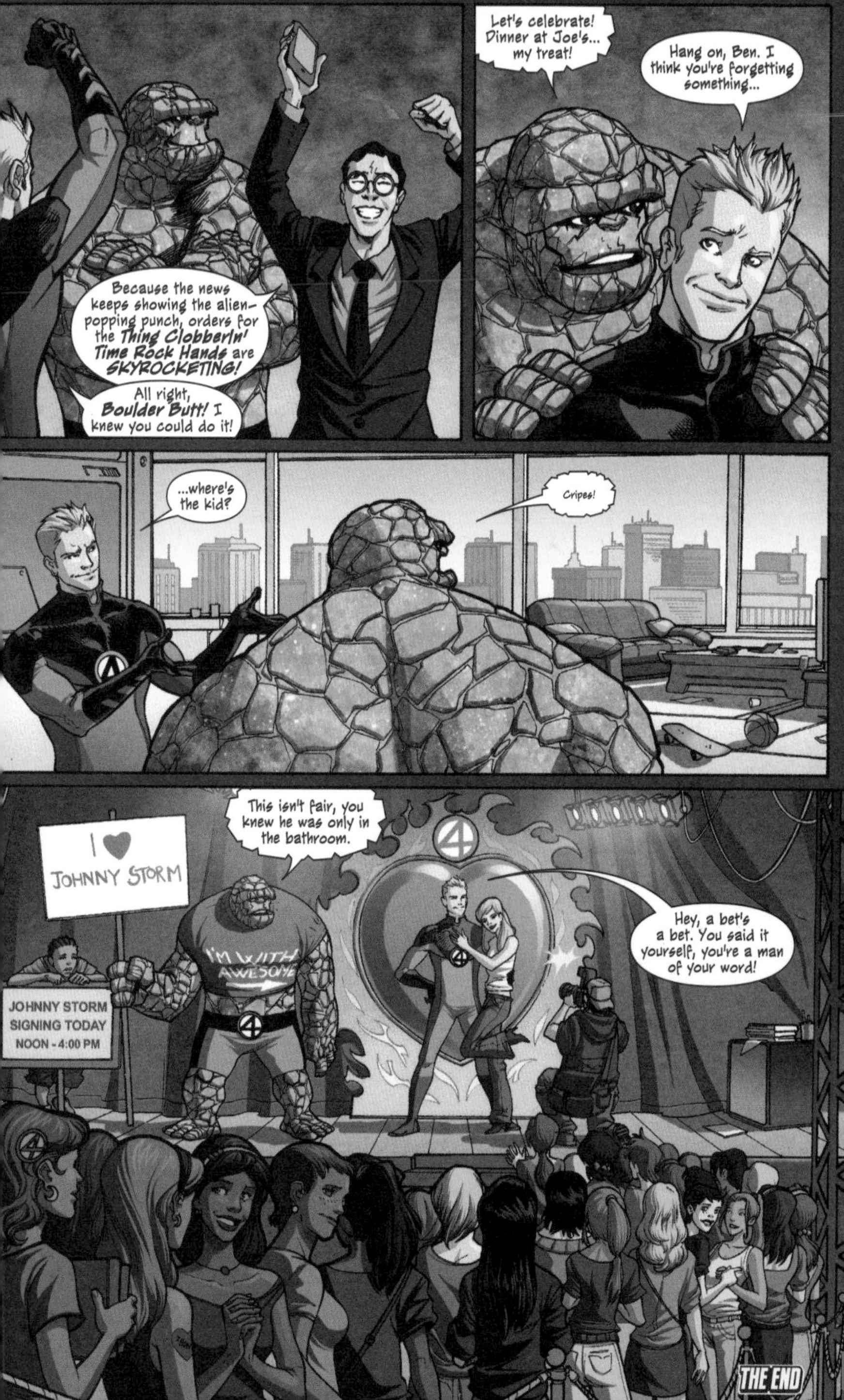
Because the news keeps showing the alien-popping punch, orders for the Thing Clobberin' Time Rock Hands are SKYROCKETING!
All right, Boulder Butt! I knew you could do it!
Let's celebrate! Dinner at Joe's... my treat!
Hang on, Ben. I think you're forgetting something...
...where's the kid?
Cripes!
I ♥ JOHNNY STORM
This isn't fair, you knew he was only in the bathroom.
Hey, a bet's a bet. You said it yourself, you're a man of your word!
I'M WITH AWESOME
JOHNNY STORM SIGNING TODAY NOON - 4:00 PM
THE END